Kincaid's Hope

by

Grace Greene

A Virginia Country Roads Novel

D1510738

Large Print Edition

Books by Grace Greene

Stories of heart and hope ~ from the Outer Banks to the Blue Ridge

Emerald Isle, NC Stories
Love. Suspense. Inspiration.

BEACH RENTAL (Emerald Isle novel #1)
BEACH WINDS (Emerald Isle novel #2)
BEACH WEDDING (Emerald Isle novel #3)
BEACH TOWEL (short story)
BEACH WALK (A Christmas novella)
BEACH CHRISTMAS (A Christmas novella)
CLAIR: BEACH BRIDES SERIES (novella)

Virginia Country Roads Novels
Love. Mystery. Suspense.

KINCAID'S HOPE
A STRANGER IN WYNNEDOWER
CUB CREEK (Cub Creek series #1)
LEAVING CUB CREEK (Cub Creek series #2)

Single Titles from Lake Union Publishing

THE HAPPINESS IN BETWEEN
THE MEMORY OF BUTTERFLIES

www.gracegreene.com

Kersey Creek Books
P.O. Box 6054
Ashland, VA 23005

Kincaid's Hope (Large Print)
Copyright © 2012 Grace Greene
All rights reserved.

Virginia Country Roads (series name)
Copyright © 2014 Grace Greene
All rights reserved.

Cover Design by Grace Greene
Trade Paperback & Digital Release: January 2012
Large Print Version Release: May 2015
ISBN-13: 978-0-9907740-9-9

DEDICATION

Kincaid's Hope is dedicated to Sarah Elizabeth, Natalie Claire and Isabella Grace—may they grow to be the people God intended and live their lives in a way that uplifts them and gives them joy.

ACKNOWLEDGEMENT

My grateful thanks to the Gothic and Romantic Suspense greats, primarily from the period of the 1950s through the 1980s, who offered readers a gentle respite from the hard knocks of real life. These novels are like old friends to me.

There are too many authors to include them all in this list, but here are a few favorites: Anne Buxton (1910–1993) pen names Anne Maybury and Katherine Troy; Barbara Mertz (1927–) pen names Elizabeth Peters and Barbara Michaels; Catherine Cookson (1906–1998); Catherine Gaskin (1929–2009); Dorothy Eden (1912–1982); Eleanor Hibbert (1906 – 1993) pen names Jean Plaidy, Victoria Holt and Philippa Carr; Joan Aiken (1924–2004); Mary Stewart (1917–); Norah Lofts (1903–1984); Peter O'Donnell (1920 –2010) pen name Madeline Brent; Phyllis A. Whitney (1903–2008)

KINCAID'S HOPE

Beth Kincaid left her hot temper and unhappy childhood behind and created a life in the city free from untidy emotionalism, but even a tidy life has danger, especially when it falls apart.

In the midst of personal disasters, Beth is called back to her hometown of Preston, a small town in southwestern Virginia, to settle her guardian's estate. There, she runs smack into the mess she'd left behind a decade earlier: her alcoholic father, the long-ago sweetheart, Michael, and the poor opinion of almost everyone in town. As she sorts through her guardian's possessions, Beth discovers that the woman who saved her and raised her had secrets, and the truths revealed begin to chip away at her self-imposed control. Michael is warmly attentive and Stephen, her ex-fiancé, follows her to Preston to win her back, but it is the man she doesn't know who could forever end Beth's chance to build a better, truer life.

KINCAID'S HOPE

Chapter One

She'd built her life before; she could do it again.

Beth Kincaid had awakened before dawn, but the memory of yesterday, of being fired, was a dark, gnarly place in her brain. She pulled the goose down pillow over her head hoping to slip back into sweet oblivion.

Not happening.

She kicked off the covers. She was an early riser and always had been. Apparently, that didn't change with the circumstances.

First, a hot shower, pounding and steaming, a brisk blow-dry of the hair and then a little makeup—a swish of the hand towel to shine up the faucet completed the morning routine.

Beth shook out her folded jeans and held them up to her waist. She hadn't seen them in a long time. She sorted through the shirts hanging in the closet, bypassing the silk shells and dressier button-downs, opting for a sky blue cotton shirt with pearl buttons.

Next, coffee, but there was no rush. She wouldn't be among the DC beltway commuters this morning.

On the counter separating the kitchen from the living room, the answering machine splashed its blinking red light onto the wall—the same as it had last night when she came home. She turned her back to it and concentrated on getting the coffee maker working.

Soft strains of Mendelssohn's Wedding March came from nearby. Beth jumped, startled, and coffee grounds scattered across the countertop. Stephen—she'd called him yesterday, but he'd asked all the wrong questions. She found her purse and dug the cell phone out of the side pocket.

"Hi."

"Hello, beautiful. How are you? Better today?" His tone dropped. "You scared me, you know, not answering the phone. I was worried."

"I didn't feel like talking." She sniffled and was embarrassed that she couldn't help it.

"Remember, I'm the guy you're going to marry."

"I know. It's just…"

"Beth, please let me help. Getting laid off is bad news and it's tough for you now, but Haddin Technology gives generous severance packages. You've been there for almost ten years."

She cringed. Stephen's mind was always on money these days. His investments had tanked and she sympathized, but….

"I can't talk about it now. I'll call you later."

Her finger hit the End button without consulting her good manners.

Beth clutched the phone. She could see him—almost as if he were right in front of her—his dark eyes, almost black, so concerned, so sincere.

He'd stopped asking her to take a loan against her 401K, but since yesterday it was severance, severance, severance. If he said that word one more time, she'd scream.

When the Wedding March began playing again, she stuffed the phone under the chair cushion. He didn't understand. No one could.

But that wasn't true. Maude always encouraged and supported her. Maude Henry, no relation and under no obligation, had rescued Beth and her brother, Daniel. She'd done her best to help them—two troubled children with no one to protect them. Years later, just before Beth left town, Maude had given her a book.

Beth stopped in front of the bookcase and ran her fingers along the spines of the books. There it was. *Clarissa's Folly*. She slid it from its spot on the shelf.

The dust jacket was gaudy and melodramatic, an illustration of a young woman in a long, full-skirted dress standing in front of a gray stone house and clutching a red cape about her, against the wind. In the background, a man stood near the corner of the house watching her. Tall and slim, dressed in black, his face was shadowed below the brim of a tall hat.

The jacket branded it a gothic romance, decades out of fashion and a misfit among her other books. Almost an embarrassment. She'd considered discarding it many times, or, at least ripping off the dust jacket. Why hadn't she?

Because of Maude. She didn't have the heart, or the lack of heart needed, to throw it away.

The inscription was the important part. She flipped open the cover to the words Maude had written on the title page in her disciplined and perfectly formed handwriting:

To Beth on her eighteenth birthday,
Make your own life. Don't let it be made for you.
Love, your Maude

Beth appreciated the advice, but had always been bemused by the choice of book.

She whispered, "Maude, I did what you said and look where it's gotten me."

A photo stuck out from between the pages. She brushed the edge gently with her fingers, then pulled it out. Michael. Dark hair, blue eyes and a smile that set her tingling from head to toe. Back then, of course. Not now. Not in a long time. They'd been so young then. Only a decade ago? It seemed like another life. And beside him, Daniel, always looking so serious, but as mischievous as his ginger hair suggested.

She reached up and touched her own hair, more gold than red, but otherwise so much like her brother's.

One page of the book was bent. Beth smoothed out the rumple and the text caught her attention.

The maidservant conducted her down the stairs and through the tall doorway of the dining room. Madam was already seated at the table to the right of a handsome, well-dressed dark-haired man. Clarissa's breath caught in her throat. Quickly, she sought to regain her composure.

The footman drew a chair from the table, opposite Madam, and waited. Clarissa approached and with each step she was surer.

It was escapist, nonsense fiction. Nothing to do with real life.

Beth returned the book to the shelf and grabbed her old comfort sweater from the sofa. She slid her arms into the loose sleeves, then pulled the front together to hold the softness closer.

So, what next?

She'd like to see Maude.

There was no employer to notify and her neighbor, Celeste, could get the mail. Why not drive to Preston and visit her?

Beth pushed open the sliding door and stepped out onto her small balcony. She breathed deeply hoping fresh air would cool her brain.

The parking lot below was almost empty. The spring-freshened breeze lightly masked the mingled odors of asphalt and stale exhaust. Beyond the parking lot and a buffer of cedar trees, most of the Route 50 traffic headed north and east, away from Fairfax and toward the DC environs. The world, the employed part, was en route to work. Her car sat idle a few rows back with the morning dew still clinging to the windshield.

Only one person was in view, a man sitting in a shiny dark SUV. He was almost invisible behind its tinted windows. The side window was down and his large, muscled arm rested on the sill. The morning sun glinted on gold jewelry around his wrist and on his hand.

He was a stranger and she was glad. She didn't want nosy neighbors speculating why workaholic-no-time-for-gossiping, all-business Beth was home at this hour on a work day.

The damp, metallic cold of the wrought iron railing reached through the nubby knit of her sleeves. Beth pressed her fingers to her face, to her throbbing temples. Her omissions were catching up with her. She'd never lied about her past, but she didn't believe she owed anyone, including Stephen, her life story.

She'd told him her parents died when she was young and that a local woman had raised her. That had satisfied him. He liked being free of family ties and emotional baggage. They both did. Romance and hearts and flowers had never been a part of their relationship, but then again, neither had regret or remorse. Until now.

Yesterday's shock had provided some kind of catharsis and opened her eyes. Their relationship, once so sparkly, had no more substance than a cheap trinket.

But breaking up? He wasn't going to make it easy. All the more reason to disappear for a few days.

Beth went back inside and yanked the suitcase from the closet and opened it on the bed. She didn't need to pack much. She wouldn't be gone long, just long enough to hear Maude's calm common sense advice. Her toiletries fit into specially-sized plastic bags and her clothing into packing cubes. Nice and neat. With a satisfied grunt, Beth closed the suitcase and carried it into the living room.

Beth pictured Maude, thin with perfect posture and iron-colored curls tight to her scalp, and with a wide smile when she opened the front door and saw Beth.

The blinking red message light caught her eye again. Time to take care of it. She flexed her fingers and punched the blinking red light.

"You have three messages. First message." There was a brief pause, then, Stephen's voice said, "Beth? You aren't answering your cell. Are you there? Call me."

Groan. She hit Erase.

"Second message." This time it was a woman's voice. Familiar. It caught her attention with the first words. "This message is for Beth Kincaid. This is Ida Langhorne calling from Mr. Monroe's office. You might remember me?" There was a pause. "Well, I'm sorry to leave a message like this, but Miss Maude has passed. A few days ago...."

Beth's mind went blank. Mrs. Langhorne's slow, southern lilt made 'a few days ago' sound like a question. The words hit her brain, but she couldn't think. Mrs. Langhorne continued speaking. Beth slapped the Stop button.

...has passed. A few days ago...

Something tore in her heart. With a

trembling hand, she pressed Play again.

"...he sent a letter, too, because we had trouble tracking you down. Your number's unlisted. Anyway, we found your phone number in her address book today. We had a small funeral service yesterday. Arranged it just the way she wanted. I'm real sorry, honey. When you get to town, stop by the office and we'll give you Miss Maude's papers. Bye, now."

Only Maude had her contact information.

There was no love lost between Beth and the people she'd left behind in Preston ten years ago. In the years since, her trips to Preston had been brief and solely for the purpose of visiting Maude.

The red light continued to blink, waiting, insisting she listen to the third message. She pushed the button.

"Third message. Beth, this is Michael. Maude gave me your number a while ago. You've probably heard by now, but I wanted to make sure you knew. It's about Maude. She's gone. If you'd like to talk, call me." He left a phone number.

One person from Preston had called, after all. His voice touched her in a way that the old photo hadn't. Her eyes hurt. She waited for the tears to start. Expected them. Wanted them. Her eyes burned, but no tears fell.

It was the effect of shock. Maude was gone. Employer was gone. Reality had suffered a sudden inversion.

She closed her eyes and concentrated on breathing. This apartment in Fairfax was her present. The small town of Preston was her past.

Look forward, Bethie, not back.

But sometimes the past returned to claim its share of the present.

She called Mr. Monroe's office and left a message on his answering machine. "It's Beth Kincaid. I'll be in town this afternoon."

She unplugged the coffee maker. She'd grab a cup on her way out of town. But she had to tell Stephen something. She couldn't simply disappear.

Beth practiced excuses and explanations as she made two trips down the stairs taking her suitcase and other items to the car. She tossed her suitcase onto the back seat and put her laptop bag on the floorboard, then stood in the open driver's side door drumming her fingers on the car roof. It wasn't his fault that, more and more, being around him made her feel trapped. Or, maybe it was partly his fault, but it was totally her fault she hadn't done anything about it.

She hit his number on the speed dial.

"Beth? I'm glad you called back. I was about to come over. I'm not angry that you hung up on me. I know you're going through a lot of negative stuff right now."

The morning damp hung over the asphalt. She slipped into the car and closed the door. She should tell him about the trip and why…as she should also tell him the truth about being fired and about Maude's death. Instead, she said, "I need time away."

"What are you talking about?"

"A few days. Alone."

"Just like that? No discussion?"

A deep breath. "I'm sorry. I'll call you when I get back. We'll talk then." She disconnected.

She backed out of the parking space, her foot powered by adrenalin, and almost ran over a man, probably the man she'd seen earlier in the SUV since no one else was around. Either she hadn't noticed him crossing the nearly empty lot and or he'd moved quickly because, suddenly, he was there, his gray t-shirt filling her rearview mirror. He was unusually tall and, thankfully, nimble. She was glad not to add manslaughter to her sins.

Come hell or high water or from the frying pan into the fire—*choose your cliché and pick your poison, Bethie*—it all came down to the same thing. Next stop, Preston.

But running away was tougher than expected.

Stephen called before she reached Starbucks and again, as Beth settled back in the car with her coffee.

She parked away from the store, around the side out of the eyes of passersby. She took a deep, cleansing breath, then dialed. He answered before the first ring ended.

"I was about to call the police."

Muted voices rose and fell in the background. Office noises.

"Why? I told you I needed a few days away."

"Because I'm worried about you. Losing your job was a huge shock."

She stopped mid-reach for her coffee. "I'll be okay. I will. But that's part of why I want to go away for a few days."

"Fine. Understood. I'll go with you. You shouldn't be by yourself right now."

"I'll be fine." She sniffled again and rummaged through her purse and glove compartment searching for a tissue.

"Talk to me, Beth. We're engaged. That should mean something."

Over the phone came the click of a door closing and the background voices ceased as he said, "Your voice sounds funny. Are you crying? No worries. You'll find a new job."

"I hope so. I have bills to pay."

"You've still got your savings, and now you have the severance monies." His voice took on a familiar, bitter edge. "I wouldn't have suggested that investment to you, or anyone else, if I hadn't believed in it. You were right not to trust me."

He was tuning up to run through the story of his investment failure all over again. She couldn't deal with this.

"It was never a question of trusting you. The market was too volatile. Outside of my comfort level." Sunlight sparked off of the side of a black SUV as it drove slowly past. She shielded her eyes. "You aren't a broker. They knew you weren't licensed. It's not like you took a percentage or a kickback." There was a brief silence. "Or had inside information or anything."

"Good intentions won't matter if they go public about it. Unlucky investments blow up into big scandals now. My employer won't want to be associated with it even if it has nothing to do with our marketing clients."

"I understand."

"And you're tired of hearing about it."

She should say 'not at all,' but it was the truth. She was sick of it. She tried to remember what had attracted her to him and came up empty. Beth took a deep breath and said, "I'm sitting in my car in a parking lot. It's not a good place for a conversation."

"Tell me where you are. I'll be there in minutes."

"No." She spoke as gently as she could, yet still sound firm. "I'll talk to you when I get back. Please understand. Bye, Stephen."

****

The train tracks divided Main Street, literally running between the north and southbound traffic lanes. Kersey's Drug 'n Dime looked shabby. On the corner of Hatter and Main, Lester's Fine Furniture was now Lester's Discount House and signs in the showroom windows promised 'Deep Price Cuts.'

The disintegration had been in progress the last time she'd driven down Main Street, but change drove more change. Main Street's vitality hovered somewhere between borderline commercial survival and going flat broke. At the end of Main, the tracks curved to the right and headed northeast around Mill Park.

Billy Monroe's law office was around the corner on Woodlawn Avenue, facing the park. The sign on his door was flipped to "Closed for

Lunch." Beth parked and walked the short distance to the office door. Up close, it was easy to see the interior was dark and empty.

She turned back toward the car. Across the street was Mill Park, unchanged. The sweep of grass beneath the tall, massive pines and the water beyond where ducks and geese reigned and dragonflies flitted, eased her heart. It always had even when things were bad.

Powell's Creek fed the lake. It had powered the grist mill more than a century earlier, but the mill was long closed. The town made an effort to keep the exterior of the three-story building in good repair, but the weathered structure was moving from picturesque to derelict. Westward, beyond the park and out of sight of the park and mill, houses backed up to the lake.

Beth got back into the car and drove along the two-lane road skirting the lake. She passed Maude's church. Well, not Maude's church, but that was how Beth always thought of it. Never Beth's church after the first day she'd sat in the pew beside Maude. Two pews behind them several girls had giggled and whispered. The same smart and pretty girls Beth didn't get along with in school. It was destined not to end well and her lack of fitting-in had grown exponentially with each service she attended.

Maude Henry's house was on the outside edge of town on the western branch of the lake. Each morning, a beautiful sunrise bloomed over the unbroken expanse of water. An exquisite sunset burnished the water and set the distant mountains afire at day's end.

The house and the old neighborhood were the same. Large and small homes were intermixed, but the lots were large and private due to the mature hedges and trees.

Beth climbed from the car and paused to shrug off her old sweater. She tossed it back into the car. With Maude gone, she'd expected the house to look empty, bereft, and it did, but the sky above was a deep blue and the smell of springtime green tickled her nose.

She sensed eyes upon her and looked up.

There was a large gap in the hedge and across the way, Mrs. Boyle stood on her porch staring in Beth's direction. Martha Boyle, and most of the other citizens of Preston, refused to let her forget her teen years, her mistakes, her hot temper. For them, it was 'like father, like daughter.' Let Martha stare.

Past was past. Let it stay there.

The key fit smoothly into the lock and the door opened. The tiny vestibule was dark, but light streamed into the hallway ahead through the wide, framed opening into the living room.

Beth paused and listened. Silence. Only the dry, musty smell of old greeted her.

The living room was on the left with the dining room behind it. The threadbare hallway rug, the almost napless fabric of Maude's Davenport, were unchanged. The tabletops wore a thin layer of dust. The tables were bare of their knick-knacks. She walked straight back to the kitchen. The fridge was empty. It had been cleaned and wiped, and a small, orange box of Arm n' Hammer baking soda was inside to absorb odors.

Stepping out the back door—now that was like entering another world. Beth breathed in the sweet scents of yellow jasmine and fresh water. The yard had always been simple, but well-groomed, bordered by massive red-tipped Photinia hedges and crape myrtle trees— mature foliage hiding this slice of property from the rest of the world.

The grass was shaggy. The planks on the weathered dock were warped and split. Overall, it didn't inspire confidence. At the gazebo, a few loose corners of screening flapped in the breeze and the white paint was peeling.

But the gazebo still overlooked the lake, the dock was more solid than it appeared and the gentle slapping of wavelets at the rock barrier protecting the shoreline was the sound of eternity.

The physical sensations tied the moments of her life together in such an overwhelming way she nearly dropped to her knees, winded by the unexpectedness. She fought it off. There were good memories, true, but they weren't worth remembering if it meant reliving the painful ones.

A boy burst through the hedge. He skidded to a stop when he saw Beth.

"Hi," she said.

He stuck his fingers in his belt loops and hitched up his jeans. "Do you live here now?"

"I used to. I just got back."

"Do you have a kid? There's not many around here."

He looked so serious Beth almost laughed. She wanted to thank him for tearing her away from bad memories, but he wouldn't understand.

"No kids, sorry. Do you live nearby?"

"My grandma lives there." He pointed toward the Boyle's blue-shingled house. "Am I in trouble?"

"Trouble? Why?"

"Because I'm in your yard." He shifted from sneaker to sneaker, postured forward on the balls of his feet, gearing up to move.

"Run through anytime you like."

Mrs. Boyle yelled from beyond the hedge. "James! Where are you?"

The boy grinned at Beth and disappeared into the next set of hedges on the far side.

That moment he grinned—he was probably about nine or ten—reminded her of Daniel. Her heart gave a twinge. No wonder she'd thought of him, her big brother, out here by the lake with the past feeling close enough to touch. And Michael, too.

This time, her heart gave a nervous thud.

No problem. If she wrapped up her business quickly, she could avoid Michael.

Back inside, Beth opened a kitchen window and then others in the living room and dining room. Some were painted shut, others were warped, but a few opened wide enough to allow in fresh air, still cool. Thank goodness it was April and not July.

She heard footsteps on the porch and then the doorbell broke the silence.

Mrs. Boyle held a bowl of cat food in one hand. A large orange cat was secured between her body and the crook of her other arm. The cat hung there, legs stuck out, eyes staring.

Martha Boyle thrust the bowl toward her and Beth took it in reflex. She did the same with the cat, nearly assaulting Beth with its massive, furry body.

"It's Maude's. I took care of it while things were getting sorted out. Now you're here, so it's sorted and it's yours."

Beth's mouth hung open. The cat twitched and settled the sharp nails of one hind foot against her arm, tensing in warning. "What–?"

"There's litter in the pantry and the box is out on the back stoop."

"Is this–? I thought..." Beth stumbled over the words.

"I don't know anything about it except its name. Teddy." She turned and walked away, her hand on the stair rail and her attention concentrated on the porch steps. Martha's only 'goodbye' was the view of her stooped back.

Teddy squirmed vigorously. Beth let him fall. He hit the floor with a soft thud and dashed up the stairs as if he knew exactly where he was going. Which he did, of course.

Beth stood at the base of the stairs, staring at the dust motes dancing in the sunlight as it streamed through the windows on the landing. Should she follow him up? No, she'd fix the litter box first.

This was way beyond unexpected. The last time she'd visited, Maude had been looking for a home for a stray kitten. Apparently, she'd found one. Here.

Maude's cat.

Her cat now.

Beth went upstairs. She had to find Teddy a new home.

The large cat was curled up on Maude's bed. He lifted his head and eyeballed her. His tail swished as if slicing the air.

"Fine. Stay there."

The furnishings upstairs seemed lean. Beth flipped a light switch on and off and opened the water tap. Power and water. All she needed for a few days.

Personal items, only a small bottle of White Shoulders, a silver-backed hairbrush and a ring holder, sat on a doily on Maude's dresser. Beth recognized the few dresses hanging in the closet and knew there used to be more.

Her own room was at the front of the house. It, too, looked stripped down.

****

Beth made a quick trip to the grocery store, both for herself and for Teddy. She was putting the food away when movement out by the gazebo caught her eye. Through the window and beyond the tattered gazebo screening, she saw a man on the far side of the structure, standing near the water.

She stared. Her breath quickened. She reached up and smoothed her hair back.

She didn't know Maude's neighbors anymore, except Martha Boyle, of course. She couldn't tell a neighbor out for a morning jog from a stranger trespassing. Yet, as the man moved along the lakeside, Beth recognized him immediately by his walk, his posture, and other attributes she couldn't name, but to which her heart and body responded instinctively.

Michael.

Chapter Two

All thoughts of avoiding Michael vanished as if they'd never passed through her brain. The slamming of the storm door behind her was no more than a faint echo of her lost resolve as she crossed the lawn to where he stood down by the lake.

Beth didn't know Michael, the adult, but she'd known him well as a child and a teenager. Surprised by a surge of strong emotion, she nearly reached out to touch him, but his eyes stayed hard. He watched her approach and his hands stayed in his pockets. His coolness squelched her impulsive rush to greet him.

His dark hair was longish around his ears and neck, but neatly groomed. A soft blue shirt matched the color of his eyes. His jeans were neat and his shoes were polished. His style said casual and comfortable, but not careless and not by chance.

"I'd recognize you anywhere," she said.

"Beth. It's been how long? Ten years? Twelve?"

"About that, I guess. Thanks for calling me."

He shrugged. "No problem. I was out of town when Maude died. She was getting weak, but she'd been around forever. Hard to imagine her gone." He looked at the house, the sweep of the lawn and out at the lake. "I didn't realize you were already here."

"I drove up as soon as I got the messages this morning. Mrs. Langhorne said they had a small graveside service. I wish I'd known in time to be here."

He frowned. His voice was harsh. "How would that happen? Did you stay in touch with anyone except Maude? If I hadn't seen her recently I wouldn't have had your number. You didn't leave a lot of friends behind when you left."

Her face heated up. "Well, I guess you get points for honesty." She turned to go, saying, "Good to see you, Michael." It never failed, did it? Expectations could always be counted on to slingshot right back in your face.

"Sorry." He reached out and brushed her arm. "I didn't come to criticize."

She gave him back silence and a stony look.

"I'd like to start over," he said.

Beth bit her tongue. Anger struggled to vent as if returning here had thrown her back into old habits, back into being that touchy, hot-tempered person she hadn't liked very much. She crossed her arms and stared at the ground.

"Welcome back to Preston, Beth. I wish it was under better circumstances."

Starting over? Is that what he wanted? She eased her tightly clasped arms apart, but then didn't know what to do with her hands. She settled them on her hips.

Michael leaned forward, touched her arm, then eased her left hand toward him and turned it over. "I see an engagement ring."

"Yes." She pulled her hand back and

sidestepped the full truth by shifting the conversation to him. "How about you? Are you married?"

Michael had been her brother's friend and both were older than she. She'd idolized them and they treated her like a nuisance, except for a few sweet moments during the summer when she was fifteen and Michael was eighteen, moments offering more promise than they ever delivered.

He grimaced. "I was engaged a few times, but none of them lasted long enough for a wedding to happen."

"Sorry to hear that."

"I'm not complaining. Even my would-be brides were happy to call it off."

What could she say to that? "Maybe you're destined to be single—an old bachelor."

Michael smiled. "Could be. I'm making a pretty good effort at it."

Warmer feelings filled the space between them and she was glad. She'd blamed him fifteen years ago when Daniel died. Or rather, she blamed Michael for surviving when her brother hadn't. It hadn't been fair to him, but grief knows no logic. And, in the end, he'd let her down, too. All ancient history.

"Would you like a cup of coffee?"

He shook his head. "I can't. I have an appointment."

As they walked up the path together, he stopped and looked at her. "How long will you stay? Will you stay?"

"Stay here? My life is in Fairfax. I can't

manage a house here while living there. Why would I want to?"

"Maybe keep it as a weekend property? It's on the lake."

"I don't see it working for me. I'll sell."

Michael nodded. "You want to get back to your fiancé and your job. Maude said you were working as a project manager at a computer company?"

She deflated suddenly. "A technology firm."

"What about your father?"

Beth tensed. "What about him?"

"Joe's living in the area."

"I'll be done with my business and out of town before he knows I'm here." She hugged her arms again.

He started to speak, then stopped. Instead, he asked, "Do you have a real estate agent?"

"Not yet."

"Ann Mallory knows this area better than anyone."

"Thanks."

"Happy to help." He walked around the side of the house and disappeared.

Goodbye, Michael. Again.

Actually, he looked good. She'd forgotten how deeply blue his eyes were. Beth walked back up the steps and into the house and heard the doorbell ringing. She hurried down the hallway and opened the door expecting to see Michael again.

Mr. Monroe stood on the porch. His dusty sedan was parked in the driveway. He was every bit of eighty-five with curly white eyebrows and sagging jowls, an expatriate from a Normal Rockwell painting. He hugged a large folder with one arm and a cane was hooked over his wrist. His eyelids looked heavy, but Beth didn't doubt his vision was as sharp as ever.

"Hello." She stepped out to the porch. "I guess you got my message?"

"I did. I have Ms. Henry's papers for you. Deed, receipts, and such. You'll want to keep them secure. Look through them. If you have any questions, call or stop by the office." He handed her a dark brown accordion folder about an inch thick, but lumpy. "There's an extra set of house keys and car keys in there."

"Thanks."

"As I wrote in my letter, Miss Maude left a small amount of money in the local bank. She directed me to cash that out at her death to fulfill bequests to the library, church and the Ladies' Auxiliary. I've done that. Her share of the house and lot, along with the contents, were bequeathed to you. The utilities will remain on until the end of the month. If you'll be here beyond that, please have the accounts changed to your name."

"Thanks for bringing these papers over. You sent a letter? I didn't receive it before I left." She hugged the folder. "Mr. Monroe, Maude used to have a lovely set of white wicker furniture on the porch. Do you know what happened to it?"

"A few months past, hoodlums tossed Miss Maude's rattan furniture into the lake."

"That's terrible."

"It's what those rascals do. After a night of floating in the lake, it was a mess. Some of it followed the current and snagged on the Hilliard's dock." Mr. Monroe shook his head. "It was unsightly, but still usable, so she gave it away."

"Did the police find out who did it?"

"Miss Maude made a report, but that was all. She'd grown frail and didn't want trouble."

"Why didn't you call me when Maude got sick? Or did she get sick? I don't even know how she died."

"She just died. Of old age. She was alone. When you reach a certain age, you've outlived most of your friends, and enemies, too. She passed during the night. Martha Boyle came over to pick her up...going to the store, I believe, and when she didn't answer the door, Mrs. Boyle let herself in."

"I see."

"I believe Mrs. Langhorne told you we didn't have a current phone number or address for you, else we would have called sooner. Miss Maude had already made the funeral arrangements, so we proceeded with the service and the interment per her wishes."

She tried to keep her focus squarely on Mr. Monroe. Emotionalism would help no one.

He asked, "Will you be speaking with your father while you're in town?"

Her lips went numb. She bit down on them.

"Consider doing so, Miss Kincaid." His faded eyes held hers for a long moment. He coughed lightly.

Beth stared back, but refused to ask the obvious. Why should Mr. Monroe care about Joe Kincaid? Her relationship with her father was none of his business. Except in a small town, everybody's business was everybody else's.

He nodded and walked to his car.

From her vantage point on the porch, she could see several houses along the road and the hedges and landscaping, but not a soul was in sight. She waved as Mr. Monroe drove away.

In the kitchen, Beth unwound the elastic string securing the brown envelope and slid the papers onto the table. The title to which Maude had added her name five years before was on top. Next were documents pertaining to Maude's guardianship. Daniel's death certificate. Her mother's, too.

Enough for now. Carefully, Beth slid the documents back into the envelope.

She went upstairs and unpacked her suitcase and put the toiletries in the bathroom. When everything was neatly squared in the drawer or lined up on the vanity she made a sandwich for supper.

In the late afternoon, the light wind stilled and the air grew stuffy inside the house. Beth walked out the back door and down the brick path. She passed the gazebo and stood at the lake's edge. The last light of day was soft and the lake breeze was sweet.

A short distance southeast of Maude Henry's shoreline a small point jutted out into the lake so that the boat dock on the point tended to catch whatever got caught in the current, including Maude's wicker furniture.

There was no comfort in memories, not for her. Sentimentality was over-rated. It was of no more use in a rational, real-life present than fairy tales, fantasy, or old romance novels.

A star popped out in the dimming sky. More would soon follow. Beth turned away and walked back to the house. Her car was parked in the driveway so she turned on all of the outside lights. No night-roving juveniles would mistake this for a vacant house.

Teddy was curled into a tight, furry ball on Maude's pillow. Beth didn't disturb him.

In her old room, she sat in the dark at the open window with the cool touch of the breeze on her face listening to the night sounds. She welcomed emotional exhaustion because it left no room for anything else.

Wood creaked in the hallway. A metallic sound came from somewhere in the house.

This was the first time she'd ever slept alone here.

Lots of firsts had happened within the past forty-eight hours, including Michael's return to her life. Thinking of him pushed the old house groans out of her mind, but brought no peace.

Ten years since she'd moved away from Preston. Twelve years since she'd seen Michael.

Twelve years older should mean twelve years smarter. Should.

****

In the morning, something glittered in the

long grass near the gazebo. Beth went outside and found a wine-cooler bottle.

She opened the door to the gazebo. Inside, discarded cans, bottles and squashed cigarette butts littered the floor. This close, the scent of jasmine and the cleansing lake breeze couldn't conceal the stink.

The debris seemed relatively fresh. As Maude had gotten weaker, human rodents had moved in and abused her property.

Her pulse quickened and rose to a low, dull roar in her ears.

Calm down, Bethie, she told herself. It's disgusting, but it can be cleaned up.

Beth dragged one of the large, metal garbage cans from behind Maude's garage and found an old broom. She swept the floor free of the litter.

The gazebo needed a bit of screen tacking, a good sanding and painting, and it would look fabulous framed by the jasmine, the Photinia, and the blue of the sky and the lake. It might make a difference in a tight market.

****

The afternoon was nearly done and when she returned from the bank, the evening stretched ahead of her, quiet and lonely. She searched for Teddy and found him underneath Maude's bed. Hard to miss those orange eyes burning in the dark below.

Suit yourself, Teddy.

Her trip to the bank had been successful. They required an account in order to rent a safety deposit box. She'd close the checking account on her way out of town. In the meantime, the papers were secure. Beth tossed the starter checks into a kitchen drawer.

She was about to put a frozen dinner in the microwave when the phone rang.

"Beth? It's Michael."

Michael?

"Hi. What can I do for you?"

"Thought I'd drop by with some takeout. Preston has a good Chinese restaurant. Opened about six months ago."

"I appreciate the offer, but..." Beth stalled, not sure whether she wanted to make nice with him or not.

"Have you eaten?"

"No, I was about to cook something."

"Well, don't. I'll be over in about thirty minutes."

Beth tossed the defrosting cardboard box back into the freezer and pulled some plates out of the cabinet.

****

"I owe you an apology. You're hardly back in town and there I was, telling you what to do and criticizing. I know you don't have good feelings about Preston, and I can't blame you, but you shouldn't judge a whole town by one man's failings." Michael moved the food containers from the carryout bag to the table.

Beth sat down opposite him. "I don't. I have more than one reason. As for Joe, I don't want to talk about him."

"He's your father."

"No, he's the man who killed my mother." It

cost her to say it bold like that, but pretending was a waste of time.

"That's harsh, Beth."

"Truth can be harsh. The way my mother died was harsh. The accident was only one of the crimes he committed. If not for him, Daniel wouldn't...he wouldn't have made bad choices."

"Daniel and I were teenagers. We did a lot of stupid, dangerous things. It wasn't the first time he drove when he shouldn't have." Michael cracked open a fortune cookie. "I can see you're angry. This is still painful for you."

The words he'd left unsaid were hanging in the air between them, and yes, still painful after all these years. But some things couldn't be gotten over easily and he didn't have the right to tell her otherwise. She busied herself with scraping the last grains of rice from the thin, white container.

"Why did you come here tonight?"

"You have to eat, don't you?" He smiled and gently took the empty container from her to add to the bag of trash.

Beth stabbed a chunk of chicken with her fork. "What's the real reason?"

"You were always the little kid tagging along. The brat. Daniel and I were pretty tough on you. Seeing you again reminded me." Michael sipped his iced tea. "I visited Maude from time to time. She was proud of you."

Not exactly what she'd expected him to say. Was he baiting her?

"Maude understood why I couldn't stay around Preston."

Michael nodded. "You were the closest thing she had to family. She missed you, but she admired your independence. Maude was proud you'd put yourself through college, even while working and supporting yourself, and had a good job."

Beth relaxed. "Maude disrupted her life for a couple of kids she hardly knew. I owe her...everything."

"It was quite a sensation at the time." Michael spoke softly.

"The town's sensation was our real-life nightmare." Maude had driven out to the Kincaid place where the two children waited for their parents to come home. Mom and Dad were overdue. If one could smell change in the air, especially bad change, they did that day.

Beth said, "The day Maude came out to the old place, she told us, 'come with me,' and Daniel asked her, 'Why should we go anywhere with you?' Maude said, 'Because there was an accident. Your mother's dead and your father won't be back for a long time. The sheriff is coming to take you to the County. Best come with me.'"

Michael grimaced, but kept his voice even, "That was a hard way to hear the news."

"Maude was always direct. You always knew exactly where you stood with her. Plain-spoken. She could be kind, but sappy sympathy wasn't her thing."

"Why was she so determined to get the two of you into her care?"

"Maude was at the volunteer fire department

that day with the Ladies' Auxiliary when the call came in about the crash. She'd known our mother and her parents, and wanted to do what she could for us. Not being blood related, Maude figured it was best to take us home and work out the legalities later. We went with her. To avoid the county home, I guess, and because we didn't have anyone else. Between them, Maude and Billy Monroe, they pulled it off and the judge let us stay."

"Never worked with Daniel."

Beth pushed her plate away. "No, it didn't. Would you like more tea? Or soda?"

"I'll get it," he said.

"Daniel was a month short of thirteen. Already wild. He spent a lot of time out at the old house, especially after Joe was released from jail." Beth gathered the rest of the dinner trash and Michael held the bag open. "Boys. Teenage boys, especially. In trouble or making trouble without even trying."

She continued, "I think some kids have been hanging out in Maude's gazebo. Likely the same ones who stole her wicker furniture and tossed it in the lake."

"I didn't know. Sorry to hear Maude had trouble."

"I want to put my car in the garage, but her old car won't start."

"You mean that little Ford?"

"The Escort? No, she sold that several years ago when she gave up driving. I mean her dad's old car."

"The Buick? That thing's built like a tank."

Michael sat back in the chair. "One of the guys on the farm is good with cars, trucks. He can fix anything with an engine. I can have him check it out."

Michael's smile was slightly crooked, one side higher than the other, as if he knew a secret, or so it had always seemed to Beth. She was pleased to see a hint of the boy he'd been, only a little disguised by maturity.

"If the Buick needs much work, I'll sell it for parts. It would be good to have someone I can trust figure it out."

"I'll bring him by tomorrow, if that's okay."

"Great. Thanks. And thanks for recommending Ann Mallory. We've got an appointment scheduled." Michael was coming back tomorrow and idiot that she was, she was happy. She tucked her fingers beneath her thighs to keep them from touching his face, his shoulder.

"Ann'll do a good job for you."

"I don't doubt it."

He left soon after. Beth returned to the kitchen to finish the cleanup and found a thin slip of white paper lying in the middle of the table.

From his fortune cookie.

She picked it up and read it aloud. "Anger begins with folly and ends with regret."

Humph. Did he leave it on purpose? As a message and a dig? She drummed her fingernails on the tabletop.

Her own cookie was still wrapped. She picked it up and tore the cellophane.

"Something you lost will soon turn up." She laughed, tried to stop, then laughed some more. An emotional pressure valve had nudged open and some of the tension around her had eased. She shoved the slips of paper into her pocket.

Despite her original plan to avoid Michael, she was unexpectedly glad to see him. It was ironic. Because he offered help, she might wrap this up all the quicker and leave. She tried to be honest with herself. Some of that old attraction still simmered deep inside. But she could handle it and it was all the more reason to welcome Michael's assistance because the sooner she returned to Fairfax the sooner she could get back to rebuilding her real life.

****

Beth was worried. Teddy had barely nibbled at his food. She stood in the doorway of Maude's bedroom peering into the near dark. No cat lay on the bed.

She went into the room and flipped up the bed skirt. Swiftly, before Teddy could evade her, she grabbed the first body part she touched. He resisted, but Beth gripped harder and pulled him from beneath the bed. His furry body slid along the bare wood.

"Enough moping," Beth said as she snatched him up into her arms. He squirmed, but she held him securely with an arm around his mid-section while she closed the bedroom door. When Beth tried to drop him to the hallway floor, she discovered he'd attached himself to her clothing with his claws.

"Teddy, hold still." Paw by paw, claw by claw, she disengaged him. Her blouse suffered a few pulled threads. Teddy didn't care. He met her eye for eye and meowed loudly showing sharp white teeth.

"I'm not who you want to see? Too bad. You're stuck with me. At least, until I find you a new home."

Teddy howled again and got in one good scratch before Beth released him. He hit the floor lightly on all four padded feet. He darted a few feet away, eyed her with hostility and twitched his tail.

The scratch on her arm had already turned bright pink. Beth rubbed the raised, stinging welt and glared at Teddy. "You might be tough, but watch out. I can handle my feelings for Michael and I can handle the likes of you."

Unimpressed, Teddy padded off down the hallway.

GRACE GREENE

Chapter Three

Michael Fowler stood in the open doorway of
the farm office watching Joe scrape red mud
from the soles of his scuffed work boots. The
blue pickup, dented and scratched, but as
dependable as ever, was parked a few yards
away. Its tire treads, too, were packed with red
clay. The familiar rich smell of earth and
manure was cut by the aroma of fresh coffee.
Joe had been out to check the cattle and now
sat on the weathered porch steps, hunched
over, engrossed in cleaning his shoes. A mug
of hot coffee was steaming near at hand. It was
early yet and the dew still clung to the thick
grass of the pastures, sparkling like fine
crystals in the early morning sun.

Michael had a dilemma.

He'd called Beth about Maude's death
because it was the right thing to do. He hadn't
expected her to rush to Preston and he hadn't
expected to run into her at Maude's yesterday
morning, but it had worked out okay.

In fact, it was good to see her.

Twelve years, ten months. That's how long
since they'd spoken to each other. Of course,
he remembered.

He'd left for Des Moines less than a month
after Daniel's funeral. His parents sent him to
his aunt and uncle because they wanted to
keep him out of more trouble. He stayed there

for his senior year and after that, it was college. His parents even paid for a summer in Europe after his freshman year. By the time he returned to Preston for more than a short holiday, Beth was gone.

He could've called her. They had phones in Iowa, even back then, but...well, it didn't matter now. It was long ago.

Beth wasn't staying. She'd been clear about wanting to sell and leave Preston as soon as possible. Probably for the best.

So, what was the problem? Beth didn't want Maude's property and he did.

Perfect, right? Maybe. His gut told him to step carefully. Some people were exactly as they seemed on the surface. Not Beth. He'd figured that out quick. She might look different, grown up, but her temper hadn't cooled any.

Holdups were expected in any project. Generally, his timing was good and luck usually hung out nearby willing to lend a helping hand. He'd been flipping houses in Roanoke when the real estate market died. Even then, luck had been with him because he'd only been caught with one house unsold. He finished the renovation, found a renter, and came away financially unscathed. But it made him cautious. He was almost relieved when Maude Henry told him she wouldn't sell her property to him. Wouldn't, she'd said, but couldn't even if she wanted to because Beth was part owner. Michael hadn't known that. No one had, except maybe Mr. Monroe, as Maude's attorney, and Billy Monroe knew how to keep private business private.

Maude had offered him Beth's phone number. He'd stuck the square of paper under a magnet on the fridge.

Seeing Beth stride across the yard to meet him at the lake side had given him a jolt. She'd been a teenager the last time he'd seen her. The scrawny kid had filled out. Back then, her hair was what everyone noticed if they could get past her temper. Or maybe it was because of her temper. Redheads were assumed to be hot-tempered, right?

One thing was true, for sure—shared childhood memories weren't always sweet.

Beth had held a grudge against him after Daniel died, but she'd been a kid with a lot on her plate. He hoped taking supper to her had gone a long way to smoothing things over, but if Beth knew who sat a few feet away from him now, sipping coffee and scraping red mud from the bottom of his work boots with a stick, she'd refuse any offer outright. In fact, the door she'd slam in his face would probably rattle the Richter scale and he couldn't blame her.

Considered objectively, for instance, as if they'd met for the first time yesterday, she was gorgeous. Too gorgeous. Hard to trust a woman that beautiful. But sharing a meal or two wouldn't require trust.

He hung a thumb in his belt and savored a long sip of coffee.

Just as well she was engaged.

Mix that hair, those dark eyes and perfect lips with her temper and their history and you got more trouble than he was willing to take on.

He owed her something, though. Not officially or anything. That last, brief meeting at the cemetery more than twelve years ago hadn't been good for anyone.

Maybe he owed her for old times' sake.

Joe looked up, "Boss?"

"Doing okay?"

He grunted and nodded. "Good."

Michael could see Joe was waiting, expecting him to say something more, but he didn't know where to go with it. In the years Michael had known Joe Kincaid, at least since Michael had been an adult, Joe always seemed tightly held within himself, but he was a good worker. Not exactly happy in his work, he always looked wrinkled and grim, but never complained. He worked. He ate. He slept. Not much else. Michael suspected he didn't trust himself enough to relax and have fun.

They'd released Joe from jail eighteen months after the accident that killed his wife. Joe had fallen off the wagon a few times since he'd come to work for Michael's dad, but not in recent years.

He settled for asking, "How's that fencing going?"

"Started the section down by the creek. It's soft there. Needs to dry out." Joe scratched the peppery gray unshaved stubble on his face.

Michael leaned against the door lintel and crossed one booted foot with the other as he chewed on some thoughts. For old time's sake, and in memory of his friend Daniel, Michael owed Beth what help he could give her. And Joe, too. He pushed away from the door frame and stepped out onto the porch.

"Joe, could you fix up the old shed in the north field? We could use secure storage out there."

Joe nodded without looking around. "Can do, boss."

"Take a few days, you think?"

"Probably."

And that, Michael hoped, would keep Joe out of town and out of Beth's way until he figured out what to do—what was best for everyone.

Chapter Four

Ann Mallory had big blonde hair sprayed to hold its shape. She swept into the house already talking.

"I've got the county records right here. Lot size. Tax assessment for lot and structures. A few comps of recent sales, well, relatively recent sales. I already looked around outside. Now, I'd like to take a closer look inside the house. After, we'll sit down and talk about numbers and reality. Sound good?"

Ann led the tour.

"Actually, you've got an interesting house here. You know how it goes? Everything old is new again? Well, these mail order houses are back in vogue. Restoration and all that."

"Mail order houses?"

"This house. Bought out of a Sears Catalog. Not surprised you don't know. Ms. Henry's house, with one quiet-living maiden lady all alone—we can call it mint condition.

"You have a great lot here. Nice-sized and private, backing up to the lake. Heck of a view. No promises, but developers appear interested in converting the old mill area into something big that will boost values from the park to the town to the lake properties—which is what you have here. So, someone might be interested in your house for restoration, or someone might want to buy your lot and replace the house with something more upscale."

"What's the real estate market like in Preston?"

"Slow overall, but the houses that do move, move quickly. Thirty to sixty days."

"What's this?" Ann's hand rested on the door knob to the small room off the vestibule. "It's locked."

"Locked? Let me try." It wouldn't budge. "Maude called it the music room, but she used it for storage. It's small. If I can't find the key, I'll get a locksmith."

They discussed price and commission. In the end, it was an obvious decision and she signed the contract.

Teddy came out to greet Ann. He tried to wrap himself around her ankles and invited her to scratch his head.

Ann Mallory's high-energy optimism was exciting, but the reference to a quick sale being thirty to sixty days was a concern. Beth had hoped for a faster turnover. She waved goodbye to Ann and headed upstairs.

Mail order houses. Beth knew about Craftsman homes, but she'd never heard of 'Honor Bilt.' Ann had educated her. Sears had marketed a wide variety of home designs by catalog from about 1910 to 1940, offering blueprints, pre-cut lumber, hardware—the works—sent by train. The cost savings made home ownership possible for ordinary people.

In Maude's room, in the top dresser drawer, next to Maude's worn Bible, Beth found a small box with her name on it. The neat, cramped, slight shaky printing on the lid of the box read, "Keys for Beth." Maude had known Beth would look here for the spare keys.

The most prominent items in the music room were a coat rack on wheels with a couple of coats hanging from it and the upright piano. Several boxes were stacked along the front wall below the one window.

The topmost box was labeled, "For Beth."

She stood silently, her hands resting on top of the box. Maude had been a genteel, gentle woman. Never married, she'd dedicated her life to her parents, to her community, and when she should have rested from her good works, she'd given two troubled kids a home.

For Beth.

Maude had deliberately locked this room and put the key where Beth would find it, and find these cardboard boxes, too, undisturbed by anyone else, even the well-intentioned.

Beth lifted the lid from the top-most box. Inside was a framed photographic portrait of a man and woman, Maude's parents. Beth remembered seeing it on an end table in the living room. The woman's tight curls belonged to an earlier age, the Roaring Twenties. Mr. and Mrs. Henry. The people who built this house. There was another photograph of Maude standing behind a store counter next to her father. He'd owned a dry goods and seed store.

She set the pictures atop the piano and took the next items from the box. A marriage certificate. Death certificates. Maude's birth certificate. All were yellowed and stiff with age. A few slight tears marred the edges.

Beneath the certificates was an assortment of softer, dearer items. A pair of women's gloves, obviously worn, as if someone had removed them upon entering the home and never had the opportunity to put them on again. Maude's mother? Beth put the gloves to her face and smelled the least trace of scent of some long ago fragrance. There was also a delicate lace christening gown with yellowed folds, and a man's wool bowler hat.

She might have to re-think Maude's lack of sentimentality.

Beth moved the second box to the piano bench and lifted the lid.

Layered inside were photographs and certificates. A diploma. A business license. A black and white photo of a young woman posing on the front porch was in a brown, embossed cardboard folder. In another photo, the same young woman posed with an older couple on the front lawn with the house in the background. Maude with her parents.

The certificates and photos were fragile. Beth put them back into the box and replaced the top. She'd look at the third box later. For now, she'd had enough of Maude's version of a stroll down memory lane.

Another box sat in the corner half-hidden by the clothes rack and on top of a pink cat carrier. The box was filled with books. Beth shuffled through them and saw a Victoria Holt, a Phyllis Whitney, and others. Most of the books were gothic romances or romantic suspense, the old-fashioned kind, by one author, Madeline Flewellyn. They wore colorful book jackets showing distressed damsels like the one in her bookcase. In fact, Beth recognized the cover of *Clarissa's Folly*. She picked it up and flipped through the pages. This copy was well-read. The one Maude had given her, had been almost untouched.

Beth skimmed the first paragraph.

The coach rattled her teeth and shook her hair loose from its pins as the wheels found every rock and root in the old, rutted road leading to the town of Woolridge. Clarissa Parrish was certain the driver was cursing amidst the louder calls to the horses to mind their paces. She tried, but could not divine his words over the noise, yet the abuse in his voice left no doubt in her mind that she should cover her ears. She waved her handkerchief delicately in front of her face to combat the dust that hung in the air in the coach interior. She felt flushed, discomforted by the driver's rude behavior and the annoyances of travel, but also because the man sitting opposite stared at her almost constantly.

Right. Sheltered heroine meets handsome rake.

Fluffy and unrealistic. Romanticized settings and relationships. Nothing pertinent to real life. Beth dropped the book back into the box.

****

Michael introduced Beth to Sam Purchase. The raised hood of the Buick hid most of Sam's top half. Only a skinny butt and long legs clad in blue work clothes were visible. The car had been rolled out of the garage. Red and black cables were strung to an old, idling truck and the exhaust fouled the air.

"Battery's dead. Sam's trying to charge it before we look at replacing it." Michael shook his head. "It's an old car. You can count on other parts breaking sooner or later. This car is a classic, but 'classics' are expensive to maintain."

"Yep." Sam's voice scratched like sandpaper.

The sound was unexpected. It startled Beth. Michael looked amused.

"It's old, but Maude took it out every so often to ride up the street and back again. The tires are only a few years old."

Again, the gravelly voice. "Try it."

Michael sat behind the steering wheel and turned the key, pumping the gas. The engine turned over and caught.

"Running. Almost purring," he said, gripping the old leather steering wheel cover. "Frankly, I'm impressed."

"For now," Sam added, stepping away from the cover of the hood. Black grease coated his fingers.

Beth gave him a quick smile and a wave. "Do you know of anyone around here who might be interested in buying it? For parts, maybe."

Sam shook his head, "Oh, no ma'am. Not for parts, not this one."

Michael trailed his fingers along the smooth, light aqua bumper. "I'll ask around. Before we turn this off, maybe we should take it for a ride. Want to come along?"

Her physical response was immediate. Her feet moved forward taking her heart with it.

"Hold up," Sam warned.

As if she'd been corrected, her face flushed hot and she touched her warm cheeks.

Michael looked at Sam, disappointed. "You sure?"

Sam picked up a wrench and the remains of a hose from the dirt. "Had to rig some of it. Rodents get into it, though this one was in good shape, so to speak. I'll be back in a few days to finish up." He added with a grin, "You can take a ride if you want. Straight back into the garage."

Michael walked around to the passenger side and opened the door.

"After you, ma'am."

She laughed. "Yes, sir."

He closed the door after she climbed in, then went around to the other side and sat behind the wheel. He leaned toward her saying, "I always had a secret wish to drive this car."

Momentarily, she was stilled by his nearness, his scent, his blue eyes. She shook herself, covering the awkwardness with a laugh.

"Now's your chance. Do you think Maude's watching?"

Michael looked up at the roof of the car, chuckled, and then turned toward Beth.

Her eyes fastened on his smile and her lips irresistibly mimicked the curve of his.

He said, "Miss Maude, if you're looking down, no worries. Trust me, I've got this."

Chapter Five

In the night, noises woke her. She lay rigid in the bed, listening.

Maybe a voice? A creak?

Beth reached for her cell phone on the nightstand, but touched only the smooth, flat surface of the furniture. The phone wasn't there. She must've left it charging in the kitchen.

Nothing in the bedroom would work as a weapon. Maybe the lamp, but to unplug it she'd have to move furniture. Beth eased out of bed carefully and tiptoed into the hallway.

Soft laughter and low voices. Distant. Muffled. Maybe from the backyard?

Beth stepped lightly across the bedroom at the rear of the house and looked out of the window. Her eyes were night-sharpened. Moonlight illuminated the open areas of the yard and the shore area, but the deeper shadows of the oaks concealed the gazebo. The spotlight by the back door covered a fair-sized area of the back yard, but not as far back as the gazebo—when the light was lit, that is. Tonight, the spotlight wasn't burning.

She'd forgotten to bring her phone upstairs with her. Had she missed turning on the spotlight?

Teddy's eyes glowed orange in the dark.

After a brief startle, Beth moved on. She was wearing cotton pajama pants and a t-shirt, so she didn't pause for a robe. Beth didn't think anyone was in the house with her, but if they were she wasn't going to be trapped upstairs.

She ran straight to the kitchen, grabbed the phone and checked the light switch almost in one motion. The switch was on, but not the light. Burned out? No, too much coincidence. She peered through the window, into the dark. She saw nothing, but heard low, unintelligible voices and saw the rise and fall of a tiny bright spot, maybe a cigarette, barely and briefly there.

Unacceptable.

Beth paused with her hand on the door knob.

Those were strangers out there. Maybe kids, maybe not. Instead, she pressed the speed dial for the sheriff's office and told the operator that strangers were in her back yard.

Within a few minutes cruiser headlights lit the night as the deputy pulled into the driveway. It was enough to send the kids, if that's what they were, scurrying. Beth walked outside to meet him. The deputy shone his flashlight up at the spotlight saying, "Bold, that's what I call it."

The bulb was shattered. No accident there.

Following the beam of his flashlight, they walked out to the gazebo and found a few new butts and spilled liquid.

"Miss Kincaid, it looks pretty straightforward. Probably some teenagers made this a hangout. That broken bulb concerns me, but it's likely an expression of resentment. Not against you directly, but what I mean is you're claiming territory they decided was theirs."

"What should I do?"

"I expect this is enough to run them off. They'll look elsewhere. You haven't had any run-ins with anyone, have you?"

"No, not at all." The damp grass chilled her feet. It was itchy.

"We have a couple of gang-wanna-be's in the area, but most of the teenagers around here are harmless." He shone his flashlight on the damaged light. "That bulb is easy to replace, but also easily disabled. Consider installing a spotlight near one of the upstairs windows. You can reach it to change the bulb, but it isn't so accessible outside of the house."

They walked back to the deputy's car. "I'll write up the report. No worries. Call in if you have more trouble."

Beth watched him drive away. What the deputy said rang true. They wanted to be private, but privacy wasn't going to be available at Maude's gazebo any longer. She was here now and the gazebo hangout was officially closed.

****

Ann Mallory's fix-it man showed up mid-morning to work on the gazebo. They discussed what he'd do and how much pay he'd want, then she went back inside and called Celeste to check on the mail and apartment. Celeste didn't answer the home phone, so she left a voicemail.

She wandered throughout the ground floor. The kitchen was old-fashioned, but had been updated several times since the house was built in 1926. Maude had a laundry installed in the pantry next to the kitchen years ago. There was only one bathroom and it was upstairs. Dining room, living room and back to the hallway. Pretty basic.

Beth opened the music room door. She returned to the second box and took another look at the contents. The papers smelled of age. They were dry and fragile. She gathered the loose photos of Maude and of Mr. and Mrs. Henry from the box.

That a message was intended for her, she had no doubt, but what? Maude had tried for years to break down her protective shell, but Beth had been hurt enough as a child. She'd never allow herself to be so vulnerable again.

Teddy jumped up onto the piano bench and meowed, then settled back on his haunches. Her cell phone rang, the noise filling the small room. "Hello?"

"Beth, it's Celeste. Got your message. I had to leave the day after you did. Got called out of town unexpectedly. Family emergency."

"I hope everyone's okay."

"My brother had a mild heart attack. He'll be fine, but I'll be gone a week or two. Before I left I saw Stephen coming out of your apartment. He offered to get your mail and check on things so I gave him your mailbox key. He said he couldn't find his."

Beth almost contradicted Celeste then

realized it was pointless. "Thanks. I hope all goes well with your brother."

He couldn't have lost his mailbox key because he'd never had one. She was annoyed Celeste had given it to him. A simple misunderstanding, but it bothered her. Maybe she should've stopped the postal delivery, but for only a few days? And it was always a hassle to get it going again. She'd planned to ask Celeste to overnight her mail. Now what?

Stephen was showing a devious streak Beth had never expected. It didn't matter. In her heart and mind, they were no longer a couple. The next time she spoke with him, she wanted it to be in person. She owed him that much. Beth didn't think either of them would be all that broken-hearted once it was done.

How long had she been living this tepid life? No intensity. No color. No passion.

She'd been living her life in shades of gray. Time to redecorate.

Beth stepped out the back door and walked down to the lake, seeking the soft touch of the breeze. The dock was in disrepair. Not derelict, but badly in need of tender loving care. The nearby shed stored the old rowboat. The lock had rusted through a long time ago. A sorry-looking rowboat occupied one corner, propped at an angle against the wall.

The distant shore was heavily-treed with homes peeking out in the cleared areas. Most of the docks had some sort of boathouse attached, some fancy. In the middle of the lake a small boat rocked gently. Looked like a couple of fishermen catching dinner.

The Photinia hedge rose full and tall on either side of the yard. Trees provided additional screening. The gazebo had its uses, but a bench would be nice in this spot, right up close to the lake. Maybe while she had this last opportunity to enjoy it.

This little piece of Preston didn't seem so bad. In fact, she loved the lake. At least, this side of it.

"Excuse me. Have you seen James?"

Beth jumped. "Mrs. Boyle?"

"You're looking well, Beth."

"Thanks. I haven't seen him today. He seems like a nice boy."

Mrs. Boyle's face relaxed. Her lips curved into the tiniest of smiles. "Do you think so? He's not always as considerate as he should be, but he's a sweet child at heart."

Since Mrs. Boyle seemed almost friendly, Beth took it a step further. "I understand you found Maude. I'm sorry I couldn't be around for her."

"Couldn't you?"

"There were reasons."

"Yes, I know those reasons." Martha Boyle sounded as though she didn't think the reasons were sufficient to warrant an absence. She turned to leave.

"Thank you."

She looked back. "For what?"

"For helping Maude. You were neighbors for many years and you don't need my thanks, but thanks anyway."

She nodded. "You're welcome." She walked away, across the grass toward her house.

"One more thing?" Beth caught up with her. "Do you know about teens hanging around Maude's property? They trashed the gazebo. I don't want them coming back."

Martha Boyle stood silently for a moment before saying, "I don't know. It's been my experience teenagers usually know what other teenagers are up to."

"The only teen I know around here is the Hilliard's son."

"Well, I don't believe Tim is a trouble-maker, but you can ask him yourself. The direct approach is the best." She paused and seemed to consider her next words carefully. "You should know there's been trouble in recent years with vandalism. Some of it with people who don't live on the lake. They park on the road and walk right through our yards for lake access. Did you notice the no parking signs?"

"I did."

"Between the vandals and the trespassers traipsing through our yards, there's sensitivity around here to strangers. Keep things shut up or locked up, especially at night. And be careful about parking on the street. Some of these folks get tow-happy."

"Okay, thanks for the warning."

Beth was almost glad not to know who it was. She didn't trust her temper in stressful situations, especially when her defenses were down.

She enjoyed project management. There

were preferred ways to manage. The methodology was carefully studied, clearly detailed, and everyone operated using the same sets of rules.

Stress due to a project delay was not a problem because it could be anticipated. Flexibility and contingency planning could resolve glitches smoothly. Personality issues weren't a problem because she'd always assembled her teams carefully, hand-picked for optimal results.

Real life wasn't like that. In the real world, people were unpredictable and that was a certainty.

****

It was quiet in the house, so quiet the inevitable house-settling noises put her on edge. Beth fidgeted with Maude's old TV, but it wouldn't do more than show her a noisy no-reception blizzard. She remembered the box of books in the music room. In an entertainment pinch they might do. There was also the library.

Beth reviewed the list in her head, like needing to pack up Maude's odds and ends. There wasn't much. Someone had already done a fair amount of clearing out.

The house would show better with the furniture in place, so shouldn't she wait before disposing of furnishings? She was hostage to the sale of the house.

Teddy was on the stairwell landing stretched out on his back in a patch of sun. He rotated his head around into an almost impossible position so that he was looking at Beth upside down.

It didn't look like the posture of a still-grieving kitty. That, at least, was progress.

****

In the morning, Ann Mallory called. "I've got a prospective buyer. Is now a good time?"

"Sure. Come on over. I'll run an errand." Beth shoved Teddy into the cat carrier. He fought her, spreading his four limbs wide so as not to fit through the carrier door. Finally, in the car, he yowled continuously until he beat her down. She unlatched the wire door. Freed, he roamed the interior of the car, sniffing. A low growling rumbled far down in his throat. He seemed to take each turn of the car, each stop and start, as a potential threat. It was unsettling.

They passed thirty minutes driving around in wasted, nerve-scratching aggravation and when they returned to Lake Avenue, Ann's car was still parked in the driveway. Beth kept going, turned around further down the street, and then parked. Teddy calmed down immediately. He flopped down on the passenger seat, purred and started grooming his tail.

The man and woman who exited with Ann were well-dressed and polished and didn't look like a couple who would happily set up housekeeping in Maude's house. If instinct was worth anything, she didn't think there'd be an offer.

As soon as the lookers had driven around the corner, Beth and Teddy were back in the driveway and inside the house. He sniffed his way throughout the ground floor like a kitty bloodhound.

There was no Internet at Maude's house and insufficient justification for the expense of a network card, so Beth drove to the library to use the public computers. The Preston Library looked more prosperous than she remembered. The librarian had known Maude well. She mentioned Maude's generosity and helped Beth get set up on a desktop unit. Beth logged into her email account and picked through the inbox. It was mostly spam, but a couple of emails came from co-workers.

Correction: former co-workers.

She sent out a few queries to employment agencies and left it at that.

Michael called in the early afternoon and invited her out to dinner. She hesitated. He was the closest thing Beth had to a friend in Preston. What could it hurt?

"Casual, I hope? I didn't bring many outfits."

"Jeans are fine."

Before he arrived, he called again. "Come out the back way through the Boyle's yard. Martha lets me use her boat dock."

"Boat?"

"We'll go straight across the lake."

"The lake?" The low sound of a motor and the background noise of wind hummed through the phone receiver.

"You're okay with going by boat, right?"

"Yeah, it's fine. Where are we going?" She wasn't familiar with any lakefront restaurants.

"It's a surprise, but I promise you a great chef. Unforgettable, in fact."

Beth exited by way of the back door. There was no sign of Michael, but then there wouldn't be if he was over at Mrs. Boyle's dock. She ducked through the slight opening in the Photinia hedge, the same one James had used. A branch snagged her hair. She cast a quick glance toward the Boyle's house, feeling like a kid again, then over at the lake and saw Michael.

He stood on the dock, wrapping a rope around a piling. He looked up as she approached.

"Ever worked as a sailor?"

"No. When did the Fowler's join the boating set?" Beth walked the dock inspecting the boat. The driver's seat was well back with seating fore and aft. "As I recall, your father owned a rowboat for fishing. Said he didn't have time for water-skiing and party boats."

He held out his hand to assist her. She stepped down into the boat feeling lighter than light. Because a man offered assistance? Or because the man was Michael? Nonsense.

As she reached the floor of the boat, she asked, "Is your mom doing the cooking?"

He groaned. "Are you asking if I live with my parents?" He pointed to one of the pilings. "Untie that rope while I get this one and we'll be on our way."

They made it away from the dock and out onto the lake. The acrid smell of exhaust blew away behind them. Beth settled into the seat nearest Michael. The windshield blocked the worst of the wind, but brisk snippets of air touched her like little gifts and the outboard motor hummed.

"Enjoy the ride. Coming back, it'll be dark and we'll go by road."

"You should've told me we were eating at the farmhouse. I could've driven myself and saved you the trip."

"Would you have come?"

She changed the subject. "So, you're a good cook?"

"No false modesty here."

As they neared the north end of the lake, they passed what used to be the Kincaid property to the right. Grasses and saplings grew wild and unkempt shielding the land from view. The only thing that marked it as a place where people used to live was the ramshackle wooden dock. She turned away and held the words inside.

Michael's truck was parked at the public boat ramp. "No dock. I have to haul it back with us. The Fowler property doesn't actually touch the lakefront."

"Do you use the lake a lot?"

"No, too many other things to do. Guess a boathouse and dock wouldn't make much sense, anyway. Maybe that's why I never did anything about it."

They drove down the narrow paved road. Beth looked straight ahead and tried to relax her grip on the door handle. The past was too near here. She breathed more easily when they turned left onto the Fowler's private road and left all sight of the land she'd lived on as a child.

Michael parked in front of the house. "Go on in. I'll be along. I'm going to unhitch the boat trailer while the light's good."

"I can help."

"Nothing for you to do. Go ahead in." Michael ushered her in through the front door and into the living room then he went back outside.

The room was little changed since she'd last been in this house. How long ago? Maybe thirteen years? More?

Beth paused by the sofa. The same sofa. She fingered the colorful, handmade Afghan folded across the back. Same Afghan. Was this some sort of time warp?

True to his word, Michael returned quickly. Beth gave him a long look. He paid no attention to her stare, but moved straight into the kitchen. The pots and pans clattered as he went to work.

Michael could cook. The kitchen was every inch a farm kitchen, big, airy and bright. The appliances looked updated, at least.

"I remember you complaining about parents, muddy fields and farm work. Did you change your mind?" Beth moved a stool near to the counter. "If you need any help, let me know. You've already set the table."

"It's all under control." Michael bounced the rotini in the colander, then set it aside while he added seasoning to the white sauce. "Dad had a minor stroke several years ago. He recovered, but they took it as a sign it was time to retire."

"I'm surprised they left."

"It was harder for them to leave their friends and church family than this place, but Mom said they weren't too old to get settled in a new church and they could always use more friends. They bought a condo in Roanoke and travel from time to time. Took a cruise to the Bahamas last year. They're doing well."

She enjoyed watching him move about the kitchen. He wore his cotton shirt and jeans well. His black hair was short, yet just long enough to appear artfully ruffled. She touched her own hair, smoothing curls back behind an ear.

"What about the farm and you? I thought you wanted to get out into the world, escape the pastures and cows?"

The smell of chicken cooking, the sauce, and rolls in the oven, seemed to mingle with generations of meals, but not stale. No, it was more the layered scents of years of happy meals around the family table.

Beth had envied him that so long ago, both the home-loving mom and the responsible, reliable dad. Michael had had it all. Memories fired up a warm rush, sending heat coursing through her chest and limbs. She rubbed her arms.

"You cold?"

"No, I'm good." She repositioned the salt and pepper shakers.

"Let me know. It's an old house. Gets drafty sometimes." He continued, "I wanted out when I was teenager, you're right about that. Sometimes I leave, but I always come back. Home, you know? Single family farms aren't always self-supporting. Too many variables. But I do alright here. Well enough for me to keep a few hands around. That frees me up to engage in other ventures from time to time that help fund the farm."

"Ventures?"

"When the real estate market was hot, I flipped some houses. Hard work, but I picked up some nice cash."

"I've seen shows about flipping on TV. Always fascinating. Speaking of old houses, did you know that Maude's house was ordered from a catalog?"

Michael brought the pasta and the braised chicken over to the table. "What?"

"Yes, Sears sold them during the first half of the 1900s."

Michael nodded. "Of course, yes. Like the Craftsman homes on the west coast. Victorian houses were popular, still are, but they've gotten harder to find."

"I was at the library today to use their Internet and I was amazed at the information on the Web about these houses. There's a whole world of mail order house enthusiasts online. I've seen houses every day of my life that I never realized came from a Sears catalog."

"Library Internet? Maude's house isn't wired, but there are other ways to get online. At the least, you could get dial-up service or a network card."

"Unnecessary expense. I won't be here that long."

He walked to the counter and returned with

a bottle of white wine. She put her hand over her wineglass.

"No?" he asked.

"No, but please enjoy it yourself."

He sat down at the table. "Do you…are you…?"

"No, I don't have a drinking problem. I just don't drink alcohol. It's a personal choice."

"Not surprising, I guess, after your childhood."

"Water or tea will suit me fine."

There were a few minutes of awkward silence. It threw people off a bit when she opted out of alcohol. She tossed out a little distraction to help the moment pass.

"It's number 227."

He looked confused. Beth laughed.

"The house. Maude's house. Catalog number 227. The Castleton."

Michael shook his head. "You're something else. You were a crazy kid, but you've grown up okay, Daniel's little sis."

"Not too bad yourself."

"I'm surprised, though," he said.

"About what?"

"That you'd be interested in the architecture of Maude's house."

"I wasn't. Ann Mallory told me about it."

"What about your work? How long are you able to stay here?"

Beth chewed the pasta slowly to buy time to think. Finally, she said, "A few more days. I have some flexibility." Not quite a lie.

"Project management, right?"

"Yes."

"No offense, but I never would've pegged you for project management."

"Why? What's wrong with it?"

"Nothing's wrong with it. You were always so energetic, so expressive. Dramatic, that's the word. I always figured you'd go into theatre, or law, you know, like a Perry Mason or something."

"You might be surprised. Project management has its own brand of excitement."

"Sure."

"No, I mean it."

"Of course." He shrugged. "So, when's the date?"

Beth frowned. "Date?"

Michael pointed at her hand. "The wedding."

"Oh. We haven't set the date yet."

"No?"

"Sometime in the fall, maybe." Stephen deserved to be told their engagement was over before anyone else. Michael was making polite conversation. He didn't need or want to know her personal business.

"I'll help you clean the kitchen."

"I accept your offer."

Michael was a neat cook and the dishes were cleared away in no time. She folded the dish towel neatly and hung it over the rack on the under-sink cabinet door.

"I had a lovely time. Thanks for inviting me and for cooking and everything."

"You sound like you're ready to leave. No need to rush off."

"I should go back now." Beth didn't know what to say to him now that the meal was over. Their dinner conversation had covered all of the safe topics. The only thing left in common was Daniel and their childhood and she didn't want to discuss either.

The ride back along the winding road that followed the curve of the lake was a lot slower than the boat, especially after dark and being careful of deer straying onto the road. Every so often there was a glimpse of moonlit water or house lights, but mostly, it was just trees. And more trees. Beth sat quietly in the passenger seat, content to share a friendly silence as she watched reflections from the moon and the dashboard play across his profile or along his fingers gripping the steering wheel.

"You okay?" he asked.

"Fine. Sorry for staring. I was watching the night. I'd forgotten how quiet it is out here."

Before they reached Maude's street, she said, "Do me a favor? When we get to the corner, stop. I'll walk the rest of the way. I turned the spotlight on in the back yard before I left. I want to see if it's still on without giving us away."

"The problem with the kids hanging out in the gazebo?"

"Yes."

"Keep the outside lights on after dark. That should be enough to keep them away."

"They came back two nights ago and busted the light over the back door. I hope it was a goodbye gift. If so, then that's that. Also, I'm paying to have the gazebo fixed. I don't want the repairs messed up."

In the eerie glow cast by the dashboard, Beth saw his jaw muscle tightened.

"We'll take a look," he said.

Before he turned the corner, Michael cut the headlights. The full moon lit the way as he drove forward very slowly. He pulled over to the side of the road still a couple of houses up from Maude's.

He said, "I'll walk down."

"What? Not without me."

"Let's go, then." Michael leaned forward and reached under the car seat. He held up a long-barreled, metal flashlight. "In case we need it."

The night-drenched landscape felt otherworldly, but not unbeautiful. The air was chilly and it was too early in spring for the noisier insects to be humming, but there was a sense of life stirring—welcome life. Yet also a sense that, in this dark world, the rules of daytime did not apply.

The back door light was burning. Michael held out a hand and gently touched her arm, warning her to stay still. They stood and listened and watched the dark. No trespassers. Only the two of them disturbed the night.

"Maybe they've moved on." Beth sighed.

He laughed, but so low and soft she wasn't sure she'd him heard correctly.

She asked, "What?"

"You sound disappointed."

"That was relief you heard, not disappointment."

"You were always ready for a fight when you were a kid."

"When I was a kid? What about when you were a kid? You weren't shy about getting into trouble."

As a light wind tossed the trees and the dark boughs fluttered, Michael touched her arm, then left her. He crossed the open area of the back yard, past the lit area, and disappeared into the deeper shadows beyond the gazebo.

Beth followed and stood beside him. The lapping of water against the rock wall was rhythmic and the moonlight echoed in ripples across the changing surface.

Michael spoke. "I understand why they liked this place."

He stared at the lake and she stared at him. In the low, reflected light, he looked like a stranger. She felt apart from the world, separate from history and obligations—two strangers sharing a moment.

Michael reached out and touched her face. When he pulled her into his arms, she didn't resist. It was a different kiss from the one he stole when she was fifteen. Their lips were the same, but now with experience in them. Happiness surged through her, sweeping away doubt and fueling passion. Her arms went around his neck and when her knees weakened, he held her more tightly. As his lips slid away from hers and found her throat, sanity returned.

Stephen. Her fiancé. She heard the words as if whispered in her ear. This kiss, too, was stolen.

But not from her. From Stephen?

She rejected that thought with an angry moan which Michael misunderstood. He tightened his arms, but she turned her face away and pushed at his chest and arms until she had his attention.

He drew back, frowning.

"Thanks for dinner...for everything." She slipped from his arms and tried to walk away casually to hide her trembling. She stopped on the porch and looked back at Michael. He still stood by the lake, staring in her direction.

If he'd taken one step toward her or had even extended his arms, she would've been right back there where she'd wanted to be so long ago, and still wanted to be, apparently.

But this interlude didn't fit with the life she'd built in Fairfax and to which she would return. She needed to wrap this moment up and tuck it back into a box, a strong box with a secure lid, before it became dangerous. But she feared it was too late.

Michael didn't move. In the shadows, she couldn't read his expression. She could only see the fists on his hips that betrayed dissatisfaction. She ran fingers through her hair, then touched her arms, her thighs. She didn't know what to do with her hands. Suddenly overwhelmed by an embarrassing need to giggle, she curled her fingers together into one big fist and pressed it to her lips. When she was back in control, she unwound her fingers and pulled the house key from her pocket.

Quickly, she turned away to unlock the kitchen door and slip inside. She closed the door and leaned back against it.

Teddy met her, meowing and wrapping his body in and around her ankles. His appetite was back.

She bent and picked him up, her fingers disappearing into his thick fur. She touched her chin to the top of his head, her heart still pounding. She cradled him in one arm as she pulled a can of cat food from the cabinet and the sight of the can set him to squirming and meowing. Beth dropped him to the floor and spooned the food into the bowl.

"Then and now, Michael is one big contradiction, Teddy. And more trouble than he's worth. Maybe. At least you're clear about what you want. And easy to please."

****

In the morning, through the kitchen window, Beth saw the shed door hanging open at an awkward angle. No doubt about it, the gazebo boys had visited again.

She found a surprise on the back porch— Michael's flashlight. It sat on the porch near the wall. Beth picked it up and hefted it, amazed by the solid feel. It was heavy and a foot and a half long. The brand read, "Maglite." He'd left it behind for her. Definitely a guy kind of gift. She put it in the kitchen next to the door, then strode across the grass to the shed.

The weathered building was camouflaged by the shade of the oaks. The rowboat now lay behind the shed, half over the rocks. Beth dragged it back closer to the shed. If those boys had planned to go sailing in this decrepit boat, then they'd better be good swimmers.

There was no point in struggling to put it back in the shed. The door was so wobbly that forcing it would likely rip it from its hinges. She'd ask Ann's fix-it man to haul the boat away before someone got into real trouble in it.

Did they come before or after she and Michael had kissed by the lake? She touched her lips. They tingled in remembrance.

"Hello there! Got some news."

Ann Mallory crossed the back yard in quick strides. Beth took her fingers from her lips and waved at Ann.

"Hi. I saw the couple you were here with yesterday. Any interest?"

"Maybe, maybe not. I think they have that potential development project in mind."

Her sneakers were at odds with her skirt and suit jacket, but sensible. As she got closer, her voice dropped to a softer level. "I talked to Mr. Markland, the man running the project. Someone contacted him about your property."

"What do you mean? Contacted him?"

"Someone suggesting they could broker a deal."

Beth frowned. "I don't understand."

"Were you working with someone before you contacted me?"

"No. Remember, I came into this late. Didn't even know about it when I arrived. Did he mention a name?"

Ann stared at her in close scrutiny. She seemed satisfied by what she saw in Beth's face.

"No, he wasn't sharing names. He might've been saying it to improve his bargaining position."

"I suppose that's possible. What's the development about anyway? What's being planned?"

"The details are being held pretty close, but the main area is supposed to be around the old mill. The interest around this side of the lake is secondary. Not really part of the development as I understand it, but expected to develop later."

"Into what? Homes or condos? Hotel? What kind of developer would be interested in Preston?" She shook her head in disbelief. It was hard to imagine who would consider Preston a potential growth location. She and Ann had begun drifting back around the side of the house, heading toward the front yard.

"I don't know, but I think it has something to do with tourism. Could inject energy and funds into the whole area. It sounds that big." Ann held up her hand in caution, "But remember, it's not settled yet. Preston is only one of the locations being considered." She stopped beside her car. "Let me know if anyone comes to you talking business. People can be devious when they smell money."

Ann's manner had warmed up again. Beth was disturbed. This seemed a lot of to-do over the sale of one old house.

"Thanks, Ann. I'll keep you posted. Please do the same for me."

"How much longer will you be in town? You don't have to stay here 'til it's sold. I'm the only licensed real estate agent left in town so it's just me bringing people by."

"I suppose that's true. I'm still hoping for a quick sale, though. It would be good if I could wrap this up with one trip."

Ann left. Beth stood in the driveway with warring emotions. She could go home now. She should go. What about Teddy?

Face it, Bethie, you own a cat now. Go home. Find a job. Take your cat with you.

If she went home, she could meet with Stephen in-person and officially call off the engagement.

Or she could stay here a few more days. Teddy was comfortable in the house. She needed to finish going through Maude's things anyway and she owed Michael a dinner.

She and Michael needed to talk.

Beth grabbed the car keys and her purse. She'd have lunch out, then drop by the library to check her email. Teddy followed her to the door, but she shut it carefully making sure not to catch a paw.

While driving, it came again—that wedding tune. It was jarring. Definitely, she needed to change the ringtone.

Beth took a deep breath. He'd been patient. Fair was fair.

She pulled the car over to the side of the road to concentrate on the call.

"Stephen?"

"It's been a week."

The complaining edge to his voice grated on her, but his words hit straight into her guilty heart.

"I'm fine. I'm good."

"I'm not. I'm worried about you. Where are you?"

"Taking care of family obligations. I'll be home in a few days."

"Family? I didn't think you had family."

"It isn't a typical family situation, but it's almost done."

He asked, "What's almost done? What are you doing?"

A semi blew by and shook her car. "I'll explain when I see you."

"Why not now?"

"I'd rather talk in person."

"I'll come to you, then. I'm dropping everything here. Clearing my work calendar for the next few days. I'm on my way."

"No, don't. I'll be back soon and we can talk." She hadn't told him where she was. That, if nothing else, would keep him away.

"Don't leave me in the dark. Tell me what's going on. Where are you?"

"I'll explain it all, I promise, but I have to go now." She added, "Leave my mail in the apartment, okay? I'd appreciate it."

"I love you, Beth."

She hesitated, then said abruptly, "You, too. See you soon." She disconnected.

She'd made a mess of it. And not only with

the conversation.

Beth resumed driving, struggling, caught between confused emotion and rational thought. She pulled into the diner's parking lot, but before going inside, she called Michael.

"Want to talk?"

"Sure. What do you have in mind?"

"Face to face. Can we meet up somewhere?"

"I'm in town right now."

"Then how about the park, beside the mill?" Beth heard a muffled laugh. She asked, "Am I amusing you?"

"Don't suggest pistols at twenty paces."

"I do sound tense, don't I? No weapons, only words, I promise. What time works?"

"In an hour?"

"I'll be there."

She didn't go into the restaurant. Stephen. Michael. Too much drama. Who could eat? Instead, she went directly to the library, did the email check, then walked down the block and crossed the street to the park.

Up close the mill's decay was obvious. There was a small parking area near a bronze historical marker in the shadow of the building. To the left, the park curved around the lake's edge with green lawn and tall pines. To the right was dense, uncleared forest with a nature trail continuing past the historical marker into the woods.

When the mill had been in operation, the water was diverted down a sluice to the huge wheel. From Beth's viewpoint on this side of the three story building, the ground dropped away beneath the sluice and wheel, left high and dry for decades. A distance to the north, the mouth of Powell's Creek emptied into the lake and kept it filled and fresh. The trail roughly paralleled the creek and the railroad tracks ran nearby, disappearing into the woods.

Beth waited near the metal railing. The barrier was intended to keep the foolhardy from falling into the drop-off below the mill wheel, but it was also handy to cling to.

The afternoon shadow cast by the mill hung heavily over where she stood, waiting for Michael.

Chapter Six

He joined her at the rail. His smile was warm and the laugh lines in the corners of his eyes creased in amusement. Her apprehension seemed foolish. This was a meeting of friends. She relaxed.

"Remember, Michael?"

"Remember what?"

She leaned back against the rail and nodded toward the path. "I used to tag along behind you two. Y'all were always trying to lose me."

Michael smiled and looked down at the waterwheel. "I guess so." He gave her a sideways look. "We were trying to keep you from falling through the trestle over Powell's Creek."

She laughed. "Like you were concerned for my safety, right?"

"Just didn't want to have to explain it to our parents. They might have interfered with our wandering around the countryside."

She put her hand against his arm and shoved. "Jerk."

His eyes examined her face. His lips moved into a smile, sort of, but it hinted of sadness. She grasped the rail to stop herself from touching his hair.

Michael said, "It was a long time ago, like another world."

"It was another world, definitely. Between this end of the trail and the other—the difference between order and chaos with the railroad trestle marking the dividing line."

"Beth," he shook his head. "Chaos? That's in the past. Leave it there."

The silence stretched between them. Before she could stop herself she spoke the words.

"You surprised me last night."

He raised his eyebrows and shifted his feet. It took him a step further away, but he recovered and put his hand back on the railing.

"It seemed like a good idea at the time." He shrugged. "Were you offended? You kissed me back."

Beth smiled and looked at the ground. "I'm not complaining. If it was no more than an impulsive moment, say so. No hard feelings."

He took her hand. "There's a ring on your finger. Why are we even talking about this?"

"Stephen and I aren't right for each other." She stretched her hand out before her. The sunlight slipping through the leaves overhead picked up the fire in the diamond. She slid the ring from her finger and put it into her jeans pocket.

Michael was shocked. "I don't understand. Is it really that simple for you?"

"Simple?" She stepped back. "No."

He reached out and touched her shoulder gently. "Cold feet, maybe? I have experience with that. No need to be embarrassed. It happens. I know."

"Not cold feet. I just don't want to hurt

anyone." Afraid of piling mistakes upon mistakes, but she kept that thought inside.

Michael drew into himself. Beth hesitated. She didn't know what she'd expected, but it wasn't this.

"This isn't the conversation I thought we'd have."

"What did you expect, Beth? What's this about anyway?"

"I keep thinking about things. You know, how it happened before. I wanted to understand..." She crossed her arms, fidgeting like an awkward kid again.

"How what happened before? I don't get it."

"Before. Like last night."

"When you say 'before' are you talking about fifteen years ago?" He looked amazed and his voice was heavy with irony. "It was a teenage kiss. You were a kid. What, maybe fifteen? I was almost eighteen. Daniel should've shot me."

"Not funny." Her eyes stung.

"No, it's not funny. You're hung up on a brief kiss fifteen years ago."

"Not fair, Michael. There was more. Have you forgotten our walks? That ride on your motorcycle? Remember how we used to talk? We'd sit by the lake..." She shook her head. "I realize they were little things and a long time ago, but then you left." She paused. "I never understood. And last night–"

He interrupted, saying, "Beth, you have to move on. Put the past behind you. Your father. Daniel. All of it." He shook his head. "You want to have some big discussion about an impulsive kiss and a walk now or fifteen years ago. Doesn't that tell you something?"

"Michael—"

He put his hands on her arms and pulled her close for a quick hug before stepping away.

"But, Michael—"

"Let it go, Beth. Let's be friends. That's what we were and what we should be. Let's not complicate it. It's my fault, okay? I'm sorry for sending mixed signals."

Mixed signals? Is that what he called it? And she was a girl on the rebound. Or would be as soon as she had it out with Stephen. Michael walked to his car. He didn't look back.

Beth stared down at the rocks near her feet. Her heart, laid bare, had been rejected with a few, easy sentences.

Humiliation. Insanity. What had possessed her?

She should've known spending time with Michael would only cause confusion. Better to have avoided him as she'd originally intended.

Maybe he was right, they were better as friends.

The words sounded good. Too bad she wasn't feeling truth in them.

****

The road into River View Cemetery followed a fold between gently rolling hills. Morning mist clung to the tops of the hills and resisted being burned off by the sun. The scene looked softly green, slowly revealed as the clouds lifted.

Beth hadn't been here in several years. It

was ironic that Maude's death and this trip to Preston coincided with the darkest day in her life.

Maude's plot was on a terraced hillside overlooking the river. Her parents had the largest monuments, obelisks pointing toward heaven with HENRY boldly carved in the granite. Maude's grave was the newest with the red earth still freshly turned.

Crushed grass and churned up mud showed where the graveside service had been held. Pastor Barnes had probably preached a short service. Someone had given a eulogy. Maybe read a few verses. Beth had left the church behind when she'd left Preston. Really, before she left. And when Beth created her new life, one of rationality and control, she'd left it out altogether.

Beyond the three Henry monuments were two stones, each marking the final resting places of Belinda and Daniel Kincaid.

Nineteen years had passed since Beth had seen her mom's smile or touched the long curly hair so like her own. Her mother had often worn it caught up in tortoise shell clip. On that last day she'd looked happy and had waved to her children as if assuring them everything would be okay. Logic told Beth even then, as a child, if it didn't end badly on that day, it would sooner or later.

Dad had a few too many that morning. When drunk, he was affectionate or irritable with no rhyme or reason and there was no way for a kid to know what action would draw which reaction.

Instinctively, she had learned to avoid him when she smelled liquor. To this day, she couldn't think of him without remembering the odor and it always triggered her anger.

There was no reasonable way to deal with the anger like that—anger over a tragedy that couldn't be fixed or resolved—except to set it aside.

Beth didn't want to think about Joe. Or about Michael either.

The meeting with Michael had short-circuited somewhere, somehow. It was a sign that her stay in Preston should come to an end. It was time to pay her respects to Maude and wrap up her affairs. When she left Preston this time, she would never return. No reason to.

Beth pulled a few untrimmed blades of grass from around the two headstones.

A slight breeze lifted a curl and brushed her cheek. She reached up to catch the errant lock of hair. She'd been totally alone. A canopy was erected across the way for a funeral service, but it had yet to begin, or was already over, because no one was in sight. Her car was parked on the roadside a distance down the slope from where she stood. Farther down the road an old pickup pulled alongside the low curb and stopped. The door of the pickup opened and a man stepped out.

He was too distant for her to make out features. White hair.

Lots of old men had white hair.

Her pulse quickened.

Beth walked, slowly at first, then faster, in a

controlled stride down the slope as if going to her car, but only the white-haired man was in her sight and he was moving in her direction.

Her vision blurred and took on a pinkish hue. It was him.

She could see him, hear him, smell him—no matter that he was twenty yards away and these were sensory memories nineteen years gone. Beth moved quickly toward him. A dark, hidden part of her brain drove her forward with dangerous intent.

She tripped, flat out sprawled into the earth and grass.

For the space of a breath, sanity returned, but only until her hand closed over a large rock half-hidden in the grass. Beth clawed at it, needing a weapon, pulling at it until her fingernails tore into the quick. Sharp pain stabbed up her arm and the brief madness subsided, leaving her bereft and gasping in the dirt. She released her grip on the rock, a pitted, ancient footstone buried in the ground.

Joe had stopped in the roadway near her car. On her knees, she stared at him. He should have had the decency to die on the day he killed her mother.

But that was then. This was now.

She could not be his executioner.

She couldn't control what happened in the past, nor his present behavior. Maude had said she could only control her own actions and Maude was right. Beth shuddered. Her deep breath, almost a sob, was audible. She repressed it. Not here, not now.

Despite a bloody elbow, torn fingernails and grass stains on the knees of her jeans, she walked the remaining distance with as much dignity as she could pull together.

His face. Beth had remembered his face from the past, but with the white hair superimposed. Before her stood an old man with weathered skin and deep lines carved around his eyes and mouth.

"What are you doing here?" She was surprised by the hoarseness of her voice. Rage built, threatening to surge again. She tried to contain it. "Stay away from me."

"Beth," he insisted.

An old man's voice. Still hated.

"Stay away from me. Do you understand?"

"I need to talk to you." His eyes were red and his voice sounded unfocused.

"No. Stay away."

Beth got into the car and turned the key in the ignition. He moved closer to the door. She hit the power lock and drove off.

A short distance from the cemetery along the main road was a turnout with a picnic table. She pulled off the road. She needed to breathe. To calm herself. To cry. She wanted to cry. Her eyeballs were red hot and swollen. Beth placed her hands over her eyes and sobbed, but no tears came. Dry, painful sobs wracked her chest. It couldn't last. After a few minutes the torture began to subside. Her shame didn't. She'd been humiliated by her own behavior two days in a row.

When she returned home she washed the

grit from her hands, the blood from her elbow and trimmed her nails. One fingernail was beyond trimming, and painful. She wrapped an adhesive bandage around the end of it.

She'd barely finished tending her wounds when the doorbell rang. Teddy was lounging on the stair landing, watching as she walked to the front door and opened it.

Stephen's dark eyes flashed. "Beth? It's been a week. What's going on?"

Beth was astounded. "I told you yesterday I'd be home in a few days. I told you not to come. How did you find me?"

"Why are you here in this town? At this house? There's a 'For Sale' sign in the yard."

She insisted, "How did you know where to find me?"

"Can I come in? Or are you going to make me stand out here?"

Beth wanted to say 'you can't come in,' but that was unfair. She was engaged to the man. She owed him an explanation before she returned his ring. "Come in."

"What is this place?" He followed her through the vestibule, into the hallway.

She saw it through his eyes—the threadbare rug, the worn upholstery, the long out-of-date draperies. Suddenly, it looked unbearably shabby.

"I lived here when I was young. With my guardian. How did you find out where I was?"

He stepped toward her with a half-smile on his face. Beth checked his approach with an outstretched hand.

"No. How did you find me?"

He shrugged. "Just getting your mail. No subterfuge. You sound suspicious."

"My mail?"

"Yes, Celeste went out of town. She asked me to get the mail."

"What mail did I get with this address on it?"

He looked aside, embarrassed. "So I opened an envelope. We're engaged, Beth. I was worried about you. Since when has it been a crime for me to look at your mail? It was a letter from an attorney here in Preston. I thought it might be important."

"Did you bring it with you? My mail?"

"Yes, it's out in the car." Stephen shook his head. "What happened? Did I do something wrong? Since when can't you talk to me?"

She wanted to be fair, but his tone pricked her nerves. He leaned toward her, too close.

"Please, we'll talk about this when I get back to Fairfax."

He stood there, immobile. His expression tense, unbelieving. He clenched and unclenched his fists.

"I could stay here with you. I could help." When she didn't answer, he continued, "You used to like my company."

"Maybe we should've talked before I left town...but I was so emotional with...everything that happened. I wanted to tell you that I...wasn't sure about us anymore."

He blinked. "Not sure. What does that mean?"

She breathed, searching her brain for how

to respond. He was staring beyond her. Thinking, she thought. Processing her words.

"I'm sorry."

"Wait." He held out his hand. "You came here, all the way here, rather than discuss this with me." He rubbed his hands across his face.

"Stephen, I'm sorry."

His hands went down, he stared at her. "No, Beth. I'm the one who's sorry. You've been through too much. I wish you'd known you could trust me, but apparently, you didn't. Now, you'll find out." He stepped forward and grabbed her hands. "You'll see. I'll prove it to you. You can depend on me."

Beth pulled her hands from his grasp. She backed away until the Davenport caught her behind the knees and she sat clumsily. She struggled to stand.

"Listen to me, please. Be honest with yourself. Things haven't been working between us for a while, but it took a bit to realize it. I don't want to hurt you."

His eyes searched her face and his expression changed, hardened. His hands clenched into fists. Beth gasped. She tried to slip past him, to the foyer and the front door. He reached out, then pulled his hands back.

He drew in a deep breath before saying, "It's up to you, Beth. Your decision. It always has been. Remember, I love you. I'll do anything for you. Say the word." He walked toward the door. "Call me when you want to talk."

Stephen pushed past the door. Beth stood there, relieved he'd gone until the car door slammed. She ran out to the porch, but he was already driving away.

Her mail. On its way back to Fairfax.

His ring. Still on her finger.

She'd tried. Maybe he needed some time to come to terms with the breakup. That was reasonable. She'd pushed too hard, too fast.

Teddy crouched on the landing with his chin resting between two rungs of the stair railing. Watching.

She'd hit some sort of wall. It was as if the bad day pendulum had swung to its greatest arc and was heading back the other way—hopefully in her favor. Hopefully, it wouldn't slam into her.

Beth sat down on the stairs, below the landing. Teddy meowed. She scratched around his ears and he stretched his neck to give her better access.

"What a day. First, Joe, then Stephen. And Michael yesterday. One disaster after another." Beth took a deep breath. "I came here to sell a house. I got side-tracked. I've behaved like a puppet reacting to the whims of these losers. I'm declaring independence from all of them. Here and now."

Ann had suggested a dealer with an auction house in Roanoke who would give a price for the furniture and haul it away. It was time to give the dealer a call.

Beth opened the door to the music room. She'd left Maude's framed pictures on top of the piano and the two boxes she'd already been through were stacked on the piano bench. She moved those boxes to the floor and set the third box on the bench. It was close quarters in this room, all the more because Teddy was determined to be in the midst of it. She picked him up and put him on the piano.

The phone rang.

Ann said, "We'll be there in thirty minutes, okay?"

"Sounds good. We'll get lost for a while."

"We?"

"The cat and I."

Beth grabbed her purse, snatched one of Maude's books from the box, and picked up Teddy. She'd left the carrier in the car.

Teddy fretted the five minutes it took to drive down the street, turn around and park, but he settled down when the car stopped. Beth picked up the book. The cover of *Joshua's Hope* showed a distraught damsel in a gray bonnet and swirling cape and dress on a cliff with a dark, brooding house behind her in the distance.

Ann arrived. There was one man with her. They went straight into the house.

Beth glimpsed movement from the corner of her eye and turned to look. Several teenagers were walking beside the lake. She was only able to see them when they crossed an open area between two houses.

Three boys and a girl? Maybe. They were dressed similarly, in dark clothing. Were they her night visitors?

Of course.

Her heart rate sped up and her hand was on

the door latch. Beth fought to relax her grip. She'd had three awful confrontations within the last twenty-four hours and was determined to break the pattern. Her life in Fairfax had been well-controlled. She'd almost forgotten what it was like to ride an emotional wave, to get caught up in the rush of it. No more.

"Isn't that right?" She reached over and scratched his neck. "And they're missing the best of the lake in those clothes. How can they feel the sun, the breeze?"

Teddy stood, stretched, then squeezed onto her lap between her stomach and the steering wheel. Ann and the man came out the front door and got into Ann's car.

Too many ups and downs recently. A crazy day today. At least her poor bandaged finger had stopped throbbing. She needed to turn off her brain for the rest of the day. She put Teddy in the house and went to see if Mrs. Boyle could spare a chair from her dock.

The lake breeze was sweet as always. Beth leaned back in her borrowed chair. She closed her eyes. The air that touched her face was warm with a hint of cool. This was April, after all.

She dozed and awakened when Michael said, "Truce?"

"Go away." She kept her eyes closed, her head back against the chair, her feet propped up, and pretended her pulse hadn't started thumping.

He leaned on the top edge of the plastic chair and said, "I see the ring is back on your finger."

"I don't want to lose it before I can return it."

"Very responsible." He walked around to face her. "Are you going to look at me? I want to apologize."

She opened her eyes. "Nothing to apologize for."

"Yesterday."

Beth sat quietly, one hand tapping the curved armrest. "Friends, right? That's what you want. We're buddies. So go away, buddy. I'm enjoying the lake." She waved her hand as if shooing a fly.

She closed her eyes again, but he knelt with his own hand on the armrest. She could feel his nearness, his chest brushed her knee. It was difficult to keep up the bored, disdainful expression on her face when butterflies were dancing in her stomach and a warm flush was working its way up her body. She kept her wayward fingers clasped around the plastic armrests.

Michael seemed unaware of her struggle. He asked, "Where'd the chair come from?"

"Mrs. Boyle's dock."

"I have a present for you."

"A peace-offering?"

"Do you want it or not?"

She opened one eye. "Depends on what it is."

Michael had a slim, green plastic bag in his hands. He held it out to her, then stood.

"Nice wrapping." She peeked inside the bag before sliding the book out. "What's this?"

"Something you're interested in."

"It's about the house. Maude's house."

"Your house," he corrected.

Beth looked up at him. "Soon to be someone else's house. It's for sale."

"Not sold yet. Until it is, it's yours."

She smiled and opened the book. "It's a reprint of the 1926 catalog?" She thumbed through the pages. "I don't see it."

"Try checking the index."

"Look at this furniture. They've got drawings of the decorated rooms. It looks like Maude's furniture. Here's her dining room set and look at this dresser. This is what it must have looked like when it was new."

She jumped up from the chair. "Michael, here it is. Number 227."

"I'm glad you like the present."

"It's wonderful. Thank you. I'll have the book as a memento after the house is sold."

"About yesterday...."

"Never mind, Michael. Forget it." She pushed her hair back. Moving on seemed the best choice for everyone.

"Anxious to get back to the city and to work?"

Beth considered how to answer. "Actually, I'm between jobs. I got caught on the short end of a re-organization about a week ago." Not precisely true, but it was close enough.

"Before coming here?" He frowned.

"What timing, huh? Anyway, I'll have another job in no time. I'd like to get all this taken care of so I can start the new job without distractions."

He touched her hand. "Understandable."

"I wasn't up front about it before. It's too new. Still a little raw."

Michael nodded. "Have you considered staying here?"

"You asked that before. The answer is still no. Preston never agreed with me. It seems to have improved a little, but it isn't exactly a hotbed of hiring."

"That could change."

"You mean the mysterious development project? No one seems to know much about it. It's all speculation and no specifics. Not much to count on so far as I can see."

"It could come to nothing, that's true, but can you blame the folks around here? The businesses are having a hard time. People don't want to spend money when they aren't sure about the next paycheck, and the businesses lay 'em off, or close altogether, and more jobs are gone. The prospect of new blood, new income and revenue generation, is the most exciting thing to happen around here in years."

"Which could evaporate. All the more reason not to hang around hoping for a job."

Michael paused before asking, "Want to take a ride?"

"Why? Where?"

"I have something to show you."

She shouldn't. She had no good reason to go anywhere with him, but her voice said, "I have to return the chair first."

"Why don't you buy your own chair?"

"I'm a budget freak. Buying a chair to enjoy a lake I anticipate not owning in the near future doesn't factor into my balance sheet."

Michael grinned and bowed. "At your command."

"Not likely." He picked up the chair. It was lightweight plastic and he swung it as he crossed the yard and disappeared through the hedge, heading back to Martha's dock.

Was he whistling?

And the world said women were moody.

Chapter Seven

Stephen Wyndham saw them in the backyard. They looked cozy and he took a quick step back. He stayed up against the side of the house, breath held and listening hard, but couldn't hear their conversation because the lake breeze carried their voices in the wrong direction.

He returned to his car, annoyed. He hadn't expected to find a man here with her.

A missed opportunity? To talk to Beth privately, yes, but, maybe there was a different opportunity he could leverage. He parked down the street with the sun behind him.

They walked out of the house and climbed into the man's blue pickup truck. The guy had his hand on her back. Touching her. He opened the truck door and waited while she climbed in.

Stephen wasn't jealous, at least, not in a physical way. The only interest he had in Beth now was financial. They had both enjoyed their relationship. It was convenient and each got what they wanted. She'd surprised him though by running off just when he needed her. Despite her refusal to help him with his financial troubles, he hadn't seen it coming.

Face it, a man couldn't be physically attracted to a woman who was willing to let him sink alone when she had the means to help.

And Beth was weak. She couldn't even leave him without having another guy lined up. Weak and a cheater.

His cell phone rang. Cole again. A low cramping twisted in his gut.

Bad lunch, that's all. Those mom and pop country diners were germ fests. Mistake to have eaten there.

He'd misjudged Jack Cole. By far, the biggest mistake he'd ever made. He'd been misled by a bland face and a guy whose taste for huge SUVs and flashy jewelry made him seem almost ridiculous. Who could take that seriously? Cole was a big guy. Steven had figured he was compensating for a small brain.

Mistake or not, he needed money. Beth was the easiest, most likely source, but to get it from her, to pry that money from her tight-fisted grip, he needed to make her care again or, at least, to play on her sympathies.

Stephen exited the car. He kept his movements casual, checking his watch and looking around like he enjoyed the fresh air and scenery. Not a soul in sight. A couple of cars on the street, but they were hard to see because of the tall shrubs.

Beth was his best chance. His only realistic option.

He wasn't an investment broker. He worked the marketing side. The opportunity had been too good to pass up and he'd done them a favor by bringing them in to it. Everyone knew the higher the payoff, the higher the risk, but their memories suddenly got iffy after the fund went broke. One investor in particular was a problem.

He strolled up the driveway and to the porch steps.

The value of the house would buy time, but there was more to be mined here. More even than Beth seemed to know.

There was also the opportunity to get a foot in the door to Markland Enterprises. Talking to them on Beth's behalf, as someone with a local stake, provided the introduction. If he could bring them in-house, even a piece of their business, he could command a greater presence at Stafford Marketing. But first, he had to shut-up the investors and secure his position.

Scandal would cost him everything.

He'd seen the lawyer's letter. He'd checked out Preston and that's how he stumbled onto talk of development. He knew how to ferret out details and those had led him to Markland.

It benefitted them both. He had Beth's best interests in mind, too. At least, he wanted to unless she made it impossible.

The 'For Sale' sign told him Beth's stay here was temporary. She'd return to Fairfax. Whatever doubts she was feeling now could be overcome, unless she was working with someone local who was up to no good.

He wanted to take a look around.

The porch made the front windows easily accessible. The wide, triple windows that opened into the living room were closed, but a single window on the other side of the front door was open a couple of inches.

"She died."

Startled, Stephen spun around. A kid was standing at the foot of the steps.

He frowned. "Who are you?"

"James. The old lady who lived here died."

Just a nuisance kid. "Sorry to hear it. Who lives here now?"

"A lady."

"I know her. I was hoping to surprise her. Can you keep a secret?"

James shrugged. "Sure."

He knelt and motioned to the kid to come closer. "Don't tell her I was here. You'll ruin the surprise. Okay?" He pulled out his wallet and found a ten dollar bill. He handed it to James.

"Deal?"

"Sure." James held the bill, looking at it.

From a distance, a woman's voice yelled, "James!"

Stephen almost swore, but then remembered he wasn't visible while kneeling. The trick was to keep the kid on his side. He winked and put a finger to his lips.

"James! Where are you?" The woman called out. "Come home right now!"

James laid the bill on a step. "Grams wouldn't like it. Thanks, anyway." He took off.

Stupid kid.

He held his temper in, but only waited a moment. He didn't want to be here on Beth's porch if Grams decided to come see who was offering money to her grandson. He stood, but kept low and backed up to the wall, the window at his back.

Stabbed in the leg—sharp teeth piercing through his pants leg and into his thigh. He yelped and jumped away still feeling the tug on the fabric.

A cat. It was a big orange cat with a foreleg and claws reaching out through the gap in window. Not teeth. Claws. He brushed at the pants leg. There were tiny holes and some strings pulled.

It was just a cat.

Just a cat and just a kid. And a cheating woman.

Stephen grabbed up the ten dollar bill and hurried back to his car.

Chapter Eight

Beth asked again, "Where are we going?"

Michael smiled, but wouldn't answer until they turned onto Main Street. There was no street parking open, so he drove up the narrow alleyway to park in the small lot behind the library. The librarian was busy at the desk. They walked past into a small alcove beyond the two microfilm readers. The alcove was brighter than the main reading room because tall, narrow windows filled the exterior walls. In the center of the small room a topographic layout of the Preston area was displayed under glass on a four-foot square table.

"Looks like someone's school project. Paper Mache? Clay? It's charming."

"The map at Town Hall is more precise, but our interest in it would probably cause a lot of questions."

"Why?"

"Everyone is hyper-sensitive about anything related to development plans."

"Look, there's the park and the mill and the path that goes through the woods." She walked around to the other side. "Even the small trestle bridge over the river."

"Here's my farm on the north side of the lake," Michael said.

"And where my family lived on the northeast side." Beth tapped on the glass.

"This is the west branch. Maude's house is here in this area."

"How cute. Look at the little mill building and the trestle. Are those made with toothpicks?" Cut down greenery used by miniature railroading enthusiasts represented the forest. Closely-packed block buildings south of the lake area represented Preston town proper.

"Not to scale, of course, but it gives a good overview." Michael drew his fingers along the glass top in a semi-circle over the area of land stretching from the north east side of the lake around to the park area on the south, then tapped the glass. "This is the primary area of interest."

"Tourism?"

"You've been speculating, too."

"Ann suggested it."

Michael leaned against the display case. "Have you ever heard of Markland Enterprises?"

"No, but it sounds familiar."

"They have their fingers in lots of pies. In this case they're seeking a location for a theme park. That's actually a secret, but it's a secret lots of folks know about. Markland will be making an official announcement any day that Preston is one of several locations being scouted and vetted—all the usual financial and marketing considerations are being tallied and analyzed."

"A theme park? Like Disneyland or Six Flags?"

"Something along those lines."

"I don't know what I was expecting, but an amusement park? Here in sleepy Preston?"

Beth couldn't make the mental picture work for her. Acres of asphalt, crowds in tank tops and fanny packs…the area infrastructure would need significant upgrading. Hotels and restaurants. Souvenir shops. Michael remained silent while she worked it out in her head. She put her index finger on the glass top over the park and mill. "There?"

"And here."

Beth watched his finger re-trace the arc he'd made earlier going back up the east side of the lake, as if felling the forest in one easy pass.

"The announcement is coming out soon?"

"The announcement that Preston is being considered, yes. No telling how long before the final choice will be made, but I thought you should know about it before you make any big decisions."

She looked at Michael. The statement seemed extraordinary. Her own interest was relatively narrow—a house on the lake that she needed to sell.

"So I get that it could increase property values. I'm not so sure about the impact on the quality of life in Preston, but then that isn't my concern, is it?"

Michael seemed to consider her words before answering, "Well, that's up to you."

"My life isn't here."

They walked out of the alcove. The librarian had left the desk and was conscientiously arranging books on a shelf outside of the alcove entrance. She looked up quickly as they passed, then away again.

Michael brought her back to the house. She didn't invite him in and he didn't suggest it.

"Thanks for the book and the tour and the information."

He reached over and gently lifted her fingers with the closely trimmed nails and one bandaged digit as if he knew how the injury had happened. She realized immediately that was impossible, but her cheeks grew warm with embarrassment nonetheless. When she looked up to meet his eyes, she saw her blush had intrigued him. Thank goodness, he couldn't see the tremors his touch triggered.

"I didn't ask about it before. The injured fingers. It's not really my business, is it? But I'll ask anyway. What happened?"

"I tripped and fell. They'll grow back."

Michael released her fingers. "Be careful, will you? Whether you stay or go. Take some time to think it out. Don't be so focused on the balance sheet that you miss seeing opportunities."

He ran his hand lightly down the side of her face, lightly brushing her cheek. "Call me if you need anything. And, Beth, please seriously consider talking to your father."

That gentle caress was a funny way to treat a friend. Annoyed, she slid from the passenger seat and stepped out into the driveway.

How quickly her senses responded to him. Her heart raced and she called herself a fool. She didn't know whether to throw herself at him or to throw stuff at him.

Michael and his broken engagements…maybe she wasn't the only one who'd gotten stuck in the past.

****

They came back in the night.

She heard the small tell-tale noises. An isolated squeak, one syllable spoken louder than the others, a low chuckle as she stood at the window and watched the lit end, the tiniest of orange sparks from this distance, going eerily up and down as someone enjoyed a smoke.

The back light shone brightly, but the beam didn't stretch to the gazebo.

She wished she could simply turn her back and ignore them, but that was impossible.

Michael's long, heavy flashlight sat next to the kitchen door. Beth unlocked the door, then speed-dialed the sheriff's office as she walked out the front door, cell phone in one hand, flashlight in the other.

She closed the front door softly, pulling it gently until she heard the latch click. She went around the side of the house, walking with care in the dark. She wanted to surprise them, hopefully only moments before the cruiser's headlights came down the street and gave warning.

Their eyes were night-sharpened, but they fooled themselves, feeling cut off from the world, shrouded by the dark, believing the night belonged to them. She understood. Yet, how foolish was she? Thinking she knew what was in their minds.

Their snippets of conversation were lazy and mellow.

She said firmly, "Do you live around here?" She switched on the flashlight, training it directly on them.

They blinked. Two boys and a girl. All dark—dark hair, dark clothing—but their faces looked white-pale in the artificial light.

The girl and one of the guys spoke over each other, "We'll go. Sorry." The other boy cursed. He looked and sounded like an adult, never mind the age.

"Y'all should know if anyone comes back to my property uninvited, I'm going to knock on every door within three blocks of here the next morning. I don't know who or where your parents are, but I'm not them. You go play in your own backyards." She used her anger, playing it out to keep the edge in her voice, using it instead of it using her, but now she'd said her piece. She was running out of steam. Headlights sliced past the side of the house and a car door slammed.

Beth expected the kids to take off and they did. The deputy found her standing alone in the dark in her pajamas, her bare feet in the wet grass, waving a big flashlight.

"Deputy. Thanks for coming again."

"Yes, ma'am. The kids came back?"

"Yes, there were three."

The deputy shifted his club back into his belt. "Don't advise you coming out to confront trespassers. You can't know who'll be out here."

The tenor of his voice irritated her. "You think I'm over-reacting, don't you?"

They moved closer to the house, into the area lit by the spotlight.

"No, ma'am. I advise caution. Call anytime."

"So, it's easy, you know, for some people to ignore them." Why did it matter what he thought? "I'm not some old woman worrying over nothing. These kids are out here at all hours, at the very least they're trespassing, at the worst doing stuff they shouldn't, including damaging property."

"Yes, ma'am. We're rural, but we've got our share of trouble and drugs find their way here, too. Next time, call, but please stay inside."

She bit her lips to keep from blurting the words. Daniel had been out all hours, all over the place, with no one but Maude to rein him in. Maude couldn't, Joe wouldn't and it had got him killed.

"My brother—" she broke off.

"Yes, ma'am. Daniel and I were about the same age. I remember. Never big trouble with him, just teenage stuff. Sorry how things ended for him."

How things ended for him. The words sounded forlorn and inadequate, even years later.

The deputy waited until she was inside the house, then drove off.

How things ended for him. On a hot July evening when the air was thick with humidity, enough to set nerves on edge for anyone who wasn't smart enough to stay in the AC or who didn't have AC—like Daniel hanging out at the old house. He kept going back, pulled like a magnet. How it ended for him when two teenage boys got their hands on some whiskey and decided to take a ride. Ended for him when the car was pulled out of the ravine with Daniel still behind the wheel of the battered car Joe had given him.

Michael, thrown clear, but scraped and bloody and in shock, standing silently on the side of the road.

She didn't want to go to bed with those images in her mind. She forced herself to remember the sound of Daniel's voice, grown faint with the years, and how he teased her, yelled at her, or put his arm around her to offer comfort when she fell and skinned her knees.

Beth dried her feet, brushing off the loose bits of lawn, and climbed back into bed, cell phone in hand. Teddy jumped up on the end of the bed. He stopped short of pushing into her area and stayed on the unused corner.

She hoped she'd done the right thing tonight and it would end, had ended, well. Time would tell.

****

She slept soundly, but not late because Stephen arrived on her porch shortly after sunrise.

Beth stumbled to the front door still half-sleep.

He arrived with a bright smile and carrying two hot coffees from the convenience store and boxed doughnuts sure to scatter powdered sugar everywhere.

Her brain groped to catch up as he passed the coffee to her and then walked to the kitchen. She followed him, staring as he tore open the box and thrust mini-doughnuts into her empty hand.

White powder flew. He didn't notice or maybe he didn't care.

"It's not fancy, but it's the closest thing I could find to pastries in this town." He turned, looking at the counters. "Where are the napkins?"

"Aren't you...I mean, didn't you go back to Fairfax?" She waved the doughnuts and coffee in the air as if trying to find the appropriate spot for them. Her brain was still fuzzy. Confused. With shaky hands, she aimed for the table and the cup had a rough landing. Coffee slopped over the lip and puddled on the table. Hot liquid had splashed over her fingers, but the discomfort hardly registered as she kept her eyes on Stephen.

"I want to be here for you. I'm going to help you." He took her hand, the dry one, and touched the engagement ring on her finger. "I won't interfere, I promise. Just support."

"Stop. I have a real estate agent. None of this is complicated. It takes some time and effort, that's all. I can handle it myself."

His voice got small. "Beth, I'm really trying, but this feels very one-sided."

She reached up and pushed her hair out of her eyes. Unbrushed and unwashed, a tangled mess, definitely at a disadvantage.

"I don't want to talk about this now. Later–"

"Later!" he exploded. "It's always later with you, isn't it? Later when you feel like it, later when it won't be ugly, when it doesn't matter anymore? Are you pushing me away until I finally give up?"

"Stop it. You can't intimidate me."

"Intimidate? I'm under a lot of pressure, Beth. I could use your support." His voice had dropped to a softer tone. "Don't you understand? I could go to prison. Prison, Beth. If anyone talks to the wrong people, maybe the Feds, it won't matter whether I'm guilty, whether I'm convicted or not. My career is over. My life, Beth. It's my life at stake."

"Sorry."

He closed his eyes, then opened them slowly as if reality was too hard to accept.

Doubt twisted in her heart. Maybe she was wrong, not about breaking the engagement but about helping him. Maybe she owed him something. Some kind of loyalty.

"I'm sorry, but I can't give you the severance money because–"

He stood abruptly and swept the table with his arm. The doughnut bag flew across the room showering white powder. The remaining coffee spilled as the cups fell and rolled.

Beth's anger flared, but instead of red-hot rage it turned cold and hard. She pulled the ring from her finger and tossed it on the table.

"Take your ring. Take it. We're done."

He stared at the engagement ring. It had

come to rest amid the spilled coffee and powdery sugar.

"When did you decide? Even before you left Fairfax? When the old woman died, were you suddenly rich enough to move on without me? You never mentioned these people but now you can't pull yourself away. You can handle it by yourself? I saw you with that guy."

"Stephen, pick up the ring and follow me." She spun out of the kitchen door into the hallway and didn't pause except to open the front door. She ran out into the yard and pointed at the car, trying not to yell, "Go. Get in your car and go." Angry, she yanked at the door handle and it swung wide.

"Is that my mail? Spread across your floor mat?" She shouted at him as she dove across the seat and scrabbled the envelopes all together into a crazy pile. She climbed awkwardly out of the car with the mess of bills and letters gathered in her arms. Pieces of mail dropped to the lawn as she walked toward him with her palm outstretched.

"My keys. My apartment key and my mailbox key. Now, or I'll call the cops."

"Do you think I care?"

She held his stare and refused to answer.

"Don't bother, I'll go. I'm disappointed in you, Beth. You used to have more dignity and self-respect than this."

"Dignity? Self-respect? You're disappointed in my dignity?"

He kept his eyes fixed on his hands as he worked the apartment key from the ring.

One of the letters fluttered from her arms, the torn edges catching the breeze. She grabbed it and saw Billy Monroe's return address. She remembered what Ann had said about the developer being contacted. Stephen had connections in the marketing world. He knew how to follow a trail. She waved it at him.

"Is this why you came? You were just looking for another way to get money from me?"

His face turned maroon. She'd pushed him too far and couldn't move fast enough. He flew from the porch, grabbed her arms and pushed her against the car. Her head slammed back against it. He held her, his grip pinching her flesh.

Shocked, she tried to regain the offensive. "Did you contact Markland saying you represented me? Was that you?"

Stephen dragged in a long, rough breath and his grasp loosened, but he didn't release her. He leaned closer to her ear.

"I wasn't the only one. At least I can claim to have had some interest as your fiancé. But another guy also talked to them about property he didn't own, not officially owned, anyway. Not yet. Although I'm sure he plans to get his hands on it one way or another."

His voice was hoarse. His breath was warm on her cheek and the stale smell of his morning coffee surrounded her.

"The other guy—you know a Michael, right? Yeah, I thought so. He told Markland he could get the property. Did you know that? He also paid property taxes owed by Joseph Kincaid.

Why would he do that, Beth? Why? Think about it. Stop being stupid."

He stepped back and Beth moved away from the car. Her knees were shaky and she trembled inside, but refused to show it. He snagged her hand and turned it palm up.

"Your keys, Beth." He folded her fingers over them. "I don't know who you are. The Beth I loved wasn't like this. She didn't scream or make threats. She was honest."

He drove away.

During their two years together, they'd never had more than a few minor fights. Stephen liked to have his way, but he'd never gone over the edge like this. Neither had she.

He was lying about Michael. He must be.

If Stephen had come by later in the day, she would've handled it better.

Had the neighbors seen them fighting on the front lawn? So long as they hadn't called the police, it didn't matter. No one cared anyway.

She knelt on the dew-covered grass and gathered the pieces of mail scattered across the lawn. The dew wet through her cotton pajama pants instantly, making her shiver. She'd had some tough days lately, but this was the lowest point.

She dragged herself back into the house wishing she could start this day over by not answering the door.

Before she turned the shower on she knew she would drive out to the farm. By the time the water was hot, she was steaming.

She didn't call ahead.

The dirt road branching off the paved road wasn't fancy, but it was well-kept. Same with the pastures and fences. They weren't decorative, but functional and maintained. Neatly kept. The dirt track going off on the other side, the east side, of the paved road was a rutted, weed-grown maze, no prettier than her childhood memories. She didn't waste a glance on it, but focused on the Fowler's farmhouse coming into view.

Would he be home? It was still early thanks to Stephen's near dawn visit. She didn't see his car, but it could be around back.

Beth parked near the front steps to the house. She needed to confront Michael while her anger was strong, before she began to doubt and make excuses for him. She slammed the car door closed and ran up the steps.

No one answered her knock. She crossed her arms and walked to the front of the porch. She stood near the railing, debating. If Michael wasn't here, maybe it was just as well. A chance for her to think it through, after all, and not confront him while riding this rough wave of emotion.

A metallic twang filled the silence. A distant sound, it came from near the barn where a man leaned over a roll of wire doing something she couldn't make out. His back was toward her. She stepped quickly down the steps and crossed the dusty yard, heading his way. Her steps scattered some gravel in the driveway. The man heard her coming, glanced back over his shoulder and then turned to face her.

She stopped dead. The pleasant 'good morning, can you help me' look froze on her face.

A few steps forward, then back. She fumbled for her keys and grabbed them mid-air.

Joe on the Fowler farm? Michael paying his taxes? Crazy. Some kind of alternate universe.

She got into her car and peeled out, her tires throwing up dust and rocks until the wheels hit the paved road with a jolt. She turned south, back toward town.

****

A truck door slammed. Beth looked out the living room window. Michael. Striding up the walk and taking the porch steps two at a time. He knocked and rang the doorbell.

Beth didn't want to answer and didn't want to hear what he had to say, but at the same time, the unhinged girl inside her wanted nothing more than to open the door and tear into him, accuse him, berate him, desperate to hear that somehow, in some way, she'd misunderstood.

She stepped out onto the porch and closed the door behind her.

Michael looked surprised and then something dark settled in his blue eyes. Did he read the suspicion and disgust on her face? She didn't care. He hadn't lied to her outright, but he might as well have.

"I went out to the farm looking for you. Joe's there."

He reached out to her, but she pushed his hand away.

"I'm sorry. I should've told you sooner. He needs to talk to you."

She was stunned. "What could I ever have to say to him? Not a chance."

"It's important, Beth. Let him talk to you. That's it. Just listen."

Beth put her hands on the door to close it. Michael stopped her.

"You're mad because he's at the farm? He needs to make a living like anyone else. Should he starve? Is that what you want?"

Yes, yes, yes. She wanted him to have died all those years ago. Him, instead of her mother.

Michael softened his voice, "I want to talk to you about why he's on the farm, but first, please meet with him. He's an old man, Beth. I can't believe there's no mercy in you, even for him."

What could he say that would make any difference? Yet, in a quiet corner of her brain, she felt a push—a go for it—to hear what he had to say and then she could close out that part of her life with no regret.

Could she sit and listen to him with her hands and anger in check?

"Come back to the farm with me."

"No. And don't bring him here."

"Where, then?"

She closed her eyes and held her breath for a few seconds. Meeting with Joe wouldn't resolve anything, but she could say she'd tried. Maybe she could handle it in a public place, not somewhere she'd feel confined or surprised. Somewhere with room to run.

"I don't know why I should do this." She

paused again to breathe. "At the park. I'll pick a bench. Tell him, and I'm serious about this, tell him not to even think about touching me. And we'll do it now, as soon as he can get into town. If I think about it too long, I might change my mind. This will be our only meeting and then I never want to hear from, or about, him again."

She read disappointment in Michael's face, and something else. Resignation? She still had questions for Michael, and she was angry, but she held back accusations. She'd get this done with Joe first.

****

The bench was smooth and cool, painted a glossy green and shaded by a large pine.

Beth sat at one end, leaving the other conspicuously open. It was a long bench. There had to be distance between them, at least beyond arm's reach.

He approached and she caught the scent of fear. Was he afraid of her?

Joe should be unsure. She was no longer a child without resources, without a guide by which to judge what was acceptable.

A tight band of tension wrapped itself across her forehead and around her head. She couldn't turn to look at him. When he sat, the bench creaked. From the corner of her eye she saw him sit upright, back straight and rigid. Then, he slumped forward, stretched his fingers and massaged the enlarged knuckles. An old man, diminished by age and reality.

"I hear you're sober now?"

He flinched, ducked his head and said,

"Yes."

There was no sympathy to be squeezed from her heart. "Speak or go."

"I appreciate you meeting me." His voice broke and he cleared his throat again. "I've wanted to say this to you for many years, but you, well, you know." He rubbed his knuckles again. "I don't have excuses. I know what I was and what I am. I can't take back what happened to your mother. I know I wasn't a good father to you and Daniel. I can't change any of that and I don't ask you to forgive and forget for my sake, but for your own. For you."

Joe breathed deeply as if gathering the frail remnants of his strength. "I did damage, I know it and can't undo it. Have to live with it. I live carefully, Bethie. Mostly sober. Fell off a couple of times. I live narrow. Not many choices. No decisions that need making."

He paused. Joe wanted something from her, even a grunt, anything to encourage him to continue. She refused.

Joe gripped his hands and rocked forward. "Don't keep the anger in you. Let it go. If that's called forgiveness, then I ask you to forgive. If it's making peace with the past, then that's the thing. Don't let the mistakes somebody else made—me, your mom, Daniel—whoever, put a scar on you for the rest of your life."

"Are you serious? Forgive you? I put you out of my life many years ago. All you need to do is stay away from me and leave me alone."

"Are you happy?"

"Not your business."

"What was between your mother and me, that was our business. I'm sorry you kids got caught in the middle of it. I never hurt her intentionally, but we made poor decisions."

A squirrel crossed the lawn in front of them and ran straight up the pine tree without slowing. Near the water, a goose honked.

"Is that what you call murder? Poor decisions?"

He shook his head. "You're wrong there, Bethie. I killed her, yes, by driving when I'd had too much to drink, but I'd have rather died myself than hurt her. Your mother and I both had drinking problems and—"

"Don't. Don't you dare blame her."

"I'm not blaming her. It's just a fact. I drove that day. It's my fault. I'm not trying to say it's not." Joe ran his hands through his hair and shook his head. "I can't give you back your childhood, Bethie. But I don't want the past to mess up your future either. Try to forgive. Bitterness is just another kind of prison."

A breeze swept across the lawn, a wave rolling across the blades of grass. Geese gathered on the lakeshore near the old mill. Suddenly, she was tired clear down to her bones. And yet, the sun overhead told her it was only noon. Beth wished the breeze could sweep the fog from her brain. She didn't want to think anymore.

"Are you done?"

For a moment she thought he wasn't going to answer. Discouragement, not merely her own, ached in her heart, but she resisted acknowledging even that much of a bond with him.

"Almost, Bethie. One last thing. It's important. To me. I hope to you. It would matter to your mother."

"Don't say her name."

"Where we lived. The old house? The land there—"

"I don't want anything of yours."

"Not mine. In my name, but your mother's father's land. She was his only child. He gave us that land when we got married. I came from nothing and I'll go with nothing. This was your mother's." He scratched his neck. "Lawyer Monroe has the papers in his office. I've signed it over to you, but you need to go by and complete the legalities."

A week ago she'd lost her job and her faith in Stephen. In herself, too. Since then, she'd gained a house and a cat. Now acreage? Life was too confusing. Her brain closed off like siege doors being secured against further assault.

"You will, won't you?" He asked.

"Good bye. We're done."

Her mother's land. There were times when her heart wept with the reality that the memory of her mother's face and voice were fading. She was forgetting the few sweet memories, with only the bad remaining. Life should be better than that—with hope, at least, for happiness.

Bitterness and anger wasn't a legacy she wanted.

Chapter Nine

The air inside the Monroe Law Office smelled of old paper and decades of dust trapped in law books and old folders that had occupied precisely the same spots for decades. But no dust marred the furniture surfaces and the office was tidy. Ida Langhorne was seated at the desk in the anteroom and recognized her.

"Come on in. Glad to see you, Beth."

Ida's hair was solid black despite being somewhere in her sixties. As far as Beth knew it had always been black, so apparently Ida liked it that way.

"Is Mr. Monroe available?"

"Will be shortly." She motioned Beth to join her at the desk. "Have you got time to wait? Shouldn't be long."

Adrift. Lost in confusion. The adrenaline driving Beth since dawn had vanished. Gone cold turkey. The idea of vegetating in the midst of Billy Monroe's clutter with nothing to do but wait appealed to her.

"Sit over here, honey. You look done in. Would you like a glass of water? Or some coffee?"

"Water sounds good."

Ida stood and crossed to the water cooler. She took a paper cup from the holder and filled it. "Here you go."

"Thank you." She didn't remember Ida as

being so nice and attentive, but again, she reminded herself, teens had their own special view of the world. Interpretations built on a whole different perspective.

"Now I hope you won't think I'm being nosy, which I am, I admit." Ida laughed. "How's it going for you since you got back? Real strange with Maude gone, I'll bet. We were longtime friends. It's odd to recall she's not there in that house any longer."

"Yes, weird, especially at first. The house seems so empty. I mean the furniture is there, but all the extra stuff is gone."

"Not surprising, honey. Lots of old folks go through their stuff when they sense their time coming, like weeding through things so others won't have to. Well, like how Maude made all the interment arrangements. She was used to doing for herself."

Beth's defenses rose a fraction, then she decided Ida hadn't intended the words as an insult, merely as a statement of fact.

"I wonder what she wanted me to do?"

"With the house, you mean?"

"The house, the furniture...."

"Well, honey, I think she just intended for you to have it. To do what you wanted to with it. Who else was she going to give it to?" She shook her head. "I guess she could've donated it to the local auxiliary or library or whatever, like she did her money, but she gave them enough. Her time, her energy, funds. She wanted you to have the house and I think she was real glad to have someone special to leave it to." She looked down at the phone. "Oh, see now, he's off the line. Give me a minute, honey."

Ida opened the office door a crack. "Mr. Monroe? Beth Kincaid's here to see you." She turned back, "Go right ahead on in, honey."

Billy Monroe's desk was exceptionally neat. The brown blotter was the only thing hiding the fine grain of the aged wood. A folder rested on the blotter. The papers inside extended beyond the folder, dog-eared. Old-looking. Mr. Monroe nodded to her when she entered. He picked up the folder and slid the papers out onto his desk.

"So you talked to your father, I see. You understand that you will now own the property, and that you'll also be liable for any taxes, etc. Everything is current at this time."

The folds of his face, the wiry hairs in his brows, nothing changed in his expression. Not good. Not bad. He stared at her.

Mr. Monroe leaned toward her. "Keep it insured. No way to keep folks off property that size. No Trespassing signs are almost meaningless in terms of liability."

Now he had her attention. Beth frowned. "How much land are we talking about?"

"Six hundred acres more or less. The original parcel was about nine hundred, but a portion was sold by your parents when your grandfather conveyed the property to them and small parcels have been sold over the years when needed to pay the taxes."

"Six hundred..." Beth wasn't sure she'd actually made a sound.

Mr. Monroe pulled out the plat. "You'll see

here it runs from Powell's Creek, to the north around the lake area to abut the Fowler property." He pointed to an area some distance from the lake. "This is the section that was sold off on the northeast side of the property. To a dairy farmer, as I recall. Both he and the Fowlers have bought parcels through the years."

"Six hun… What am I going to do with six hundred acres?" She was astounded.

"Precisely."

"What? I don't get it."

"I encouraged your father to complete this transaction now. He's old and has abused his health. He's not up to the stress of making decisions of this kind. He has no use for the property. Only headaches for him."

Now it was her headache. Was it a good headache? Did this mean her future was secure? Or was she land poor?

She stared at the plat hoping for inspiration.

"I have copies of all the paperwork here for you. I'll register the deed with the change of ownership. You aren't keeping important papers in the house are you?"

"No, I have a safe deposit box."

"Good. Also in that folder you will find the tax assessments and receipts of payment of property taxes."

She looked at the assessed value and the tax receipts. She was stunned. "I'll have to sell it to pay the property taxes."

"They've been paid for this year. Also, there are transfer fees, but there's cash to cover those. You'll have some time to decide what's best. You are a sensible young woman."

She didn't feel sensible and this made no sense to her. "Mr. Monroe, I never knew my grandparents. Not even one of them. Who was my mother's father? Did you know him?"

Billy Monroe re-situated his glasses on his face. The eyebrows bristled over the frame. "Of course. Evan Stewart. The only child of an only child. A quiet man. Had been ill as a child and never got past it. Lung ailment, I think. He married a local girl who died shortly after your mama was born. He had no taste for farming. Let the land go wild. Hunted here and there for sustenance. He died a handful of years after his daughter, your mother, Belinda, married Joe Kincaid. I knew Evan well." He paused for breath and looked at her closely.

"You look confused. No doubt this is a surprise to you. When families become estranged, well...that's beside the point. Your father refused to sell off any of the property through the years, even when he wasn't sober and when he needed cash, except to keep the taxes paid. He's held onto it and now there's all this folderol about big development and such, he's been getting pressure about selling."

"From who?"

"From more than one. Some from that corporation and some from folks with foolish ideas about what he should do." He adjusted his glasses. "You may not know right at this moment what you will do, and you are young and inexperienced, but you have backbone and won't let anyone snooker you out of your property or pressure you into something you don't want. If you have any questions, come see me. I may not know the answer, but I'll help you in any way I can."

Ida was on the phone as Beth exited through the anteroom. They exchanged a quick wave. Beth kept moving. She wasn't ready for more talk.

She stood on the sidewalk in front the law office. She'd left her car over by the park, but she was thirsty now. Two doors away was an ice cream shop, she bought a bottle of soda. Not diet. A full-bodied sugar and caffeine rush was needed.

It occurred to her any development figuring around the old mill would surely take the park land and maybe this very sidewalk and shops.

An amusement park? It would take the heart of Preston town. Her blood sugar must have sunk to super low depths for her to be feeling so sentimental about Preston and the future of the Mill Park and Main Street.

****

Beth drove home. She pulled into the driveway and realized she'd thought 'home.' Not Maude's house, but home. She sat for a moment with the engine idling, feeling like she'd experienced some sort of reality shift. No wonder. It had been an exhausting day and it was barely afternoon.

She walked up to the house and unlocked the door. Her door. Teddy greeted her in the hallway. Her cat.

In the kitchen, the pile of mail had spilled out across the table. Bound to be some bills in among the junk. She wasn't up to it dealing with it yet.

She filled a glass with tap water at the sink. Beyond the kitchen window, down by the lake, were a pair of white Adirondack chairs with a small table between them.

Her home. Her cat. Her chairs?

Beth went around the house opening windows to bring April inside. Then she walked back to the kitchen sink and looked out the window. The chairs were still there.

"Well, Teddy, it looks like I have a rendezvous lakeside."

She was pleased with the way the white chairs echoed the white trim of the gazebo. The chairs were wooden and heavy enough not to blow away with a lake-borne wind gust. Each chair had matching white wood ottomans.

The chair fit her beautifully, needing only a small pillow to support her lower back. Next time she'd remember to bring one. She laid her weary head back against the smooth, painted wood and closed her eyes. She visualized the lake breeze blowing through her head, cooling her fevered brain.

Fresh water smells. Springtime smells. Hints of jasmine and lavender in the air.

She slid her fingers around the smooth edges of the armrests.

A gift by the lake.

It was perfectly obvious where the chairs had come from.

It soothed her battered spirit.

The events of the day flowed through her head like Scheherazade stories seen from an emotional distance. Not her heartache. Someone else's. She was merely an observer. She dozed off without realizing it, but when she understood she was dreaming and therefore, must be asleep, she embraced it.

Daniel was sitting in the chair next to her. He was grown. A man in his thirties. His hair still glinted gold and copper in the sunlight, but he'd grown a close-cropped beard. She was surprised to see he wore glasses. She held the image closely, wishing simple dreaming could make him flesh, but he vanished. It was bittersweet, yet a small treasure to have seen him as he might have been.

With no idea of how much time had passed, Beth breathed deeply and opened her eyes, refreshed. If not perfectly at peace, at least much more even-keeled than before.

Brown leather shoes were propped on the ottoman. Her eyes followed the olive khakis to where long slim fingers curled around the end of the arm rest.

"Stephen." She groaned. "No, not again. Please go."

"It's nice out here. No wonder you like it." He sighed. "I couldn't leave town without talking to you about this morning." He ran one hand over his face. "I'm embarrassed. It's not how I wanted us to end. We had something good."

"We're done. Done." She slapped the armrest lightly with her hand.

"Agreed. Seems like our chemistry changed overnight. Too volatile. I never saw it coming."

Beth listened to the calm, faintly regretful tone of his voice and tried to read it. "You sound sincere, but I've never known you to be sorry about anything. Anything, Stephen. What does that say about you? And me, too, that I could live with that? Saying you're sorry is not the same as meaning it, not if you don't really feel it."

"Because I control my reactions and how I express my feelings, it's wrong to say I don't have them, Beth. I'm like everyone else. I do try to view setbacks and mistakes as rational events. Something to learn from and then to move on." He took his feet from the ottoman and leaned forward, his elbows on his thighs, his hands clasped.

"Did you never know me? Never understand who I was?" He shook his head. "That's how I feel about you. The woman I loved did more than leave town a week ago. She left my life and I didn't find out until yesterday. Yes, I knew it yesterday, but I couldn't accept it until this morning."

Hot tears formed, prickling her eyes despite herself. Was she going to cry over this? Not over Maude. Not over her father. But over Stephen? Unacceptable. She didn't speak, afraid her shaky voice would breach the dam.

He continued, "I had to try once more. This morning it went bad so quickly. I don't know what hit me. It's not easy for either of us. You're different now, Beth. It's not that I didn't know you before. You're just different. As if you'd shed a skin. That sounds odd. I'm not trying to imply you're a snake." He chuckled. "Let me try again. You have more color. More vibrancy." He looked at her directly. "What I'm trying to say is I don't think you should come back. You are more alive here. You should live it while you have it."

Beth was amazed. Was he right? Had she never known him?

"What about you? Are you living the life that's right for you?"

"Yeah, I think so. I like the thrill of the chase, a chase that might look boring to others, but to me it's a living, breathing chess match with high stakes."

"You've always been on the lookout for opportunities."

He nodded, smiling ruefully. "I guess I'm a predator, Beth, but in a suit, and my preferred prey is acquisition, marketing at the front end before it becomes business as usual. To do that, you have to have a cool exterior or the competition will eat you alive.

"Let me say one more thing. I'll leave you alone as you've asked, but promise me you won't let pride stop you from asking for help if you need me. I'll be there for you. No strings attached."

He stood, offered her a hand and she took it in reflex. He pulled her to her feet.

"Thank you." Gently, she touched his shoulder. "Good luck, and I really mean it."

A lawnmower roared to life and the harsh

sound of its motor grew quickly louder as Ann's handyman pushed it into the side yard.

It was a natural break, the opportunity for them to walk toward the other side of the house, to where he'd parked in the driveway. She welcomed the peaceful resolution. She didn't need more drama or negativity soaking up the energy of her life.

"Do you think you'll stay in this house, Beth?"

She checked a step.

"Polite conversation, Beth. Just asking."

"Sorry. Yes, maybe, no...I don't know. For a while, I think."

"If you don't mind me saying so, I think you're making a good decision. There's something—I don't know what—but something agrees with you here. You look so much happier. But what about a job? This place seems pretty lean for job prospects."

"I'll take it one day at a time. The house is for sale and I'll make a decision when an offer is made."

Stephen looked earnestly into her eyes. "Take care, Beth. Remember, call me anytime."

"Travel safely." She stayed in the front yard to wave him off. Something that could have been nasty had, instead, ended well.

What about her plans? Was staying here a real possibility?

Until an offer came in for the house, there was no point in worrying over it.

Michael had left a message while she was outside. She didn't want to return his call. He hadn't been honest with her.

Restless and unable to settle, she drove back to town, to the library, to finish out the afternoon.

Beth received some interesting emails from former associates who heard she was looking. Some thoughtful, some curious. One mentioned an opening at their workplace that might be perfect for Beth.

Good news, right? She replied to both and told the second one she'd send a resume.

She looked up to see the librarian standing discreetly a few paces away. Her eyes were glued on Beth and a tentative smile was fixed on her face.

"Am I interrupting?"

Beth stopped, fingers still poised over the keyboard in mid-tap.

"What can I do for you?"

"I saw you yesterday with Michael Fowler." She nodded toward the alcove. "At the map?"

"Yes." She looked at the woman's soft appearance, the silky hair, gently rounded facial features, and the matronly pantsuit, and tried to guess what she wanted, but the best she could figure was that it was related to the development plans. Wasn't everything?

"Did you hear the news?" The woman looked around and dropped her voice. "It was announced this morning we are definitely in the running for the amusement park. Two other towns were also named, Winchester, and a town in North Carolina."

"Interesting." Was that why Michael had

come to her house earlier in the day? Not because she went to his farm and found Joe?

The librarian continued, "So, I don't know if you've heard the talk around town, but people are wondering if your father's property is going to be the site. Without it, if Preston's chosen for the amusement park, most of the town will be lost. Many folks don't mind, they think we need to come into the new century, new businesses and all that, but not everyone agrees. I heard your father was giving the land to you and I was wondering whether you planned to sell it to Markland Enterprises?"

Beth was stunned. There was no privacy or anonymity in a small town. She couldn't control her expression or reshape her facial muscles back into a polite arrangement.

"I don't know what I'll do. I haven't heard from anyone connected with these developers." She stood and gathered her stuff, ignoring the embarrassment on the librarian's face. "What did you say your name was?"

"Kim. Kim Stebbins." She stood, fumbling with her chair. "I'm sorry. I'm nosy. I saw you talking to Michael about it. I thought you wouldn't mind me asking."

"Michael was showing me the map. I know nothing about the rest."

"Michael didn't tell you–," she broke off.

"Tell me what?" Beth tried to soften her approach as it occurred to her that Kim might have information she needed.

"Well, it's just that it's the only thing people have been talking about. Ed Mason, the mayor, was talking about that eminent domain thing. I saw it on TV on one of those news shows. You know where the local authorities declare property is needed for the good of the area and take it? They pay you, of course, though probably not as much as if you sold it yourself."

Kim crossed her arms. "They want the Kincaid property for the amusement park. You have plenty of land out there for the park and still have an ample buffer between it and the town and farms. It's not like anyone's doing anything with the land now. It's just sitting there."

"It's sitting there doing what nature does, and minding its own business. Do we really need to pave it?" She was surprised at her reaction and the vehemence of it. Selling it was one thing. People talking behind her back about forcing her to sell was infuriating.

"Kim, if anyone talks about my land and what I should do with it, you tell them to come talk to me."

"They talked to your father, I'm pretty sure. And Michael, of course."

"Why Michael?"

"Well, your father's working for him and Michael's working with Markland trying to bring them to Preston."

Sickened, Beth walked away from Kim and crossed the library to the alcove. She put her hands on the glass top and looked at the crude, yet artistic layout of the lake, the mill, the hills and farmland. And her land. She saw the plat in her mind's eye—east side of the lake, north side of Powell's creek and running north northwest around the lake.

Should she talk to Ed Mason? She might do better to retain a lawyer to speak with him on her behalf. The amusement park might evaporate. If so, the interest would pass. Given time, she might find a buyer for the land who could create something profitable, but less invasive, less destructive.

Kim had followed her. She looked downcast. "Sorry I upset you. Maybe I shouldn't have told you, but it's all everyone is talking about around here."

"Actually, I'm glad to know this is going on. I had no idea. I should thank you."

"If there's anything I can do, please let me know. I don't want to lose the library. My heart is in this building. A new one wouldn't be the same, but sometimes we have to move on, don't we?" Kim's eyes got bright and shiny. "Anyway, I don't want something happening to someone else that I wouldn't want happening to me."

"Thank you, Kim."

Beth went directly to Billy Monroe's office, annoyed he'd left significant details out of their discussion about the property conveyance. His vague warnings didn't do justice to the facts.

The law office was already closed for the day. It was only four o'clock, yet the sign was turned. She leaned against the door lintel, wondering what to do. Ann might know more than she had shared, but if she did, Beth didn't want to tip her hand. After all, Michael had recommended Ann. They could be working together. She didn't know who to trust.

She couldn't reconcile the Michael she knew with a Michael who was trying to manipulate her for his own betterment. Surely, he meant well. Not everyone was ill-intentioned.

"You're deep in thought."

"Michael."

"Are you speaking to me after this morning? I'm sorry I missed you at the farm. I was out and about early. I came to your house to tell you the news and then, well, you know what happened. Did you hear Markland made the announcement?"

"Yes, I heard the news. And no, I'm not sure I'm talking to you."

Hands in pockets, he glanced down at the sidewalk. "Sorry to hear that."

"There's so much I don't understand."

"Like?"

"Like why did you pay property taxes for Joe?"

Michael nodded toward the park. "Want to take a walk?"

He touched Beth's arm and guided her across the street. "Jay walking," he said. "It's always good to break a rule or two." When they were safely away from traffic, including people traffic, he stopped and watched her expression as he said, "I inherited Joe and his problems from my father."

"You...what?"

"My dad gave Joe a job several years after he got out of jail. For those first few years, Joe couldn't stay sober."

"I remember. That's one of the reasons I hated for Daniel to be out at the house with him." She shook her head and her voice sounded a little lost. "I never understood why he wanted to be out there. Maude tried to make a home for him."

Michael answered, "Somehow your father and mine got together and one day Joe was suddenly employed doing odd jobs at the farm. Dad told me to mind my own business. He said Joe could stay in the small house out by the east pasture, but only if he stayed sober. Mostly, I think he did.

"I didn't find out until I was actively managing the farm that Joe worked for the roof over his head and food, and not much else. He asked Dad to put his wages toward the land taxes. That wasn't enough to cover the taxes in full so Dad helped him sell off a bit here and there when needed. Joe didn't want the cash because he didn't trust himself with it."

They had walked the open area between the street and the lake and veered off to the right, toward the mill.

"Why did he bother?"

"Do you mean, why did my father help him?"

"That too, I guess. Why did Joe bother to keep hold of the land? Why not sell it off and be done with it? He couldn't have had any hope I'd ever come back for it. I didn't even know."

"He had a Will, so you would've inherited regardless. Maude knew."

"She never said a word."

"I can't speak for Maude, but she might not have wanted to tell you, just in case."

"In case he decided to sell it after all?"

"Maybe. I think she helped pay some of the land taxes, too. I think, in fact, though my father has never admitted it, that she had something to do with Dad hiring him on."

"What about eminent domain?" She aimed the words right between his eyes.

Michael moved in closer to her. "Where did you hear that?"

"Does it matter? More to the point, why didn't I hear about it sooner?"

"Because it's only talk. This is a small town in Virginia. Most people here are individualists and won't put up with local officials trying to trump property rights. It's one or two people, and they're speaking out of desperation because they're afraid this town is dying. They want to keep the town as it is and still bring in the tourists."

"That's stupid. If one of those theme parks gets built here the town will change beyond recognition no matter how large the buffer."

"If I thought it was something you needed to worry about, I would've told you, but you'd only just arrived and didn't know about the land. You had your hands full trying to deal with grief and history. I'm glad you talked to Joe."

They sat on the bench at the head of the nature trail. As daylight faded, dark encroached from the fringes of the forest. They sat together in silence. Beth didn't understand what the feelings were between them. Drained by the emotional upheavals of the past few days, she wasn't sure she'd recognize a genuine feeling even if it came labeled.

She gave herself permission to put her doubts about Michael aside for an evening. If he was working behind her back with Markland or the town, one evening of denial wouldn't make much difference.

Beth leaned against him, her head on his shoulder. She sensed a moment of surprise in him as his posture stiffened before he brought his arm up behind her and held her close. The cotton fabric of his shirt brushed against her cheek. She liked the feel of it. As if Michael were hers, someone whose shoulder she was entitled to find comfort against.

One evening of denial…

His arm rested along the back of the bench and his fingers pressed against her shoulder. The tips of his fingers moved downward slightly, tracing small circles on her arm. He shifted his body toward her ever so slightly.

"Beth–"

"Don't."

She refused to change position, but settled in more comfortably. His chin came to rest on the top of her head. When he spoke again, she felt his breath on her hair.

"I–"

"No." She said it nicely. "Not tonight. No talking, please. Just sit for a little while."

He moved his head and kissed her hair. He tightened his arm around her.

Beth allowed herself a small smile, then

placed her hand lightly on his thigh near his knee. The denim was rough, yet smooth as only well-worn denim can be.

They sat together and watched the first stars appear in the twilight sky.

"That's Orion." She pointed at the night sky.

"The Big Dipper and the Little Dipper."

"And the North Star. Reminds me of another evening by the lake a long time ago sitting with someone special."

She moved away from his warmth and stood, extending her hand.

"Walk me to my car?"

****

The representative from Lowery's came in the morning. He walked through the house making notes and muttering under his breath. He had salt and pepper hair and an impressive belly. She tagged along behind him, not quite certain whether to let him roam on his own or to keep an eye on him. He wasn't likely to abscond with a sideboard or nightstand, and in truth, didn't even seem aware that Beth was at his side. He didn't speak to her until they'd been into every room.

"It's nice, not spectacular," he said, still making notes on his list.

"Maude took good care of her furniture."

"Yes, but not high-end, you know. In this market that's a plus. The condition is very good. We'll work up a price for the lot and let you know."

"What if I decide to sell part of it and keep a few pieces?"

"That'll require extra calculating. Which pieces are in question?"

She had no clue, really. "I'll try to come up with a short list."

"Call our office when you know. Be specific. You don't want to have to buy it back from us. Cheaper to keep it. I saw an outbuilding. Anything in there we should list? Old tools or farm implements? Anything like that?"

She led the way to the garage. The man from Lowery's got a glint in his eye when he saw Maude's aqua Buick.

"I'll have a man come appraise the vehicle, shall I? She's a beauty."

"Okay, great."

"Anyone else coming to see?"

"Not yet."

"Well, anyone does, let me know. No promises, but we're interested.

****

The third box waited and she tackled it immediately after lunch. Beth set the box on the piano bench.

The box was filled with personal items. Daniel's old beat-up compass. They'd practically haunted the woods when they were kids. Mostly, Daniel and Michael. Beth, too, when she could keep up with the boys. She ran her fingers over the scratched metal. Dirt was ingrained around the edges of the glass face.

Her old Barbie lay atop a child-size shoebox containing the doll's wardrobe. Bumping around beneath the doll clothing was a daisy ring, a ten-cent trinket from the drugstore.

Daniel bought it for her eighth birthday. She could squeeze it over the tip of her adult-sized little finger.

Maude had packed an assortment of things into this box. Nothing more than odds and ends of a young life.

Beth picked up a woman's hairbrush with a rounded wooden handle, the shellac half worn off. Golden hair was entwined in the bristles. Her breath rushed into her lungs in one gasp and hung there. Her mother's. She looked in the box again and saw a red and blue silk scarf. She pressed it to her face and breathed deeply. Did a trace of her scent still linger?

Beth closed her eyes and exhaled slowly, willing her heart to slow to a saner rhythm.

She would have to go through the items one by one. Maybe in small doses. The stuffiness of the room magnified the emotion and the sensations.

Below the jumble she found something box-shaped wrapped in a soft cloth and below it, a leather album. She slid the top one out from under the loose items. The cloth fell aside and she found she was holding an old Bible. The brown cover was flaking off and the edges were frayed.

Why was a Bible packed in this box of things from her past? She flipped it open.

Names and dates were written on the opening pages. Some in a large uncontrolled scrawl, others in a tight, compressed hand. Much of the ink was faded.

Stewart? Yes, Evan. She looked closer and

could definitely read, Belinda. The Bible was old, with yellowed pages and loose binding. She set it carefully on top of the piano.

A thin, small white envelope was pushed up against the side of the box. Beth slipped it out and saw her name printed in pencil on the front in a youthful hand. She stuck her finger in and pulled the valentine free.

A valentine—a small heart cut from red construction paper and folded in half. The giver had drawn a little arrow broken by a squiggly line. He'd written Beth + Michael.

The memory made her smile. She'd only been six and Michael had slipped the valentine into her backpack. But later he'd ignored her. She figured he was embarrassed and when she told him she'd keep it a secret, he blushed bright red and pretended he didn't know what she was talking about. Some things never changed.

The last item was a photo album. It was long and caught against the box edge as she pulled it out. Her hands jerked and the album tilted. Photos slid out and fluttered to the floor around her feet. Some black and white, some in faded color. She dropped to her knees.

Mama and Daniel on the porch. Daniel with their mutt. Daddy leaning against the car.

Touching them, dropping them, picking them back up, closing her eyes against them, then opening her eyes again because she had to look. Each small square paper held a fragment of her life. The shaking started inside, then spread. The room spun.

Too many sensations. Memories swamped her. Beth heard a high, soft wailing and knew it was her own voice.

Teddy jumped from the piano into her lap. She fell back against the bench. He meowed, twisting in circles in her lap as if he couldn't get comfy. He butted his head against her arm, and began to purr like a freight train.

The spell was broken. Beth was grateful and scratched his neck before pushing him off her lap. She gathered the photos and slid them back into the album.

She hadn't known about any of these keepsakes or photos.

Beth carried the Bible and the album into the kitchen, placed them on the table and forced herself to fix a cup of hot tea before sitting down for a closer, more composed look at her old family photos. She needed to find a safe place for the fragile Bible until she figured out what it was supposed to mean to her.

What other secrets had Maude kept?

Chapter Ten

Stephen took the call on his cell while still sitting behind the steering wheel of his BMW, parked in the motel lot. His instinctive, panicked reaction to the number on the Caller ID was calmed by the Camellia Motel sign blinking vacancy, reminding him that distance bought time, especially since no one outside of Preston knew he was here. Correction: no one in Preston, except the motel clerk, knew he was still here.

Jack Cole said, "Where's my money?"

Cole's voice was disturbingly matter-of-fact. Not a particularly deep voice, but resonant, hinting at his size. He sounded good-natured, as if willing to be amused.

"I told you I'd do my best. Relax, okay?"

"I've been relaxed. Now I want my money."

He started to contradict Cole, to tell him the choice to invest his money had been his, but they'd had that conversation already. He'd made a mistake with Jack Cole. He'd read the open face as literally open, not realizing Cole had an open face because he wasn't bothered by the tangled emotions which troubled most of humankind. If he'd had any inkling of what actually lay behind that bland façade and the crazy blue eyes, and he wouldn't have touched Cole's money under any circumstances.

"It's handled. It's a timing issue. I'm

managing it."

Cole's voice dropped to softer, wheedling tone. "Where is that, Wyndham? Where are you managing it?"

He paused for only a split second, "Fairfax. Where else would I be?"

"I know you aren't home."

"How–," he stopped mid-thought.

"Or at your girlfriend's place." Cole disconnected.

Stephen's blood moved like sludge. His fingers were icy and his brain activity slowed to a crawl. But his stomach and bowels had suddenly gotten active. He clutched his room key. His palms were wet. Had he left anything in his apartment that would guide Jack Cole to Preston?

His breath returned. At his place…nothing. At Beth's apartment, if Cole got inside, he might find out about Preston. Not likely, but not impossible.

Suddenly, the timing issue became critical.

He did still have time. Beth's house wasn't going to sell quickly enough to help, but she could borrow against the land and the house, too. If he couldn't persuade her…then it'd be the backup plan. Not what he wanted to do, not if he had a choice.

Now Beth had become demanding— demanding he leave. It had thrown him off-stride and he'd been impulsive. But he hadn't lost total control. This afternoon he'd been able to return and smooth it over.

His insides had settled down. He could do

this.

He hit re-dial and heard surprise in Cole's voice. He would like to have found some satisfaction in it, but couldn't. It was hard to influence someone who had no dimension to his thinking, no imagination. Cole's brain operated only one level and even that only went simply from point A to point B.

Stephen was accustomed to using his wits to land on his feet. He'd never considered the possibility of physical danger, of getting his bones rearranged. Same with his professional reputation, his intellectual flexibility always kept him ahead of trouble. The problem with Jack Cole was that he didn't have intellectual depth. If he couldn't persuade him to back off, maybe he could turn Cole into a resource.

"What is it, Wyndham?"

"Cole, this will work out, but only if you're patient and give me a little time."

"I've been patient. Now I want my money."

He drew in a deep breath and focused on the number on his motel room door. He said, "And I know how to get it, but that's if you don't do something stupid and screw it up for us."

"Maybe there's hope for you yet. Details?" Cole paused, then added, "That's not a request, Wyndham."

Chapter Eleven

Beth parked on Main Street near Billy Monroe's law office. Mr. Billy Monroe was the one person in Preston whose integrity she didn't doubt. She needed to ask him about eminent domain and what he knew about Michael's involvement.

His office was still closed.

She didn't want to go home yet. She'd been sitting around too much. Beth crossed over to the park. The geese honked loudly. The gaggle looked at her speculatively. Hungry. She turned and headed in the opposite direction, back toward the mill and the bench she'd shared with Michael.

Afternoon light filtered through the trees along the shaded path, tempting her. The idea of her land, her acreage—how imposing that sounded—had caught her attention and now her imagination. She had no special wish to visit the old home place, but she'd like to see the land with her new understanding. That unpainted house had been her grandfather Evan's home, and his bride's, the lovely Emma. Wasn't that how Billy Monroe had referred to her?

And her mother's home for her entire life. A short life.

Her purse, slung over her shoulder, bumped her hip rhythmically as she walked along.

Where the asphalt ended the atmosphere of the trail seemed to change, becoming heavily shadowed. The trees were tall and narrow, closely packed, with the pines having all of their branches high above.

She passed a familiar landmark, a large rock, and beyond that, followed a weedy, overgrown path branching off from the main trail. This was the path to the trestle.

Powell's Creek ran swiftly under the trestle, about a fifteen-foot drop when the water ran high. The creek was relatively narrow here, only about twenty feet wide. A pink strip of plastic hung from a branch above the far bank looking incongruously decorative.

Crossing the trestle had been deliciously scary when she was a child.

She didn't recall feeling a sense of vertigo fifteen years ago. She remembered being light-footed, not light-headed. And fleet and flexible, not this awkwardness adulthood had given her. Not a big deal. She stepped out over the water rushing below.

****

Beth stood in the semi-clearing with itchy weeds scratching her bare ankles and gnats dive-bombing her face. And, ugh, perspiring. Right through the shirt, front and back and underneath and in-between. She plucked at the shirt where it was stuck to her skin.

The house had nothing to offer. A tree had fallen and crushed it into a jumble of rotting wood. Shards of glass and broken roof shingles littered the rough ground.

One of the pictures had showed the smiling family on the porch. What had gone so wrong? How could her parents have allowed such bad stuff into their lives?

Not her parents. Her father. Yet, her mother had been smiling in those pictures, too.

Beth turned her back on the house and picked her way through the weeds and prickles and saplings until she found the remains of a wrought iron fence hidden by an overgrown stand of crape myrtle.

Evan Stewart's stone was easy to read. Emma's was pitted, but readable. Beth walked carefully, wary of areas where the ground was crumbling over older, unmarked graves. What would happen to them now?

If she hadn't found out about the land—if Joe hadn't conveyed it to her and Billy Monroe hadn't told her about her mom's parents—she would never have come out here. She wouldn't have given them a second thought, nor yet a first thought since she'd forgotten they'd ever existed or mattered to anyone.

She'd gone from no family to a bunch of them, and every one of them dead and gone.

Beth stumbled over a small rock, picked it up and sent it flying into the woods beyond.

This desolate land. Land she couldn't even afford to pay the taxes on. She'd have to sell it, either piece by piece or all at once. Why not an amusement park? Why not?

She stepped back, caught her foot in something, and fell hard. She threw her arms out and twisted to avoid the iron spikes of the fence.

Beth missed the spikes, but pain shot up her calf. Lying there amid the crumbling graves panicked her. Her foot was stuck in a...heaven knew what kind of hole. She yanked her foot from the hole in alarm, disregarding the pain. She pushed up to her feet and with most of her weight on her good ankle she hobbled out of the cemetery. Only able to go one halting step at a time, she forced her foot to take her weight and fell. Back up again. Was there nowhere decent to sit? No, not in this forsaken spot. No security back then and no comfort for her now.

Unable to sustain her balance on one foot, she tried to sit, but instead, dropped onto the ground and landed on her side in the weeds. She pushed back up to a sitting position and unzipped her purse's side pocket to pull out her cell phone.

No life. No energy. Her indrawn breath, rough and abrupt, wouldn't release.

Relax, Bethie.

She eased the air out of her lungs slowly and forced herself to think.

Dense, almost untouched forest surrounded the clearing. Preston was well into the foothills of the Blue Ridge Mountains and the elevation was enough to cause cool temps in April and guaranteed cold at night. She wouldn't worry about a chilly night because she'd probably die of fright in the dark long before the frost settled on her.

She could crawl. Undignified, yes, but there was no one here to see. Crawl where? To the road? A long trip on all fours, but more do-able than navigating the grown-over path and the trestle.

The rutted dirt track led to a paved road out of sight from here. It was a lonely road that followed the property line with the Fowler farm, but a more likely place to find help than this isolated clearing.

She'd never tried to crawl with a purse dangling from her neck.

High above some satellite was surely taking pictures of her butt as she crawled on the ground because she'd had some stupid, sentimental idea—*admit it, Bethie*—of seeing the old place, of wanting to see the people in the photos looking happy and whole in this place and on that porch, even if only in her imagination. Here she was, all alone, weeds and sticks pricking her palms.

She was angry and glad of it. Anger kept the fear at bay.

Beth crawled toward a thick, straight branch near a thicket. If it would make a good cane, she might be able to manage on foot.

Her ankle was swelling like a melon and throbbing with pain. She loosened her shoelaces a fraction, but only a little, hoping the structure of the shoe would provide support for the injury.

If she removed the shoe, she wouldn't be able to put it back on.

She heard the sound of motors. Her view was blocked by the thicket, but the noise grew louder. She moved a foot over, to where she could see through the branches.

Rescue, was her first thought. Her second thought was who would be driving out here? Two vehicles. One was a car and the other was a pickup truck.

Beth stayed still and low, peering through the weeds.

The car was white despite the dust cloud. The pickup in its wake looked familiar.

She didn't know the two men who stepped out of the car. They wore dark, pressed slacks and crisp white shirts, sunglasses and perfectly styled hair, exotic in this weedy, despairing place.

The third man, from the pickup truck, joined them.

Michael. Yes, Michael.

What was he doing here with these strangers, pointing this way and that?

The temper she'd worked so hard to control bubbled in her veins like hot lava. She breathed deeply in and out, as slowly and controlled as she could, forcing herself to think.

One of the men walked toward the shattered house. He stopped in front of it and shook his head, then picked his way around to the back, stepping carefully.

Her life, or what had been her life before her parents died, was stripped bare. Looked at and dismissed as so much rubble. A pile of trash. By a stranger.

She grabbed the stick and used it to push herself to her feet. She yelled, "Hey, who are you? What are you doing here?"

Michael and the man both turned. The third man came back around the house, but stood apart. They stared at her, an irate, disheveled woman who'd appeared seemingly out of nowhere.

Michael moved first. "Beth? What are you doing out here?"

"This is my property. The question is what are all of you doing out here on my land?"

"What happened to you?" Michael ran to her, disbelief on his face.

The other men came closer too, and suddenly Beth saw herself, as if from that satellite high above, leaning on a stick, one foot held off the ground, dirty, and heavens above, with a purse hanging from her neck like a freakish adornment.

Michael grasped her arm and then released it to kneel down and touch her ankle.

"Stop, it hurts. Who are these men and what are you doing here?"

The man who'd walked around the house stepped forward and extended his hand. "You must be Beth Kincaid. I'm with Markland Enterprises."

"My hands are dirty." She stared at his proffered hand with no hint of courtesy, and kept her own to herself.

He withdrew his hand comfortably as if not noticing the insult. "It looks like you've had an accident."

Unflappable. This Markland representative was a cool character, but Beth was still simmering.

"What are you doing on my property?"

"Looking at the land. I'd like to speak with you about it personally, but perhaps we need to get you some medical attention first. Can we offer you a ride to town?"

Unflappable, for sure, and yet, Beth noticed there was a quirk to his smile. He was laughing at her. How dare he?

"You talk to me before you set foot on my land again. Understand? I alone represent my interests. No one else."

The man nodded imperceptibly and removed his sunglasses as if to see her more clearly.

Beth saw deep, expressive eyes and met them stare for stare.

Michael cut the meeting short. "Beth, your ankle could be broken. You can explain later."

"Explain? Me? I have nothing to explain."

"Put your arm around my shoulder and I'll support you. Let's get to the truck. Ryan, I'll catch up with you later."

"Hey, wait a minute..." She resisted his arms, his hands. Full of orders, he was.

"Okay, I'll carry you, then."

"What? And trip and kill us both? No, thanks."

"Work with me, Beth. Cooperate." His voice sounded weary. "You can't stay out here."

"Alright, but don't grab at me," she complained. She grasped his arm on one side and the stick on the other.

He helped her hobble about halfway to the truck and then lost patience, stopping and picking her up. "Don't fight or I might drop you. By mistake, of course," he huffed.

Her anger lessened as relief edged in. She wasn't going to spend the night in the wild, after all. But in the truck and driving down the dirt track, it came back like a wave.

It wasn't smart to put the anger aside because she wanted life to be different. Wanting didn't make it different. But she needed to manage the anger, use it like a tool, an asset.

Cultivate cool, Bethie.

Pink streamers tied to branches waved in the breeze at the side of the road, exactly like the ones over by Powell's Creek. Understanding hit her.

"Someone surveyed this property recently." She grabbed Michael's arm. "Who's surveying my land?"

"Hey!" Michael jerked away. "Watch the claws. That hurts. You want to crash?"

"You owe me an explanation."

He scowled at her. His face looked hard. "We'll talk later. Where do you want to go? The walk-in clinic? I can drive to Roanoke if you prefer the hospital."

"The clinic is fine. It's just a sprain. Drop me off at the door." She pushed her hair back behind her ears and a twig caught in her fingers.

"I know you were Daniel's friend, not mine, but I thought we had something going on between us. Whatever it is, or was, apparently doesn't involve honesty and mutual respect."

Michael's jaw clenched, but he said nothing. Beth sank back against the seat. Pain wrapped around and through her ankle, her foot and lower leg.

They rode in silence.

The walk-in clinic was south of Preston. It was still light when they arrived, but near suppertime and the waiting room, lit against the coming night, was empty. When Michael maneuvered to pull into a parking space, Beth said, "No, I'll get out here."

"How will you get home?"

"I'll call a cab."

"There's only Town Cab. Warren Smith operates it."

"It'll do. Thanks for the ride. I can manage from here."

She could almost manage. Michael parked the truck at the curb and helped support her as she limped into the building.

"Beth—"

"Bye. Thanks and goodbye."

"I'll—"

"Just go."

It was a bad sprain. The doctor wrapped it tightly, gave her some crutches, and told her that if she wanted it to heal properly, she should stay off of it for at least two weeks. Then she could get around with crutches.

Yeah, sure. She was a lone woman with a cat and she needed to sell a house or, if not, then she needed to clear out the apartment. This was now possible. If she sold the land she could easily take the next few years off. Travel.

Leave the aggravations behind.

Was that what she wanted? Unless, of course, she'd scared off the only likely buyer an hour or so ago, in which case it was pointless to speculate.

"Miss Kincaid? Did you hear me?" The doctor spoke more loudly.

"Two weeks. I understand." There was no point in spelling out reality to the doc.

They insisted she exit via a wheelchair. By now, it was fully dark outside.

Beth asked the nurse, "Can you call a cab?"

"Oh, no need. Your friend is here."

He was sitting in the waiting room with his long legs stretched out across the floor, boots crossed at the ankles. His usually neat hair was mussed and he looked like he'd been napping.

"I told you to go."

He stood up and jangled his keys. "I'll get the truck."

She couldn't find the energy to argue.

Grimy and disheveled, it galled her to lean on Michael for assistance to climb into the truck, and then again, the porch steps to the house. She stopped him at the door.

"Go home now."

"How are you going to manage?"

"It's not your problem." She shut the door.

****

Having the kitchen on one floor and the bathroom on the other was inconvenient. Beth hobbled around with the crutches despite the doctor's orders because after this long, emotional, discouraging day, she had a great empty pit called a stomach suddenly screaming for food. Her stomach competed with Teddy's and Teddy was howling in outrage about his empty food dish.

Her crutches kept snagging on chair legs and banging into cabinets. It was a relief to drop some snacks into a plastic bag, abandon the crutches at the base of the stairs and climb up on hands and knees. This fascinated Teddy who accompanied her the entire way, running ahead and coming back, as if encouraging and coaching her.

She needed a soak, badly. Had to keep the bandaged ankle dry, of course. Maude's tub was an old claw foot with high sides. She started the water running and ditched the clothing. Bits of dried weedy stuff littered the linoleum floor. Dirty laundry. Dirty floor. Even the least annoyance seemed insurmountable because everything she did would have to be done while dragging the injured ankle along with her.

****

She called Ann in the morning.

"I sprained my ankle yesterday and I can't get around too well."

"Sorry to hear that. Anything I can do?"

"No. I wanted you to know in case someone wants to come by and see the house. I'll try to be unobtrusive, but I can't go anywhere. I'll be here at the house."

"No problem. If I can bring you anything, let me know. Who's helping you out?"

"I appreciate you asking, but I'm fine.

Thanks."

She was managing with the crutches, but couldn't entirely stay off the foot. The biggest headache was the bathroom being on the second floor. The foot hurt, of course. She wanted to get off of it and prop it up somewhere.

For sure, she wouldn't be able to check her email at the library for a while. Luckily, it wasn't her accelerator/brake foot, so it wouldn't keep her from driving after the pain was no longer a distraction. The greatest obstacle would be moving around outside of the car.

Celeste called.

"How's your brother doing?"

"Better. I'm home now."

"Can you send my mail?" But Celeste had given Stephen her mailbox key. "Sorry. I forgot. You don't have the key."

"I can get it back from Stephen. Or go to the management office. I think they keep spares. What about the mail he collected? Or did he already send it?"

She bit her lip before finding the words. "I already got it from him."

"Okay." She sounded non-committal.

"He won't be getting my mail anymore."

"Oh, okay. I see. I think."

"Would you mind taking care of it?"

Celeste gave a little chuckle. "Don't mind at all. Happy to. The rental office might want to confirm with you." There was a brief hesitation, then she asked, "Are you coming back, Beth? You've been gone a while now."

Beth paused, and it was telltale, especially to herself.

"I'm not sure," she said. "Just have them call me."

****

Mr. Markland's assistant called at noon to inquire about her injury.

How odd that someone would call and express sympathy on behalf of someone else, both equally strangers. It was easy to be cold on the phone, if only to his assistant, and even if it was petty. Mr. Markland had no business discussing her interests with anyone but her, and he had no business being on her property without asking first.

"Mr. Markland will be glad to hear you're better," he said.

"I'm so glad he'll be relieved."

There was a long silence. Beth waited.

"He'd like to come by your house. Would this evening be convenient?"

Now he had Beth's attention. Evening seemed an odd time to drop by to discuss business.

"What does he want to talk about?"

"I'm sorry, I don't know. He's leaving the area tomorrow and asked me to arrange a meeting with you for today. Would late afternoon or early evening be possible?"

"Yes. I mean, either is fine." She shook her head in confusion. Did she need Billy Monroe present?

"Do you prefer beef, chicken, or vegetarian?"

"I don't understand."

"I'm sorry, Miss Kincaid. Mr. Markland will bring dinner with him. You're confined to home, correct? Did I misunderstand?"

"No, I am. He's bringing dinner?" Oh, why not? "Beef is fine." She could play his game, whatever it was. She was tired of harassing the assistant. It seemed unworthy.

"Will six o'clock be convenient?"

Chapter Twelve

White linen spanned the area between them. It was more like a catered meal than takeout, and Ryan Markland of Markland Enterprises was seated opposite her.

She was profoundly glad she'd made the effort to dress up despite the struggle with the stairs. She'd thought she was arming herself for a business meeting, but instead, found herself in the midst of something with much more dimension, with intriguing, fascinating undercurrents.

Her skin tingled. She'd forgotten about her ankle—the pain, the wrappings and the inconvenience—all of it. He had that kind of aura. Without the distraction of the dust and insects, and her natural annoyance at the situation when they'd first met, it was as if a veil had dropped. Her vision was clear. As silly as her reaction seemed, even to her, she wanted to reach across the expanse of white linen and touch him, his hand, maybe his face. He had beautiful skin, lightly tanned, and lovely small pores.

She restrained the impulse and, instead, picked up her glass of iced tea and took a sip, and then a deep breath. He smelled good, too.

Ryan's eyes were dark and deep and his manners were perfect.

Could he read her mind? The warmth of a

flush touched her face.

They'd almost finished the salad course and yet the dinner still had a fantasy feel. The idea of someone bringing the equivalent of a restaurant to her humble catalog home was intoxicating. Maude would've loved it. She would've dabbed that White Shoulders behind her ears and donned her pearls. Her furniture, her good china, the faded table linens, everything seemed to have picked up a special glow. Nothing looked threadbare or worn out in the soft light of the fancy lamps on the sideboard.

Teddy stayed in the kitchen with the chef. The chef. She said the word out loud again to feel it roll off her tongue in the same sentence as 'my house.'

"You brought a chef to my house." Oh, yes, she was impressed.

"Not exactly a chef, though Frank is very capable."

"He's probably accustomed to more modern kitchens."

"Give the credit to Olive Garden. Frank found one near Roanoke. They were great about arranging takeout. The food was already partly cooked. Frank will finish some of the items and warm the rest."

"This house has never smelled so delicious."

"This house is amazing."

"Mr. Markland, you are charming, but now you're overdoing it. Amazing?" She tried to sound serious.

"Please, call me Ryan. And, yes, when I

arrived I thought I'd walked right back into great aunt Eileen's house. I had a host of great aunts and she was my favorite."

"Big family?"

He nodded as Frank walked in bearing the entrée.

"Beef Gorgonzola-Alfredo. I hope you like it."

"Of course." She had no doubt she would.

Mr. Markland. Ryan. Who was this magic man, anyway? A hard-headed, hard-hearted businessman? His voice was smooth and cultured, yet slightly rough, as if not too far removed from humbler roots. Educated expensively by the sound of it. He'd made this lovely scene materialize in her lonely home, had pushed her recent miseries from her brain, and she didn't know how to think of him. She was sure her pleasure showed.

"I'm serious about this house," he insisted. "It's a page out of history. It's a history many of us experienced and remember among the memories that make up our lives."

"I've been reading about them and you're right."

"They make an interesting tie between many towns and cities across the country, including Preston. Preston and Newark." Ryan poured iced tea from the pitcher into his glass. "My great aunt had a pale green sofa like that one. I remember it well because she didn't allow us children to sit on it for fear of dirt." He waved toward the living room. "What did she call it? Not a sofa…"

"A Davenport?"

"That's it. I haven't heard that term since I was a child."

"I don't want to spoil the mood and the meal, but I asked you a question when you arrived and you avoided answering. I have to ask again. Why are you here?"

"To speak with you. To apologize for offending you."

"To size me up?"

Ryan smiled and buttered a bread stick. "When we met, it was under difficult circumstances. Not the best way to be introduced."

"Why was it like that? Why didn't you contact me sooner?"

"You weren't the owner of the property."

"Well, yes, that's true." Too much had happened too quickly. The timing was fuzzy.

"Mr. Kincaid didn't want to discuss it. Now I understand why. He wanted you to have the property and make the decisions regarding it."

She tried to sound cool. "Do you want the property, Mr. Markland?"

"We are sitting here sharing a meal in your dining room and I believe we are enjoying each other's company. I know I am absolutely enjoying your company."

Beth tried not to grin—*lose the dimples, girl*—and settled for a nod that she hoped was dignified.

"As I told you earlier, I'm not *the* Mr. Markland. That's my father. I'm the legs of the business. He doesn't enjoy travel and isn't about to walk through fields and such. My brother has a family and prefers the city."

"The city?"

"New York."

"He has a family?"

"Wife and children."

"But not you." Fencing. Parrying light thrusts. Thrusts, not dangerous lunges. It was fun.

"No family."

He sat still, but relaxed. No fidgeting. No knuckle-cracking. And with a benign half-smile that intrigued her.

"You travel around checking out properties Markland is interested in acquiring?"

"Yes, that's part of it, but there's more than land to consider in any project."

His nails were manicured. Their satin perfection mesmerized her for a moment as she watched his hand grasp and lift his glass.

She shook it off, forcing herself to re-focus on business. "What else are you considering?"

'Demographics, community and economic studies, local government...'

"I'm actually surprised big projects like this are happening. Aren't things tight right now? Financing and such? Isn't tourism down?"

"Projects like this span years. They don't happen overnight. They stop, start, mutate. Sometimes they go poof." He turned his hands palms up in understated emphasis.

"And this project? Do you want to buy my land?"

Ryan laughed. "Do you want to sell it?"

"I don't know. I'm still trying to grasp that I

own it."

He leaned forward. "You live and work in Northern Virginia. You arrived here and found unexpected...opportunities. You need time to think about it, but also want to divest yourself of it and go back to real life. Is that right?"

Beth re-arranged the napkin in her lap. "This isn't real life?"

"Not for you, I think. I look around the room and see no change. Unless I'm wrong and you've re-decorated back to pre-1950? This has the temporary feel of someone passing through."

Beth was silent. She'd been thinking more and more of staying, yet she hadn't changed even the location of a crystal ash tray. Was this just another way of running and hiding?

"I'm unemployed. Stay or go? I'm not sure what I want to do, but I don't like the idea of acres of asphalt and tourists practically on my doorstep."

"Fair enough. The Not-In-My-Backyard syndrome?"

Beth waited while Frank picked up the emptied plates, then asked, "What about 'for the greater good'? I understand there's been some discussion along those lines."

Ryan sat back. "What do you want? That's what you need to decide. Let the other things take care of themselves. They'll fall into place."

Frank interrupted. "Would you like chocolate sauce or strawberries on the cheesecake? Or both?"

"Both?" She laughed softly in delight at the

entirety of this evening. "I think I'm in love. Thank you, Frank." She looked at Ryan expecting to find laughter and instead, caught surprise on his face. And something else, admiration? Not for her character, surely. They barely knew each other. Still, it was flattering to be thought attractive. She focused on Ryan, continuing the conversation as if nothing had distracted her.

"While I'm not watching out for my business, will someone else be taking care of it for me? With or without my permission?"

He spoke, carefully weighing his words, "There were persons who were interested in representing your business."

"Without my knowledge or consent."

"You have friends and there are always third parties who perceive an interest. It isn't unusual. Any kind of change, especially where profit may be involved, brings out the best and worst in people."

"Well, it's a new experience for me. Who contacted you regarding my land?"

"Many people contact us when they hear about possible projects. Some have legitimate interests. I respect their privacy as I do yours."

Sounded like a pre-programmed speech.

"Michael Fowler. What about him?"

"Alright." He held up his hand in mock surrender. "One. It's the least I can do since he was there on your property with me. Michael Fowler was unofficially speaking for your father. As an adjacent property owner, it was natural for us to talk."

"For a finder's fee, maybe?"

"If he played a pivotal role in finding and assisting us in acquiring the land, then a fee would be reasonable. He never attempted to negotiate for the land."

"And who else?" Stephen's name was on the tip of her tongue, but she didn't want to offer it up to Ryan Markland. Maybe there was still a tender memory left, after all. Still a hope that her judgment hadn't been totally wrong.

Ryan smiled and shook his head slowly. Silence was his answer.

He lingered after the meal ended. Their conversation continued beyond dessert as Frank whisked away the last dishes and a soft rattle came from the kitchen from time to time as he cleaned up. At one point, her ankle began to throb and she must have grimaced because Ryan insisted she prop up her foot. He maneuvered a chair into position and placed her foot on the seat, his fingers careful to avoid pressure on her ankle. Beth was speechless.

Ryan spoke. "It's time to say goodnight. If I return to Preston, may I visit you? By then, your ankle will be better."

Her cheeks burned. She was pretty sure Ryan was used to this sort of reaction because his voice grew warmer.

"You're flushed. Are you okay?"

She looked up quickly and met his eyes. His dark eyes sparkled in the low light of the lamps. Was he mocking her?

"I'm fine. You are just...not what I expected."

He furrowed his brow. "This meeting was

rather last minute, but I thought you were okay with that."

He left an opening for further explanation that mesmerized like a jeweled chasm. Dangerous, but inviting. "That's not what I meant."

He stared, politely and patiently, waiting her out. She jumped back in to fill the gap.

"I thought you were planning to tear up nature in favor of asphalt. Everything sacrificed for corporate development. I was prepared not to like you."

Ryan laughed out loud. "I'm glad you found the reality better than the assumption."

"Frank's probably done in the kitchen by now. He must be excruciatingly bored without a TV or anything."

Ryan didn't answer.

She called out, "Frank?"

"I imagine he's done and out in the car, probably relaxing and listening to the radio. Don't worry about Frank. He's fine."

She was reluctant to see him leave, as if a rare and special light would go with him, but she was also ready for him to leave. He should go now while she was still charmed by his charisma.

He left with a handshake. With his departure—the removal of his physical presence—the attraction wasn't extinguished, but it diminished to a more comfortable level. She stood, propped on her crutches, and smiled at the closed door.

Ryan was a man who could make any

woman feel desirable simply by looking at her, even one hobbled by crutches and bandages. It was easy to respond to him. Why? Aside from the obvious, that Ryan Markland was a rare, exotic creature who had delightfully and unexpectedly passed a few hours in her catalog home, it was all about the present. There was no inconvenient history to trip over with Ryan as there was with Michael, few expectations and much less risk to her heart.

Chapter Thirteen

Late-morning, Michael called to say he was bringing lunch. Beth gave him credit for courage, or maybe he was just foolish. He couldn't know Ryan had cleared him of insinuating himself in her business, nor that she was still in a glowing good mood from the evening before.

Beth set the table, cheerful despite the annoyance of dealing with the crutches. She folded the napkins perfectly and added knives and forks.

When she answered the door, Michael's demeanor seemed serious, but once inside his mood brightened. He walked straight back to the kitchen and deposited the white paper bags on the table.

"I'm glad you've decided not to be mad at me," he said. He opened the bags. "I brought salads and cheeseburgers."

"And fries?"

"And fries."

"Good, because I'm working off extra calories fighting with these crutches and I'm starving."

He held the chair for her as she sat, then situated her injured ankle on the opposite chair.

"You're supposed to keep your foot elevated. You shouldn't be 'fighting' with the crutches or anything else. Didn't the doc tell you to stay off the ankle?"

"Gotta live. I'm a single girl and don't have a lot of choice in the matter." She waved at the far end of the table. "Shoo!"

Teddy's pink nose was showing above the edge of the table and his whiskers twitched. Beth started to rise.

"I'll get it. What do you need?"

"Push that chair in all the way to discourage Teddy."

"Okay."

He slid the chair up close to the table. Teddy vacated the chair and parked himself near the stove, still keeping a steady eye on the table and floor beneath it.

"Pearl's has the best burgers and fries. This was a great idea."

"It's not fancy, but I agree it tastes good."

Something had changed in Michael's mood. He appeared subdued again, as if distracted by unvoiced thoughts. They ate in silence and the food was soon gone. Beth started gathering the plates and trash, but Michael stepped in. He put the plates in the sink and disposed of the trash.

Beth insisted on doing the dishes. "This will only take a second."

"I'd have been happy with just the paper wrappers."

"But I have these others dishes, too. I'd love it if you'd dry." She smiled and handed him the towel.

Michael was wiping the first dish when he asked, "What did you think of Ryan Markland?"

Deliberately, she kept her eyes on her task

as she swished the utensils with sudsy water.

"He was here for dinner last night. How did you know?"

"The whole town knows."

"He's such a gentleman." Beth breathed the words. She sounded like a silly teenager and she didn't care.

Michael stared, shaking his head. "I don't know what you mean by that. He didn't spit in public? What?"

"Ha, ha." She laughed sarcastically, then saw Michael was really bothered by her statement. "Look, you've been around him. Didn't you notice anything special? I can't believe it's just a girl thing."

"He's...he's just some corporate guy."

"Oh, come on. You were practically his tour guide."

Michael's blue eyes had turned frosty. Okay, so she was teasing him, maybe, but what she was saying was also true.

"Well, if you don't understand, then I don't think I can explain."

Michael stayed silent. How annoying. Why should he care if she found Ryan Markland attractive? Michael had made it clear he wanted to be just friends. Buddies.

Jealous? He didn't have the right.

She turned her back and busied herself at the sink. She was getting better at the crutch stance—a crutch in each arm pit, one foot down, injured foot up, swish the dishcloth in the glass, rinse and hand to Michael to dry—but Michael was no longer there. He'd moved a few feet away.

Beth twisted partway around and balanced with one hip against the counter, still holding the dripping glass. "What's up with you? Have you got something on your mind? Get it out or drop the attitude."

"How do you feel about me?"

"Do you really want to know?"

"Yes."

Her heart stopped for a beat and her lips went numb. For that moment, she was unable to respond and, truly, she didn't know how to respond. The truth crystallized in her brain as if it and her heart were, at long last, communicating.

Her words fell softly into the quiet room like a confession, or an indictment. "When I left Preston behind, I left more than a town, more even than my father. I left you, too." After a pause to calm herself, she said, "I put you behind me forever. I thought I'd succeeded until..." She forced her eyes to meet his. "I love you. I have always loved you, Michael. I think you know that."

Beth waited. Michael stared at her as if trying to read a code he couldn't decipher. For one, long horrible moment, she thought he might not say anything at all, but then, when he did, she wished he'd kept his mouth shut.

"No, I don't know it. You had a crush when you were a kid. Maybe I did, too. But love? What does love mean to you, Beth?"

Fire rushed up to her face. She tried to speak without anger, but without the heat, anger sounded like, felt like, despair. She took a deep breath.

"Love is something that happens to people regardless of common sense or preference. I have loved you since the first moment I saw you. I was four. Daniel brought you over to our house after school. I was waiting for him on the porch and the two of you came walking down the road, kicking the white dust in the air. Do you remember?" A cold, hard lump formed in her chest.

Michael said, "First day of second grade. Daniel and I got off the school bus together. Instead of walking up the road to my house, I went with him. My father whipped me good when I got home because I made mom worry."

"You looked so tall. You and Daniel both seemed so grown up to me." Still balanced on the crutch and leaning against the counter, Beth folded the dish towel. The towel was cool and damp. She wished she could press it to her face. She'd summoned every speck of rationality in her being to present this calm exterior, but it was all a front. Michael had rejected her attempt to talk about their feelings for each other a few days ago at the mill when he told her to let go of the past, so what was this about?

She laid the towel on the counter and reached for the second crutch.

"The past, Michael. You told me to put it behind me, but how can anyone really do that? We bring our past with us wherever we go. We—you and I—have a shared history. I look at you and remember Daniel, Joe... Mama. I remember those awful days. It isn't your fault. It's just how it is. I was naive to hope it could be different."

"Different?"

"Yes, I wish I could be different, and you, too. But we are who we are."

"Do you really want it to be different or are you just afraid?"

That bothered her. "Me? Afraid of what?"

"Of facing the past and putting it aside."

"Now see, that's what I mean. It's so much better when people meet and fall in love as adults. No history. No messy baggage to work around." She thought of Ryan. The lack of bad history together made it so much easier to simply relax and have fun, not constantly trying to avoid pushing each other's buttons.

"Was that the secret of your success with that guy in Fairfax? What's his name? Stephen?"

Stephen. Beth gripped the metal tubes of the crutches. She squeezed her hands around them until her nails bit into her hands. "Not every relationship works out."

"Have you ever had one that did?"

She spoke, keeping her focus on the linoleum floor. "You should go." Without looking up, she raised her voice, "You aren't any better. Where's your soul mate? How many women have you left at the altar?"

Michael ignored her accusations and shot back. "The past. History. It's part of who we are, but not all we are. Not all of your memories are bad. You were a happy kid. Don't act like your childhood was one long tragedy that should cripple you for a lifetime."

"My mother—"

"Yes, I know, she died. That was a tragedy, but what about the rest?"

"My father was an alcoholic."

"He drank. A lot. Way too much. Sometimes he got angry. I remember. Alcohol and anger don't mix well. And it was worse toward the end. But I also remember how he spoiled you. When he was sober, he treated you like a princess."

"That made it more of a nightmare. I knew how good a father he could have been."

"But it wasn't all bad. Maude gave you a good life. She cared about you."

"Maude did her best. It wasn't the same."

"That was a long time ago and you've got a lot of years ahead. Why can't you enjoy the good memories and not dwell on the bad?" He shook his head. "I don't get it, Beth. Are you still looking for someone to blame or punish?"

She'd had as much humiliation as she could handle. "You think I'm all about self-pity, is that it? It's all about me, right? Then why don't you go? Just leave. I haven't asked you to keep coming 'round, but you show up with food and gifts. I was willing to accept you on your terms, as a friend, but I don't want your friendship if all it means is lectures and put-downs. Go before you destroy whatever good remains between us."

Michael's face had flushed red and he hit the wall with his hand, pulling his punch at the last moment and instead, pressed his open hand against the wall as if holding it in place.

"You have to learn to forgive. No one's perfect, Beth. Forgive your father, forgive me."

"You?"

"Everyone, I mean..." His voice dwindled off.

Beth waited, wondering, as he took a deep breath and open his mouth to speak again, but the doorbell rang. Michael stared at her crutches and headed to the door. Beth clunked along behind him.

The stranger at the door held a blue glass vase filled with white roses.

Michael cast an angry look her way, then accepted the flowers. The vase was large and hefty. He glared at her between the half-open buds. "Do you want these on the kitchen table?"

"Thanks." She glared back at him.

Michael reached into the roses and pulled out the card which he handed to Beth as he stalked past to the kitchen.

She slid the note card out of the small envelope never doubting who'd sent the roses. It was absolutely his style. She read aloud, "Thanks for the wonderful evening and for allowing me into your home. Ryan."

Michael watched her from the kitchen. Even with the length of the hallway between them, she sensed his question and the heat of his emotion.

"It's a thank you. He has good manners."

His voice was low. It smoldered as he said, "He's a businessman."

Did he think she'd forgotten why Ryan had

come to Preston? "He's too smart to think a vase of roses would have any impact on land transactions. In fact, he doesn't even know if Markland will want the land."

Michael walked toward her. Their eyes locked. Beth refused to back down. He strode past her and out of the door, closing it as he went.

She was disappointed and sad. Frustrated. She didn't want to be at war with Michael. There could be no winner, only victims. Somehow, they had to get their acts together even if that meant accepting they were better apart.

****

Mrs. Boyle brought over a casserole. "I heard about your fall. Different people are coming and going around here. It seemed a good idea to check and make sure you're okay."

People as in male people? "Thanks, can you put it in the kitchen?"

"Certainly." She went down the hallway.

Beth waited by the front door for Mrs. Boyle to return.

She said, "I'm going to the grocery store in the morning. Do you need anything?"

"That's very nice of you, Mrs. Boyle. I think I have what I need."

"Here's my phone number." She held out a small square of paper. "Was that Michael Fowler who left a short time ago?"

"Yes. Do you know him?"

"Of course. A nice enough man, but you're an attractive young woman. He has a reputation." Mrs. Boyle pursed her lips signaling 'nough said.'

"What sort of reputation?"

"With women. Fear of commitment. Dr. Phil talked about it. He's a smart man, Dr. Phil is. One of the few."

Beth opened, then closed her mouth. She'd been about to snap back regarding Michael's reputation, but the last remark almost choked her. Mrs. Boyle meant well.

"I understand. Thank you for your concern. Michael and I are friends from childhood."

"Well, then. Call if you think of anything you need from the grocery store."

Mrs. Boyle left. Beth crutch-walked back to the kitchen avoiding Teddy who tried to weave his body in and out, around her ankles and the crutches.

"Teddy. Quit it. You're going to trip me and who'll be here to help me? Not you. You'll just purr me to death."

She fixed a cup of tea and sat at the table, thinking of Maude. Had Maude ever been in love? Beth had asked her a few times, but Maude would only say times were different when she was young. Was it true? She'd been very young, barely sixteen when Pearl Harbor was bombed. About twenty when the war ended. What about Rosie the Riveter? Maybe it had been different for a young woman in a small town.

Beth pulled the photo album across the table to where she sat. Someone someday might care. Someone had cared enough to keep the photos together even if the project hadn't progressed too far.

The black corner triangle pieces were tucked into the folds of the book and a tube of glue was stashed in a kitchen drawer. She took another look at the photos and spread them across the table, arranging them. Some of the photos had names and dates written on the back in an old-fashioned script.

She pulled the old Bible closer and opened it carefully. The Stewart Family Bible. Beth studied the handwritten entries on the first pages and tried to match them up with the oldest pictures. Teddy climbed up on the table, but she fussed and swatted at him until he settled for a nearby chair.

The beauty and scent of the white roses was uplifting and easing.

Regarding matters of the heart, Martha Boyle's words about Michael and commitment issues kept coming back to her. Maybe Martha had something there. Every time they started getting close, he became touchy and full of lectures. It was something to consider.

He accused her of hiding behind bad memories. Maybe he'd found his own way to hide from love and risk.

After a while, she pushed the project aside, planning to come back with a fresh eye.

Beth picked up Maude's book and sat on the Davenport where she could prop up her foot. She'd done enough thinking for today. Plus, she'd tested the emotional waters by going through the photos again and was pleased she was handling it better. Now it was time for a break. It was time to discover what the gray lady on the cliff was up to that caused her such distress.

Chapter One

Joshua's Hope was well-known in the vicinity of Lancashire for the tempestuous nature of its inhabitants. For generations, the Joshua family was admired or feared by the gentry, as well as the general populace thereabouts, depending upon the nature of their relationship with the ancient family. Some said it was due to the sea from which the first male Joshua was reported to have sprung, struggling ashore when his ship was struck down in one of the vicious storms spawned by the Irish Sea. He refused to go back to sea, cursing its dark, treacherous nature, and 'twas said the sea cursed him back, condemning his descendants to share its torment.

She had heard all this and more, from her guardian and others. The stories, true or not, likely contributed to her state of unease, as did her lack of food. Indeed, her guardian had left the vicinity many years ago at odds with his difficult, imperious son. His departure had taken him abroad and brought him into contact with her own father, also an ex-patriot Englishman. Her father sickened soon after. His death was sudden and unexpected and, before he died, he pressed his new friend to watch over his young daughter and her estate—a sad estate that did not long survive the beginning of the guardianship.

The grey-stoned Joshua manor home was imposing. It sat atop the hill like a bejeweled crown surrounded by extensive grounds and pristine forests. Denied sight of the sea, yet the wind from the west bore the smell of the sea that served as lure or reminder of the first one— the progenitor of the current family. Maggie saw the distant stone edifice framed in sun and shadow and wondered at its cruel reputation.

The last man to speak of it to her, the master of the hostelry where the public carriage disembarked the local travelers, had glowered when asked the way to Joshua's Hope such that she trembled and dared not ask the favor of free conveyance. Her purse was empty and she could pay no hire, so it was only left for her to walk the rest of the way.

She clutched her dark, worn cloak more closely about her slight, yet buxom frame and shivered. Her shoe leather was so thin that each stone in the road was an instrument of torture. But her walk was nearing its end and she must summon her courage and put aside fear and pride. Her desperate need outweighed her personal inclination. She must overcome her weakness. She must traverse that dusty drive and brave the imposing door for there was nowhere else for her to go. Joshua's Hope was her last hope.

Maggie was in the shade of the elms lining the drive when she heard a distant thunder that shook the ground. Suddenly, rounding the curve in the drive and bearing directly down *upon her, came a black, lathered stallion. Its monstrous hooves pounded a rhythm that echoed in her terrified heart. She could not move so greatly did she fear, as if the devil himself were bent upon her destruction, until the last moment when she fell aside, agony striking her head and shoulder. The world spun in pain and darkness, until gratefully, Maggie succumbed to unconsciousness.*

Beth turned the book over to check the cover flap. The author's black and white photo showed a middle-aged, dark-haired woman, distinguished, yet pleasant looking. She flipped back to the opening pages and found the copyright. 1966.

Beth returned to reading and followed Maggie's limp form as it was carried into the house by her rescuer, the reckless man who'd almost killed her, though not through the front door, but instead through the servants' entrance.

Beth was halfway through the book before she put it aside. She was surprised at how much time had passed, but in a good way. She'd stayed off her foot, hadn't she?

Not great literature, maybe, but she'd willingly stepped into Maggie's life for a couple of hours. Maggie's difficulties were more appealing than her own and she was happy to abandon her worries for a while as Maggie accepted food and a dry bed in the attic in exchange for maid's work, while of course, her obvious beauty, genteel manners, and intelligence could not escape the notice of the dark, brooding master of the house, nor the bed-ridden spouse who couldn't produce an heir.

Good stuff. Beth hadn't realized what she'd been missing. Given that the book was published in 1966, Beth felt assured of a happy ending, at least for Maggie, maybe not for the invalid wife.

Beth was hungry. Teddy's warm, purring body was wedged between her side and the Davenport's back. What had been cozy, was now cramped. She tried to edge away, but he woke immediately and jumped lightly to the floor, looking offended.

He'd forgive her when she fed him.

Feeding herself was more difficult. She examined Mrs. Boyle's casserole, but saw green specks that looked suspiciously like broccoli and slid it back in the fridge. Her cabinets were pretty empty. If she'd known she'd be sidelined with a sprained ankle, she'd have planned ahead better. No warning, of course. Bad news rarely gave advance notice.

Mrs. Boyle had offered, but Beth had turned her down. A reflex. She never needed anyone's help, right? It wasn't too late; she could still call her, but that wouldn't help her this evening.

Supper with Michael two nights in a row. Fine dining with Ryan. Lunch today with Michael. Enjoyable in retrospect, even with the subsequent drama, embarrassment and heartache. For a woman who hadn't sought drama or male attention, she was staying pretty busy. But where did she and Michael stand now? Was he just pouting or gone for good?

She settled for crackers and peanut butter.

A lot of emotional storms lately. It reassured her that when the storm passed, calm and rationality were still in control. She was glad she'd told Michael. Now, it was out in the open. The next move was Michael's—if he chose to take it.

Chapter Fourteen

Joshua's Hope had fallen to the floor during the night. Beth had taken Maggie's story to bed and couldn't stop turning the pages until Maggie had survived the murderous attempt of the invalid wife's childhood nurse turned lady's maid who was determined to keep Maggie from succumbing to the master's dark charms and breaking the wife's heart. Maggie wasn't out of danger yet because the evil doers avoided being found out, but Beth's need for sleep had won eventually.

Mid-morning, she was still in bed when the realization she'd been in Preston for nearly two weeks hit her. The phone rang. Ann wanted to bring someone by to see the house.

"Not too early, I hope. I need a little time. I'm slow with the crutches."

"Stay at the house. Ignore us while we're walking around."

"Can you give me an hour?"

"Two hours. I'll put you at the end of the list."

Whew. It didn't even bother her that the buyer might like one of the other houses better. She'd barely dressed when Lowery's called.

"We've got an estimate for you, Ms. Kincaid. I'd like to set up an appointment for our rep to come out and go over it with you."

"Can't you tell me the price?"

"He'd like to bring someone with him to look

at the vehicle."

"Okay. When?"

"Tomorrow morning at ten o'clock?"

Beth took Maggie and the cell phone and went out to sit by the lake. It was an interesting exercise to navigate the back steps, but the hand rail made it possible and the brick walk kept the crutches from sinking into the ground. The air outside was comfortable, warmish for April, but she'd forgotten the grass would likely be damp with the morning dew. She concentrated on keeping her bandaged foot lifted to keep it dry, not noticing the dark figure already seated.

The girl heard her almost at the moment Beth realized she was there. She stood abruptly, glanced at Beth, then quickly turned away and walked off.

"Wait. Hey, wait. I can't move fast."

The girl stopped and looked back at her, expressionless. Her face was pale. Dark, thick hair frizzed around her head and gave the impression she'd spent damp, chilly hours by the lake.

"You weren't out here all night, were you?"

She shook her head. She was wearing some sort of drab jacket shirt with multiple pockets and her hands were shoved into the lower ones, her shoulders rolled forward. "No. Just since dawn. I didn't mean to bother anyone."

"You didn't. Were you one of the kids here the other night?"

"The guys didn't come back. I told them not

to. They didn't mean to cause any trouble."

"Maybe not, but it's still wrong to trespass on private property."

She shrugged, turning away again.

"What's your name?"

"Sorry. I'll go."

"I wasn't asking so I could get you into trouble. I only wanted to know what to call you."

"Elise."

"I'm Beth Kincaid. Did you know the lady who lived here before?"

"Yes. No. I knew who she was, but she didn't come out here at night. I think she went to bed early and we tried to be quiet. Didn't want to scare her or anything. She never said anything to us so we figured she didn't mind."

"Trash was left in the gazebo and someone tossed her wicker furniture in the lake."

Elise didn't answer. She stood awkwardly, caught between leaving and staying. "Was she your grandmother or something?"

"No, she was my guardian. She took me in when my family fell apart."

Elise looked at the ground, drawing her eyebrows together in thought. Finally, she spoke, "I have to go now."

"Okay. Thanks for staying to talk. You can sit out here when you want, but if anyone else wants to hang out, they have to ask me first."

"The guys found another place to go. They won't be back." She looked down, her hair falling forward like a curtain, and walked away.

Her demeanor was disturbing. Vulnerable. Teenage moodiness? The problem of the gazebo kids appeared to be solved and she was relieved, but the memory of the dark-haired teenager lingered.

****

Ida Langhorne showed up in the afternoon. "Mr. Monroe told me you'd had a mishap."

Beth backed a step on the crutches. "Hi. Come in."

The visitor walked straight back to the kitchen. She sat a plastic grocery bag filled with food items on the table. "Lovely flowers." She leaned over them and breathed in. "Oh, my. Well, looks to me like you've got yourself an admirer."

Beth kept her lips clamped together while trying to smile politely.

Ida smiled back. "You got any iced tea, honey? Never really had a taste for hot tea."

"Sorry, no tea. How about a glass of water or a soda?"

"Diet's fine, if you've got it. You sit, I can get it myself."

She helped herself to a glass and a can of soda and settled herself at the table. She flipped open the photo album. "Mind?"

"Go ahead. Maude kept the photos…for me, I think."

"Oh, my. Look at that. I remember your mama. What a beautiful girl she was. They were quite the pair."

Beth's curiosity stirred like an unsatisfied appetite. She wanted Ida to continue talking, to see her parents through Ida's eyes, from an adult's perspective.

"I remember how quiet she lived with her daddy out in the woods. Wouldn't say 'boo' to a mouse, that is, until your daddy came to town. She was a teenager by then and they took to each other right off. I guess her daddy, Evan, wasn't too happy about the match, but he was always so concerned about his health. Never was a healthy man. Not a day passed but what he thought he was checking out permanently. I expect he thought Joe would be better than no husband at all, leaving his daughter unprotected, you might say, so he signed for Belinda to marry. She was underage, you know. Did your mama ever tell you?"

"No."

"Not surprising. Probably didn't want you going in the same direction. Marrying young and all that. A real sweet girl, she was. It's nice you're putting together the photo album."

"Not sure who'll care."

Ida sat back and gave Beth a look. "Why, you care, else you wouldn't be doing it."

"Have to do something with the photos. Can't have them falling all over the place."

"Real tidy of you." She shook her head. "You're an attractive young woman. You'll get married and have yourself some kids one day before long. You'll want to have this for them."

Beth laughed. "Well, no one's asked recently. I did have a fiancé, but I ran him off."

"Any fiancé who lets himself be run off isn't the right one anyway."

"Did you marry, Mrs. Langhorne?"

"Call me Ida, honey, you're a grownup now.

And yes, ma'am, I did. My Robert and I were married thirty-four years. Lost him to a heart attack. Out cutting the grass, he was. I came out to bring him a drink of water and there he was."

"I'm sorry."

"It was early, but quick. We had good years, but I miss him. You learn to live alone...although," she laughed, "even after more than ten years, I still talk to him almost every day right out loud."

"You were lucky. You got a good one. Lots of women aren't so fortunate."

"Well, honey, yes, he was a good man, but he wasn't perfect. He had his flaws." She picked up a photo of Beth's parents. "Were you thinking of your father when you said that?"

Beth's jaw tightened. "I'm sure you know about all him."

"Well, I know about lots of things. And yes, I know about your father's problem, but nothing's ever as simple as it seems. Or as simple as we'd like it to be. It's a lot easier to know what to do when the problem is somebody else's trouble. Folks are full of advice then, aren't they? When your mama–"

"It wasn't my mother's fault."

She reached over and touched Beth's hand. Beth started to pull away and Ida's gentle touch turned to a steely grip. "Honey, your mama's head was turned when your daddy came to town. So was his, for her. He'd lived wild for a long time, but Belinda never had much experience with life. She went giddy with it and with the attention he paid her. Sometimes when folks take things too far, they don't know how to pull back."

Ida released Beth's wrist and closed the album. "Never mind me, honey. I'm a nosy old woman who should mind her own business." She pointed to the bag. "A few odds and ends. Snacks and such. If you need anything, give me a ring."

"Will Mr. Monroe be in the office tomorrow?"

"Likely in the afternoon. His sister down at Lake Gaston took a bad turn. Likely, she caught the cold he just got over. He and Mrs. Monroe went to check on her." Ida stood and smoothed her slacks. "I'll be on my way. I'll see myself out. Stay put and keep off that ankle or it won't heal properly."

The whole day passed without sight or sound of Michael.

Regardless of their argument, he'd be back. They weren't done with each other yet.

Beth finished Maggie's story in bed that night. The story had become clichéd over time, but she enjoyed it nonetheless.

Maggie survived the murder attempts of both the nanny and the invalid wife who showed surprising spunk in the attempt to rid herself of the girl to whom her husband had taken a fancy. It was hard to hold it against the invalid wife. On the other hand, she'd made her bed— her invalid's bed—and was now dealing with the consequences. When accused of theft, Maggie revealed she was the ward of the brooding Master's half-crazy father who had wasted most of her legacy. She'd come to Joshua's Hope to beg for some of her inheritance, had been mistaken for a servant girl, and had humbly served as a maid until the final act.

Maggie stood aghast at the foot of the great spiral staircase, gazing upward in horror. The staircase followed the curved wall of the entry hall, and stopped where it met the third floor gallery. Generations of the family lined the gallery walls overlooking the spot where the current mistress was poised on the topmost stair, swaying perilously, clad only in a silken negligee. Her feet were bare. There was something about the Lady Lisanne's stance and expression that made Maggie suspect she'd been dosing herself with laudanum again.

Maggie called to her, "Madam, please take care. Please step back."

Maggie thought of the interlude in the library with Lord Carleton earlier that day when his hand on her own had sent delightful shivers coursing through her frame, yet her wish for happiness with him was wrong, and could never be right, if it came at the cost of his wife's life. Yet, alive, the unhappy woman stood forever in their way.

She repeated, "Please, Madam, step back carefully."

A dark form emerged from the shadows of the gallery behind the Lady Lisanne. Maggie saw it was Smithers. The former nurse took her ladyship by the arm and attempted to cajole her back to her rooms, but Lisanne struggled. Maggie stared in horror as the stair rail broke and Lisanne fell to her death on the polished marble floor below.

Maggie screamed at the macabre whim of fate and swooned. She was caught up by the strong arms of her beloved who gently laid her upon the hall settee. He whispered, "My darling Maggie, you shall always be my darling. Please rest here and I shall return to you."

Lord Carleton joined the group surrounding the broken body. He knelt and gently touched Lisanne's cheek. A single tear slipped from his eye as he said, "Once we were young and thought we were in love. We should have taken better care of each other. 'Tis folly to think that love can survive without tender, assiduous care." He rose and returned to Maggie. He spoke so softly none but she could hear, "This time I won't make that mistake."

Chapter Fifteen

Lowery's offer was substantial. A week earlier Beth would have accepted it immediately. She found her current lack of resolve embarrassing. Confusing.

The man who came with the Lowery's guy took one look at Maude's old Buick and asked if he could check it out more closely. He touched the smooth, still glossy paint on the fender, the shiny fixture on the hood.

Beth watched him, noting the hunger in his eyes. And moisture. His eyes appeared to be tearing up. Could that be? It was an old car. It was good to know, and encouraging, too, to see someone appreciated it.

"1953 Buick Roadmaster. Mind if I look inside?"

"Feel free. Here's the key."

He looked inside and out. Over and under. Beth grew bored and walked back to the front porch to wait with Mr. Lowery and discuss his offer for the house contents.

"If I delay a week, will it make a difference to the amount?"

"Can't promise. One week, probably not."

"The house isn't selling so far and I need furniture while I'm here."

"Is that your only concern? There isn't another auction house around who'll give you a better offer."

"It didn't occur to me to call anyone else. Should I have? But, no, that's not it. I need furniture while I'm here, at least some. I'm reluctant to leave the house, you know, empty and unsold."

He made a growly noise deep down in his throat, clearing it. "You have to do what you have to do. I know that's true. Houses aren't made to be empty. Somethin' happens to them when they are. I've seen lots of foreclosures and estate auctions in my time. The longer a house is empty, the quicker it deteriorates."

The man finally left the Buick in the garage and joined them on the porch. He said, "Have you got the title to the car?"

****

The title was in the safe deposit box at the bank. Very handy because the man was able to have the cash transferred directly from his account to Beth's. Should she have held out for more?

Thanks, Maude, your Buick did me one last good deed by buying me many months of budgetary peace of mind.

In the afternoon, Billy Monroe knocked on her door. "Mrs. Langhorne said you wished to see me?"

"Thanks for coming over." She stepped aside and invited him in.

"I see you're managing well."

"I'm getting comfortable with the crutches. The ankle is better every day."

Mr. Monroe looked up and around as if

searching. "It's quiet here. Maude liked a quiet house, but most young people keep the TV or radio blaring all day."

"I won't lie to you. I miss my cable and the Internet." She sat on the chair, laying her crutches on the floor near her feet. Teddy jumped up onto her lap.

Beth felt vaguely embarrassed as Mr. Monroe paused near the Davenport and stared at the book she'd left lying there. She was immediately annoyed. It wasn't porn, for heaven's sake. There was nothing wrong with a little light reading. Even so, she couldn't stop herself from blurting out, "It's Maude's."

He leaned his cane against the arm of the Davenport, picked up the book and held it as he sat. "Ah, I see you know. I didn't think she'd tell you."

"Tell me what?"

Mr. Monroe's mouth opened, then closed. His lips pressed together in a tight line that deepened the web of wrinkles in his face.

"So, what is it?" Beth shook her head. "Don't even think about not telling me. Ever since I arrived back in town I've been discovering Maude kept secrets from me."

"I don't think she intended anyone to know. She kept it a secret for fifty years."

"What?"

He held up the book, "Miss Maude was a romance writer, in secret."

"You mean Maggie's story?"

He looked at the cover and frowned. "It says *Joshua's Hope*."

"Are you telling me Maude Henry was Madeline Flewellyn?" Absurd. Maude? Writing silly love stories about mysterious, vaguely dangerous heroes and ripe, fetching damsels?

"She started writing around 1960, shortly after her father's health declined. She didn't want him, or anyone, to know. She was embarrassed about the, hmm, lack of intellectual and literary merit and did not want anyone to know the family financial situation. She had to supplement their income. She stopped shortly before you came to live with her."

"But her father provided well for his wife and daughter. Maude didn't live lavishly, but she was comfortably set."

"Due to her initiative. I say this privately to you, Frank Henry made poor business decisions. He was given to impulsiveness and gambling."

"You're kidding"

"Regrettably, no. He had little money or other assets at the time his health forced him to retire. Miss Maude had never held a paying job. Volunteer activities and such, but she was a great reader. I didn't find out about her vocation until she sold her first book and came to me for advice."

"You've known all these years."

"Yes."

"And kept her secret." Beth saw in his eyes, more than respect for Maude, but also a loyalty that was rare in her experience.

"She published her last book the summer

before you came to live with her."

"Maude always acted as though she felt only love and respect for her father, so much that she never left home. It always seemed strange to me that she lived such a quiet life."

"A gentle life," he corrected her. "She respected and loved her parents. She honored her mother and her father."

He paused and Beth wondered if he was suggesting she'd failed in giving honor to her parents. To her father, certainly. She tried not to take offense.

"She was devoted," he resumed. "Disappointment comes to everyone, but one doesn't stop caring. Miss Maude had a great capacity for forgiveness. And love." Mr. Monroe shifted position. "Past is past. What can I do for you?"

The switch was too quick for Beth. Her head was still half in that box of old books and the rest of her gray matter was synapsing about the bowler hat in the music room and the tall obelisk at the cemetery.

"Ed Mason. Eminent domain. Is this a problem for me?"

"I don't believe so. Not at this time. I doubt Markland Enterprises will choose Preston for their big plans and that will suit many of us. We want growth, but not at any price."

"I'm glad to hear that."

"Down the road, if this area becomes more attractive for development, the situation could change. Of course, no telling what the laws will be in that regard in the future, but you will likely have either disposed of the land or developed it in some way yourself by then."

"Me? Develop it myself? More likely I'll have sold it to pay the taxes."

"Miss Kincaid, don't borrow trouble. That's what my mother said when I was a young man in the caveman age." He laughed pleasantly. "It's still true."

"I can't thank you enough for everything you've told me."

"Miss Maude was private. In her mind, it wouldn't have done to embarrass her father regarding finances and it wasn't quite seemly for an unmarried lady to write such novels. Yet, Miss Maude had her hopes at one time. A fine young fellow. A year or two older than she. He was from somewhere up there." He waved his hand toward the street. "Up north. Unfortunately, she lost her young man in the War. The second one. At Omaha Beach."

Suddenly, Beth wanted to cry for Maude. Her eyes watered, but she shook it off. "I understand. I'll keep her secrets."

He nodded and added, "I don't suppose you've visited the D-Day Memorial in Bedford? I drove Miss Maude out there one day to see it. Several years ago. A beautiful day."

After Mr. Monroe left, Beth reread the dust jacket bio about the author. Prolific writer...lives in upstate New York with her husband and three children...an Irish setter named Rose. None of the details resembled Maude's real life, any more than the author's photo was of Maude. Pen name. Pseudonym. Madeline

Flewellyn. The life she'd wanted? The life she'd given up hope of achieving? Did no other man come along to replace her lost love?

Beth looked at the box of books with new eyes. She picked up the framed photo of a much younger Maude standing in front of the house. Slim build, wavy pin curls tight to the head, a shy smile....

****

One week left in April and Beth still wasn't mobile outside of the house. Her injury was five days old and she was happy with her recovery so far, but it wasn't helping her find a job.

She called the utilities company to put them in her name to keep the juices flowing.

Beth tidied the roses, twisting off a dead leaf or two and wiped up the litter from the table. The satiny white was mellowing to a creamy tone and some of the edges were tipped with brown. She wanted to keep them as long as she could. Who knew how long it would be before someone sent her roses again?

Thunder rumbled in the early dusk and gusts of wind rushing across the lake slammed into the house, rattling the pictures on the walls. No rain yet, but the air was thick with violent potential. With each blast of wind, the lights blinked. Beth crutch-hopped through the house double-checking the windows. She dropped towels near the windows on the back side of the house. If the rain drove in horizontally, they would leak. She and Maude had done the leaking-window-mad-towel-scramble many times.

Something was hitting the backdoor. She pushed the curtain aside and saw a figure huddled up close to the door. Instinctively, she opened it and Elise was pushed through by a strong wind-burst that tore branches from trees.

Her black hair was straight and sticking out at angles, wild from the wind. Her hands touched her flushed face. She reached up and snagged her fingers in the crazy hair.

"Sorry. I got caught out. It came up so fast."

"It happens like that on the lake. I'd forgotten."

"Sorry. I guess I freaked."

"I almost didn't hear the knocking over the wind."

The house was slammed again and they both jumped. Beth put her hand to her heart and they laughed as the pounding rain, almost a solid wall of water courtesy of Mother Nature in a vile mood, forced its way under the door and around the window sashes.

Beth tossed Elise several bath towels and said, "You get these windows. I'm going upstairs."

Beth lost her crutches somewhere along the way, took the stairs on two hands and a foot, faster than she thought possible. With the towels already waiting in place, it was quick work to shove them up against the streaming runnels of water.

The horizontal onslaught was brief and the rain settled into a vertical downpour. Elise came into the bedroom hesitantly, carrying the crutches and dry towels. She helped Beth pick up the soaked towels and they wrung out the soaked towels over the bath tub, then Elise carried them down to the laundry. Beth followed more slowly down the stairs, leaning against the railing and carrying her crutches.

"Are you hungry? I'm famished."

"Maybe."

The power had stayed on. In the bright kitchen, Beth took eggs out of the fridge.

"Scrambled or fried?"

"It doesn't matter."

"Do you eat bacon? I have the microwave kind."

"That's fine."

Beth stopped trying to stir up some conversation. Elise could talk when she wanted. Beth pointed to the cabinet. "Dishes are there." She turned back to cooking.

They ate to the sound of rain. No conversation, but it wasn't uncomfortable. She let Elise finish eating before asking, "Anyone you need to call?"

"Like who?"

"Parents? Mom and/or dad?"

"No, Mom works in the evening."

This wouldn't be the first teenager to be left home alone, but Elise looked about fourteen and vulnerable despite the dark makeup and clothing.

When they were done, Elise put the dishes in the sink and paused in front of the darkened window. The beat of the rain had diminished to a lighter rhythm.

"I'll give you a ride home."

Elise looked at Beth and back at the window. "Okay, thanks."

Beth wrapped her bandaged ankle in a large plastic bag to keep it dry. Elise held the umbrella over the both of them as best she could as they crossed the yard to the garage. The exterior lights broke the gloom enough to see their way, but branches of all sizes littered the ground, so footing was tricky. The crutches wanted to sink into the mud. It was relief to have the garage available for her car. At least, she hadn't had to worry about car damage from hail or large branches.

She pulled carefully out of the garage and onto the paved road, careful of debris and possible high water. Elise directed her further north along the lake and then around several residential streets. The house she identified as hers was dark with not a light to be seen.

Beth said, "Are you sure…"

"Sure, yeah, it's okay. She'll be home in a little while."

"Do you want to come back with me until she gets home?"

Elise looked startled, then quickly resumed her deadpan expression. "No, it's okay."

"Wait." Beth leaned across her and scrounged a piece of paper and a pen from the glove compartment and scribbled her number. "Here. My cell number. Call me if there's a problem."

Her fingers closed over the proffered slip of paper in reflex, but she wouldn't meet Beth's eyes as she tucked it into her pocket. She paused partway out of the car door. "I can come by tomorrow, if it'll help you some. To clean up and stuff, you know."

"What about school?"

"We have the day off. Maybe I'll see you then. In the morning."

Chapter Sixteen

It was the first true lake storm of the spring season and all of winter's leavings, dead branches, even live ones, were ripped off and strewn across the neatly cut grass along with any trash the wind could find. The yellow vinyl cover from someone's lawn furniture hung from a crape myrtle like a shipwrecked survivor's distress flag.

Beth stood on the porch in the morning light and wondered how she'd manage the cleanup while on crutches. Maybe she could hire Ann Mallory's fix-it man.

She finished her coffee and breakfast and the next time she looked out the window she noticed the storm debris was disappearing. She opened the door to see who was responsible.

A teenage boy looked up at her from near the garage as he tossed a branch onto a pile of debris. His face was sullen. He turned away and went back to work.

Elise walked around from the side of the house. Her expression was brighter this morning and her step was light.

"Aaron came to help. Hope you don't mind."

"Of course not." Beth had brushed off the offer last evening never expecting the teenager would follow through. "Thank you, Elise, and thank Aaron for me, too. I appreciate the help."

"Sure." Elise went back to gathering the

storm litter.

Beth watched them from the window for a while. Even though Elise and Aaron hardly spoke, she was certain Elise had a crush on Aaron. That might account for her perky mood. And Aaron's presence? Maybe he returned her feelings.

She should warn Elise to be careful. Beth remembered the breathlessness, the taut anxiety of looking for Michael everywhere she went when she was a teenager. Reality was different. Love's potential was better than the actuality.

****

Beth ditched one of the crutches permanently and was now using a crutch and one foot to get around. This was especially handy because when she answered the doorbell two days later, she was able to receive the delivery of the crystal vase of long stem red roses and carry it back to the kitchen in the crook of one arm. The rose petals and lady's breath tickled her cheek.

Who? Not Ryan. Not so soon after the white roses. There was no reason for another flowery thank you. She drew out the card in wonderment.

Please join me for dinner tonight. I'll pick you up at six. If you don't want to go, don't come outside and I'll leave quietly with no hard feelings. Michael.

It was clumsily phrased, but she wouldn't hold that against him. He sent red roses. This must be a real, genuine date.

He hadn't said where they'd go. There were one or two nice restaurants in the area, neither especially fancy, but jeans didn't work for every occasion. Beth clunked upstairs with the crutch. Teddy decided it was a game and he batted at the rubber-tipped end. She tried not to crush his paws and not fall either.

Her closet was nearly empty. The few odds and ends she'd left behind over the years were encased in one, slim garment bag. She laid the bag on the bed and unzipped it. A blouse. A skirt. A pair of slacks. A simple dress of dark green jersey that might work. It was loosely tailored. Her size hadn't changed much so it should fit. As to shoes...well, her slip-ons would have to do, on the one usable foot, of course. Maude had an old-fashioned boucle sweater in shades of white, cream, and linen. She could take it along in case she needed it. It was vintage and chic in its own way.

She was amused by the sight of her own flushed face as she stood in front of the mirror with the dress up in front of her. That first date feeling? What had Michael's card actually said? Dinner at six?

She faltered, dropping the dress to the bed. She should stick to the jeans and not act like this was important to her. If he let her down this time, she'd let him have it once and for all. Her suspicions about whether he was dishonest in his business dealings with her would be the least of his troubles. This time he'd leave with bruises.

In the end, she was an independent woman.

Not sure about her heart and without a job, maybe, but the upside? She owned a house on the lake and six hundred acres of potentially valuable property, undeveloped, also on the lake.

What was wrong with that picture?

Not one thing.

Her optimism surged. The smile in her heart reflected on her face. What was that feeling stirring in her heart? A sense of freedom?

She still needed reliable income and there were property taxes to be concerned about, but as Billy Monroe's mother said, 'Don't borrow trouble.' Things would or wouldn't work out with Michael. Regardless, she was making a new life for herself and while her savings were limited, she had some real assets to work with.

She picked the dress back up with determination and put it on the hanger.

Let it be said, that in the end and when it mattered, Beth Kincaid stepped forward and took a chance.

Chapter Seventeen

Michael paused in front of the mirror on his way out of his house. He flexed his shoulders and tugged on the jacket lapels. He wanted to look like he'd made an effort. More than his boots and jeans.

He hadn't chased a woman since his last almost-marriage didn't happen nearly three years ago. Over the previous twenty-four hours, he'd thought a lot about Beth. For fifteen years she'd been his friend's little sister, and then the almost girlfriend, too young for anything serious.

Beth was an adult now, but still with that hair that was always slipping out of whatever clips or bands she used to control it. Hair begging to be touched, to be smoothed back from her cheek. But she'd lost her teenage spontaneity and picked up a load of worries. He felt an instinctive warning—a reverse siren call: be careful.

He walked past the truck and unlocked the car doors with an electronic beep.

"Relax, it's just a date," he said aloud, as he settled into the car.

Beth said she loved him, and she probably did in her own way, but what did that mean? He'd give her the opportunity to come up to speed, to the present, to put the past behind her. Maybe they'd be friends. Maybe more.

When he'd called to place the flower order, he'd asked the florist about the white roses Markland had sent. She said they symbolized purity or secrecy. Obviously, Ryan Markland didn't know Beth at all. Not like he did.

Red roses meant respect, courage and love. Beth had guts. He chose red.

He covered the miles quickly, oblivious to most of them. As he turned the corner onto Lake Avenue, he relaxed his grip on the steering wheel. She'd be there on the porch, he was sure.

She wasn't.

Michael pulled his car into the driveway. His grip on the steering wheel became white-knuckled. Finger by finger, he purposely eased his grasp. He and Beth hadn't parted on good terms. Had he assumed too much?

He didn't see her car. Had she left town? Or parked in the garage? The front door opened.

She maneuvered around the front door and the storm door with a crutch, a purse and a sweater draped over her arm, all the while trying to keep her bandaged ankle off the porch floor. He was stunned once again by her beauty, the red-blonde lights in her hair and the green dress that clung to her.

Mesmerized. He knew the word. Had never thought of it in connection to himself. The shape of her legs were perfect. The dress, some kind of knit, sort of wrapped itself around her body— sort of like what his mind and imagination was doing.

She looked down at him and smiled.

Michael was out of the car in a flash and up the porch steps, intending to take the purse and sweater and assist her. Instead, when he reached Beth, his arms went around her. The crutch clattered to the wooden boards of the porch and the purse dropped with a thud as her arms responded. He pulled her close and kissed her as if a fifteen-year drought had finally ended.

Chapter Eighteen

Beth could hardly breathe as Michael crushed her to his chest. She didn't need to breathe. She needed only his lips, his kisses, and the strength of his body. Welcome and warm. Desired. His lips on her throat, his hands on her back pulling her closer and tighter, they could never be close enough.

First, it was a whisper, then louder and more persistent was that little voice she attributed to Maude, urging her to think things out. She resisted the voice, not wanting to spoil this wondrous moment. She pressed her forehead against his shirt and fought for clear-headed thought. He ran his fingers along the side of her face, teasing and tempting her to look up again. She took a deep breath and held very still, but couldn't bring herself to release him.

Michael's hands stopped moving.

"Beth?"

"Yes?"

"Are you okay?"

She spoke into his jacket. "Don't I seem okay? Where are we going for dinner?"

Michael stepped back. He picked up the crutch and her purse and took her arm. "You're hard, Beth." Without another word, he helped her down the steps.

She let the remark pass because she had no

idea what he meant, but she paused near the car and tried to give him her sweetest smile. She touched his cheek and said, "Thank you."

Beth saw confusion or something like it in his eyes. Let him make of her 'thank you' what he would. She was beginning to see it was important to keep Michael on his toes.

The ride was silent. Every so often, Michael turned his head and moved his mouth, but then shut it and looked forward again. Beth fought her own annoyance, but she couldn't complain. She'd asked for this. Or had she? Her fingers tapped the armrest on the car door. This date was his idea. He'd kissed her unexpectedly. In fact, this was the third time in their lives he'd done this—kissing her without warning.

Not her problem. It was Michael's problem. He needed to manage his expectations better.

She found herself staring at him until he turned toward her again and met her eyes. Her lips curved into a slight smile despite herself. Neither spoke, but the atmosphere in the car warmed.

They ate at a Mexican restaurant. Colorful serapes and sombreros hung from the frescoed walls. The lighting was low enough to soften expressions. The guitar music playing softly in the background filled in the awkward silences. There were many.

"Nice music."

"Yes, it is."

She wished he hadn't kissed her. It had started the date off all wrong, backward, and she couldn't think of anything intelligent to say and he didn't seem to be managing any better. She reached across the table to touch his hand, he stiffened and she sat back.

The waiter took their orders and they settled the napkins in their laps. His foot brushed hers under the table and she perked up, hoping it was on purpose.

He moved his foot away.

"This is so awkward. Why?"

Michael scanned the room as if someone might be eavesdropping. "I don't think you're supposed to ask that."

"What?"

"It's a first date. No one is supposed to admit it feels awkward. At least, not this early in the evening."

She examined his face. Was he making a joke? "It's your fault."

He raised his eyebrows. "Why?"

"The kiss. Too much too soon. The rest of the evening has to go downhill."

He smiled after a short delay. He got the joke. Beth relaxed. She could breathe again.

Beth said, "There's something I'd like to ask you. It's personal."

Michael waited until the waiter placed the food on the table and left before speaking. "No promises, but you can ask."

"I'm interested in what you've been up to for the last few years."

Michael coughed gently, then sipped his drink. "I know what you want."

"What do you mean?"

"You want to know about those broken

engagements. You're not supposed to ask stuff like that. You could scare a guy off."

She laughed, happy to go along with the change in mood. "Well, I'd never ask any other date a question like that, but...well, you're different."

"Fair is fair. What about you?"

"What about me?"

He took her hand and ran his fingers along hers. "The ring is gone. You returned it?"

Her cheeks warmed up fast. "I did."

"Good." He touched her hand again. "My former engagements ended when we disagreed over where we'd live or how we'd live. Nothing big or insurmountable."

"You could've worked it out?"

"If we'd tried? Probably. But we didn't try. That's why I say it was just as well."

This time when she reached over and touched his hand, he wrapped his fingers around hers. She ate one-handed as if it were the most natural thing in the world while they chatted.

"Do I get a question?" Michael asked.

"Sure." She didn't mind talking about Stephen. Not now and not with Michael.

"How do you feel about Joe?"

It hit her unexpectedly—a blow from out of the blue. She waited for the sick stomach feeling to rise and the roaring to begin in her ears, but the physical sensations that usually heralded thoughts of Joe had diminished. Some were even missing. She felt vaguely guilty about that. But also hope.

"What should I think about him?" She amended, "Why should I think of him at all?"

Michael observed her. "You seem less reactionary. Less angry."

"Maybe, but he and I are never going to have a relationship, you should understand that. We're never going to a father-daughter dance." Beth shook her head in emphasis and several strands of red-gold dropped to brush her cheek. She pushed them back behind her ear.

"Okay, it's progress. At least, you didn't blast me for asking."

"Give me time. I could blast you yet." But she said it with a smile.

****

Michael escorted her to the door, one arm around her while she helped to support herself with a hand on the railing. His mood had gone quiet.

"I overdid it with the ankle." It was an excuse. She was afraid of upsetting a delicate balance by saying or doing the wrong thing. They might never have a chance like this again.

They stood on the porch in the moonlight, the moonlight Michael always seemed to find so tempting.

"Are you glad we did this?" He didn't wait for her answer. "I am."

Pleasure trilled through her, tickling her heart and making her smile. "I am, too."

Beth stepped forward into his arms and stood on tiptoe to touch her lips to his. A quick goodnight kiss. His restrained response surprised her and he didn't try to stop her when she pulled away.

She moved to open the door. Michael grabbed her hand.

"Beth, please. I have something I want to say to you."

It was a mistake, she knew it. The edge in his voice gave her a cold shiver. They'd come so close to having a really nice evening…but it wasn't in her to refuse if he needed her to listen.

"Go ahead."

He pulled her over to the porch rail. They leaned back against it side by side. He continued holding her hand.

"You're scaring me, Michael." She was only half-joking.

"When we talked at the mill, you said I left. I knew what you meant."

She couldn't respond at first, remembering Daniel's funeral and Michael's disappearance soon after. Twelve years ago. She laid her head against his shoulder. "I was angry at you, blaming you for Daniel's death, even though I knew I was wrong. I went to your house to tell you, but…."

"They sent me away to keep us apart."

Beth closed her eyes and took a deep breath. "Your parents. I know."

"And I let them. The shock over Daniel's death was no excuse. They said 'go' and I went to Aunt Bernice and Uncle Bill. I thought I'd call, but…then, after so much time had passed…I didn't know how." He whispered into her hair, "I'm sorry."

Forgiveness was an extra special gift in that

the receiver and the giver were often the same person.

Beth was speechless, caught between his admission and the realization he'd carried feelings of...regret...guilt...and remembering how devastated she'd been when she found out he was gone without a word or a goodbye. She struggled to find the right thing to say, afraid he'd misinterpret her silence.

"What's that poem? No, not a poem...a psalm? To everything there is a season?"

"Ecclesiastes." He paused. "Wow. I'm surprised I remembered that. It's been a long time."

Beth nodded. "I'm impressed." She moved her free hand to his arm and held on. "It wasn't our season. In a way, your parents were wrong—maybe in the way they did it—but they also were right. We weren't ready. And with the emotional crunch of losing Daniel, we were both at risk." Beth drew in a deep breath. "When I remember the girl I was...well, I have a sort of admiration for her gutsiness. Is that a word? But she was also wild and rude, someone who had a lot of growing up to do." She shook her head. "Still does, it seems."

Michael brought her hand to his lips and kissed it softly. "Goodnight."

She watched him walk away. Her heart felt so huge she thought it might burst in her chest, but her arms had never felt so empty.

Once inside, she changed for bed, but the evening, filled with such promise, left her restless. Managing with one crutch, she wandered back into the kitchen and poured a glass of ice water from the fridge. It was time to kick procrastination to the roadside and actively resume the job hunt. She would update her search area to include communities in the Preston area. Fairfax was still on the table, but had ceased to be the preferred option.

She wandered to the music room and Maude's box of books. Teddy followed closely because he had plans for her lap.

Maude had written late at night. She must have; otherwise, she couldn't have kept it secret from her parents, as well as from Preston and the world. She couldn't have done that without Billy Monroe's help.

Funny, though, when she thought about Maggie's story—*Joshua's Hope*, that is—she could hear the echo of Maude's voice now that she knew the truth.

She selected *Clarissa's Folly*, the same book Maude had given her on her eighteenth birthday. The red-headed woman on the cover clutched the corner of a building, her skirt, shawl, and hair blowing in the wind, while a dark haired, shadowy man with a cane watched her from the distance. She checked the copyright for the publication year and saw it was one of Maude's later books.

Clarissa's Folly by Madeline Flewellyn.

Chapter One
The coach rattled her teeth and shook her hair loose from its pins as the wheels found every rock and root in the old, rutted road

leading to the town of Woolridge. Clarissa Parrish was certain the driver was cursing amidst the louder calls to the horses to mind their paces. She tried, but could not divine his words over the noise, yet the abuse in his voice left no doubt in her mind that she should cover her ears. She waved her handkerchief delicately in front of her face to combat the dust that hung in the air in the coach interior. She felt flushed, discomforted by the driver's rude behavior and the annoyances of travel, but also because the man sitting opposite stared at her almost constantly.

She averted her eyes once again and pretended she was not aware of him. She smoothed her skirt, tugged at the sleeve of her bodice, and fingered the small pearl buttons that fastened the demure garment at the base of her throat. Finally, she met him boldly stare for stare. Her hazel eyes challenged the dark, almost black depths of his gaze, appearing still darker obscured by the shadow of his hat brim. She tried to penetrate the depths until she looked away, bested by the churl. No matter that he wore the coat and hat of a gentleman and presented an attractive appearance—his manners were less than the boot boy who, at least, tipped his hat and called her 'mum.'

The mail coach was lightly occupied. Woolridge was not on the main coach route, but a spur that the coach traversed twice monthly when weather permitted. The current travelers had joined at the last stop, a somewhat larger town at which the other travelers had disembarked.

Clarissa sat next to a small, elderly man who took very little space and spoke almost not at all. Occasionally, he made clicking sounds while moving his fingers in counting motions. The rude, well-dressed man opposite her was likewise silent. She had never traveled in a less agreeable manner. But no matter. The trip would soon be over and she could not complain even had she found a sympathetic ear. It had been her decision to accept the post as companion and she would see it through regardless of doubts and hindrances. She was an enlightened woman, and wished not to be dependent upon the kindness of relatives.

The approach into Woolridge rounded a hill and sloped sharply down into the town area. The driver held the horses back and thus Clarissa had a good view of the town before the carriage stopped. She was dismayed by the small, poor quality of the buildings and conveniences, but not surprised. Her uncle had warned her that this small town in the north of England would be very different from her accustomed surroundings in Hargreaves Commons. When the coach jolted to a stop in front of a tavern and rooming house, Clarissa made as if to rise and was astonished when the gentleman himself arose, cutting her off without explanation or apology.

She read until Clarissa exited the coach, disdaining the staring stranger who was bent in close conversation with the little, counting man, and stepped into the tavern seeking the person who was supposed to escort her to the Bellingame estate.

Beth's tension had eased. Teddy was wedged, impossibly, into the narrow space where her hip met the mattress. She pushed him to the foot of the bed and rearranged her covers.

Miss Clarissa Parrish was prim and proper, yet the author hinted at the qualities of courage, determination and independence. Maggie, of *Joshua's Hope*, had been proper and genteel, through and through, and a bit dim. Beth suspected Miss Clarissa had a strong layer of steel-rimmed common sense hiding beneath her delicate manners and flounced petticoats.

Chapter Nineteen

Ed Mason sat on the edge of Maude's Davenport, bolt upright and legs bent at the knee in perfect right angles. His short hair was peppered with gray.

"Miss Kincaid? Excuse me, but I was saying–"

"Call me Beth, please."

"Certainly, Beth. I hope you'll call me Ed. How long will you be staying in Preston?"

"I'm not sure." She turned to face his wife. "Mrs. Mason, would you like something to drink?"

Mrs. Mason had chosen the chair in the corner, near the front window. "No, thank you."

"Well, Ed, I'm not sure how long I'll stay. This house is for sale, but the market is slow."

"Have you considered what you'll do with–"

"Then, too, it's been pleasant seeing the area again and seeing familiar faces."

"Miss Kincaid, Beth, I sense that you don't want to discuss–"

"The Kincaid land outside of town?" She nodded. "You're correct. It's no one's business but mine."

"Markland–"

"Markland Enterprises has decided nothing at this time. When they do, we'll see what they have to say."

"If we made it clear the property is available–

"

"If Markland's plans fall through, I may have some development ideas of my own."

Ed's ears perked up, his knees snapped together and his back straightened. Beth was sorry she'd mentioned development plans. It had come out of nowhere, or from somewhere in that conversation she'd had with Billy Monroe.

She wanted to cool Ed's enthusiasm a bit. "When Ryan Markland came to dinner—"

Ed leaned forward. "Oh, yes. I heard he brought a meal to you. Quite unexpected. Very sorry, by the way, about your injury. Did he talk specifics? Any inside info?"

"He was reluctant to discuss business. We talked about Michael and—"

"Oh, yes. What could be more natural?" He smiled broadly. "Certainly, Michael has been working with Markland and the Fowler and Kincaid properties adjoin. There's lots of land out there and yet away from town. That would please many of our citizens, let me tell you."

"Ed, this is very much up in the air. We're a long way from any...we should wait and see what Markland decides before jumping too far ahead."

Up in the air...jumping too far ahead...how many clichés could she mouth in the attempt to sound like she was saying something about nothing. Beth sensed Mrs. Mason was hanging on every word. This conversation was likely to be a hot topic at the Ladies' Auxiliary. Well, the misinformation hadn't been intended, but it would serve them right to sound foolish. These people had spent entirely too much time discussing her and her business.

"Are you thinking recreational? Or convention-type?"

Beth shrugged eloquently to encourage him to draw his own conclusions. "Too soon to be talking details."

"This is very exciting, Miss Kincaid. Beth. Preston is fading away and while we love it as we always have, it won't have a future without new life, new business. In short, growth."

Ed and Hilda left soon after. Beth waved goodbye. Had she done a bad thing? She'd been toying with Ed by cutting him off whenever he seemed about to mention her land, and then he'd turned the tables on her, whether deliberately or not. Most of what he took to be truth, she hadn't intended to imply at all. He'd taken the threads of the conversation and run with it. His concern about Preston was real. To give him false hope was bordering on cruel, wasn't it?

Bethie, my girl, you may have done yourself and others a bad turn.

Ann's fix-it man had cut the grass the day before. The sky was blue and the chairs by the lake looked inviting. The house-shoppers had all but ceased coming by. Maybe it was okay.

It was time to give up her apartment.

It had nothing to do with Michael. This was about her. Not about her and a man.

She'd call in the morning and set the process in motion. They'd want the notice in writing and she'd have to give thirty days, so she'd have time to work out what should go into storage and what should come down here.

Unless the house sold. Then, where would she go?

She took *Clarissa's Folly* down by the lake, but didn't read. Instead, she put her head back against the chair, closed her eyes and enjoyed the feel of the fresh breeze and the soft sound of the water against the rocks. How could she move away from this? Surely, there were jobs to be had somewhere in the area. After the Fairfax traffic, any other commute seemed easy. She could look as far afield as Roanoke and still live here.

"Hello."

She jumped. James was sitting in the other chair. "Where'd you come from? Long time, no see."

"I was at home. Now I'm back at Grams' 'cause mom's going away for a few days."

"What about school?"

"No diff. I live a few blocks away. Same school, different bus."

"Nice."

"I was looking at your boat the other day."

"That?" She pointed to the partial view of the rotten rowboat stashed behind the shed.

"Yeah." He fidgeted in the chair. "I was thinking I might fix it up, you know?"

"James, its seafaring days are done. It's no good."

"I mean, well, if you don't want it then, I could work on it. Maybe learn something about building ships. I wouldn't go out in the water. 'Course not."

"I don't have any tools for you to use."

"Grams has some."

"Would she mind, do you think?" I had a feeling Grams wouldn't think much of this idea.

"Nah, she won't care so long as I don't drag it into her yard."

Beth had no experience with children. She stalled, trying to think of the potential problems and hazards. "You could get splinters or hammer your finger."

He gaped at her. She'd insulted him. Beth struggled to control her expression. Let Mrs. Boyle have the last word on it. "Clear it with your grandmother. If she agrees, then work on it behind the shed, out of my view. Okay?"

"Cool. Thanks."

"Don't hurt yourself. Don't make me regret it."

"Oh, no ma'am. I'll be careful."

She had to laugh. James was ecstatic over a broken boat? Apparently, guys got harder to please as they got older. Beth shook her head and picked up Maude's book.

Madam Bellingame received Clarissa in the morning parlor. Madam's plump figure appeared uncomfortably and solidly corseted, encased in a tight black silk gown. The expression on her round face was well-bred and unreadable.

"You slept well, of course," she said.

"Indeed. The accommodation is more than

adequate." And very welcome, Clarissa thought, having arrived at the estate so late with only the butler and housekeeper to welcome her. A cold welcome that was, indeed.

"Adequate?" Madam sniffed in disapproval. "May I hope that you will continue to find it so."

Her new employer was offended. To attempt to remedy it would only compound the slight. It was best to move forward as if unaware. "I cannot imagine that it should ever fail to please."

"Humph." Somewhat mollified, Madam continued, "We must discuss your duties."

"I am to be your companion."

"Your duties as my companion, yes. I would speak frankly with you, Miss Parrish, but I must be assured of your discretion. You are young and attractive in a…a robust way, but I was assured of your breeding and good sense."

"I am gratified, Madam."

Madam Bellingame nodded graciously. "As to the companion duties, I am quite sufficient to myself only occasionally requiring assistance. That need is well met by Agatha, my personal maid."

"Ma'am?"

"I presume you have not yet met my son."

"No, ma'am."

"My son," Madam breathed deeply to steel herself for the admission, "is blind. He has only come to this state in recent years. Because of this he is much withdrawn into himself. He is my only child. I wish him to marry one day and produce an heir. For his own happiness, of

course, and for the good of the family."

"Of course."

Madam straightened in her chair. Clarissa was intrigued. A blind son was tragic, indeed, but what had that to do with her?

"He has grown shy of women and society. It is my wish that you will stay here under the guise of my companion, and rendering certain assistance to me so that it will be believable, meanwhile occupying yourself with Edward."

"Occupying? What are you suggesting, Madam?" Clarissa was shocked. Was she drawn here under false pretenses? Was this respectable house not as it appeared? She felt the warmth of a flush rapidly spreading from her bosom up through her face.

Madam Bellingame sniffed again. "I am not suggesting anything untoward, aside from the deception. The small deceit will be well worth it should it make him at ease and revive his interest in feminine society. You can read to him, engage him in conversation. You will eat at table with us."

"Madam, are you suggesting I act as companion to your son?" It sounded quite scandalous and brought to mind a parting warning about men from her uncle's cook. Firmly, Clarissa said, "I am inclined to think I should remove myself immediately from this situation."

"Miss Parrish, I am pleased my estimation of you as a virtuous young woman is correct. I do not seek a paramour for my son. You are not here to entice him in any way. As he is blind, *your appearance will not tempt him. I merely wish to accustom him to female society so that he may grow in confidence and marry a suitable woman of his own class."*

"I must consider." The proposal was unconventional and less than honest, yet, its purpose was well-intended.

"You should join us for lunch, Miss Parrish. You may make your decision afterward. If you choose not to stay, I shall pay you a month's wages and your return fare, but I remind you I expect absolute confidentiality and discretion. Indeed, 'twill be a fortnight before the coach runs again, but I will have you driven to the main coach line if, at any time, you find the position unacceptable."

Back in her room, Clarissa spoke to her reflection in the mirror. "In conscience and charity, I can do no less than stay to lunch with Madam and her son. In daylight, with servants all about, any unwelcome activities are unlikely." Indeed, should she return to Hargreaves, her uncle would, as always, be the kindest of men and say not a word in reproach, yet she owed it to herself to judge the situation on its merits and not merely by society's convention. She considered Cook Hattie's departing words, "Miss Clarissa, men will look at you, at that hair and figure, and will not think of marriage first. Guard yourself, my girl. Don't give 'em one without getting the other first." Her aunt and uncle, had they heard Cook Hattie, would've been shocked. Clarissa suspected Hattie's advice might be pertinent, if improper, for her maidenly ears. She had observed the bawdy practicality below stairs was oft times more sage than the delicately phrased hints of decorum, both proper and not, that her aunt shared.

The maidservant conducted her down the stairs and through the tall doorway of the dining room. Madam was already seated at the table to the right of a handsome, well-dressed dark-haired man. Clarissa's breath caught in her throat. Quickly, she sought to regain her composure.

The footman drew a chair from the table, opposite Madam, and waited. Clarissa approached and with each step she was surer.

"Miss Parrish, this is my son. Edward, I would like to present Miss Clarissa Parrish. Miss Parish had recently arrived to fill the role of my companion."

"Madam Bellingame. Master Bellingame." Clarissa inclined her head courteously. She took her seat at the table. She saw Madam's son had turned his head in her direction and, if staring could said to be done by a blind man, then Edward Bellingame was staring.

As he had stared at her in the coach on the way to Woolridge the day before.

Chapter Twenty

Beth affixed the corner pieces onto the pages and placed the photos. Chronological order seemed best. Whoever had started the project had put Evan and Emma's photos on the first page. She would continue that pattern.

She held the photo of her parents on the porch of their house, laughing and hugging. Mama and Joe. Dad. Daddy. She had adored him. Her heart had soured as his drinking worsened, then turned to active dislike when her mother died. She wanted to say to those happy people on the porch 'you should have been more careful of our family,' but it was too late and always would be. Her anger had softened to reproach and regret. It was hard to face hurt dead on, but not impossible as she'd once thought.

****

She picked up her crutch, her purse and car keys, and successfully descended the front steps without damaging other body parts.

Driving was no longer a problem. She parked in the small lot behind the library. Kim Stebbins saw her struggling up the cement steps and held the door open. Beth settled at her favorite computer. She had a lot of spam, but also an email from a prospective employer. She was asked to contact their Human

Resources department to arrange for testing if she was interested.

Beth groaned. A battery of tests and a grueling day of interviewing and test case studies to show she was qualified and psychologically competent were standard in the industry. She remembered the days when she had loved the challenge, knowing she'd excel and prove herself. No more. Those days were gone.

She wished those days were gone, but they were back because she needed a job. This job was in Fairfax, and if it was good, she'd be a fool to walk away. Project management was where her education and experience were.

Hadn't she decided not to return to her life in Fairfax?

Finally, she shut down the computer, but before leaving she went to the fiction section and walked along the alphabet until she reached where Madeline Flewellyn was shelved. There were ten different titles and all looked well-read.

"Miss Kincaid?"

She jumped. "Kim?"

"Sorry I startled you." She laughed. "I guess I did sneak up on you. Can I help you find anything? We have some wonderful women's fiction. I've read most of them."

"Have you read these?" She pointed to Maude's books.

"Oh, sure have. They were real popular around here for a while. You know how it goes, one person reads something, says it's good, her friend reads, then two friends, and so on. Would you like to check some out? You don't have a card yet, but I can issue one in no time."

"Not today. I've got a couple of books back at the house, thanks."

"I'm glad you're getting better and able to get around. That was quite a story about how you got hurt out there in the middle of the nowhere. How fortunate Michael Fowler and Mr. Markland came along." She leaned in closer. "And so good looking."

Beth had been edging past Kim. Now, she paused. "Which one?"

"Both of them. A girl couldn't go wrong with either one, now could she? But then, with your looks, I'm sure you have lots of handsome boyfriends. Oh, but I didn't mean…I mean…"

"No problem." She smiled to show she hadn't taken offense, but inside she shook. Not at Kim's words, but at her own behavior. If she'd had half that glow when she was talking about Ryan to Michael, no wonder she'd angered him.

As she exited the library, the strap of her purse caught on the doorknob, throwing her off her feet. She lost her crutch as she grabbed for the iron railing. Her good foot slipped from the top step and she felt it all going, going, going…until large, sure hands grabbed her.

Brown loafers, hands on her arms, and then a concerned, smiling face were suddenly there. The man was unusually tall with short-cropped hair and bright blue eyes. The eyes caught hers and she smiled back. A stranger, but he looked familiar.

"Whoa, ma'am. You almost lost it there. Are you all right?"

"I am now. Thank you so much." Did she know him? Her eyes kept going back and forth between the startling, unnerving eyes and the flashy rings on his hand. She searched her brain, but couldn't place him.

"Glad I was in the right place at the right time." He handed her the crutch and held her arm lightly as she descended the few steps. "Are you steady now?"

"I'm fine, thanks to you."

"Any time. My pleasure." He nodded and walked away.

Beth watched him stride down the sidewalk. Nice, polite. Her skin tingled, but in a creepy way. She looked down and saw goose bumps the full length of her arms. Maybe it was the eyes. Bright blue. Compelling.

If she'd met him before, she would've remembered those eyes, if nothing else. And encircling his wrist was a leather band with gold studs. Memorable.

She walked up the narrow, paved road between the library and the next building and around back to the parking lot. Isolated. She'd been here several times and never felt that way. Why now? Because she was still shaken by the near fall?

Driving home, she passed Maude's church on the corner. This time her foot eased on the gas. On impulse, she turned into the empty parking lot.

Just curious, of course. No one was here.

The building would be locked.

Across the crisp, green lawn was a small cemetery, not wild like the one on the Kincaid property. This one was well-kept. She remembered sitting on a black wrought iron bench in the shade of the oak eating an orange Popsicle. She'd been very young. Was it Vacation Bible School? Probably.

It was a nice memory and she tucked it away with some of her newly-renovated ones.

****

Noises from the backyard were audible in the kitchen. Teddy was nowhere to be seen when she entered the house, but materialized within seconds meowing for dinner. Through the window, Beth saw James step out from behind the shed as he moved around the rowboat. More surprising, Elise was sitting in a chair watching him. He walked over to her, his posture indicating a question and Elise leaned toward him, moving her hands as if explaining. Beth's heart warmed.

She opened the back door and a man rose from the other chair. The chair's back was toward her so she hadn't seen him sitting there.

Stephen.

She stepped out onto the porch.

"Beth. Hi." He waved.

Didn't he leave Preston more than a week ago? Nine days? Stephen was never random. It put her on guard.

Goodbye to mellow.

She stayed on the porch and waited for him. James had returned to his boat building, but

Elise watched them. When she saw Beth looking her way, she sat back in the chair, but her face stayed tilted toward them. A curious girl.

Beth hoped her face reflected her attitude—unyielding.

"I know you're wondering why I'm here. I hope you're not angry. We parted on good terms, I thought, with everything okay between us."

"Why are you here?"

He shrugged his shoulders, cast a quick look around and lowered his voice. "I need to talk to you. It's serious. I hope this is unnecessary...not necessary to bother you, I mean, but I can't take the chance."

"What are you talking about?"

"Could we talk inside?"

"Why?"

"Beth. Please."

She relented. How could she leave Stephen standing in the grass with kids watching?

In the living room, she took the chair and left him Maude's hard Davenport.

He did a slow look around the room. "This is where you grew up?"

"In my teens. What is it you want to tell me?"

Stephen fidgeted. "I don't want to worry you or scare you."

"Scare me? About what?"

"The investment that tanked."

"Okay. What?"

"The investors all said they understood the risks, although no one anticipated the extent of what happened in the market. No one could have. But one is insisting I pay him back. I think I told you about him."

"You did. Can you pay him back? Should you?"

"No, I shouldn't and no, I can't. I lost, too. I don't have that kind of money and it's not my obligation to pay him."

"Is he threatening you?"

"The threat is implied. Nothing I can call the cops about. But this guy, well, you have to know him to understand. Physical violence is possible."

"If that's true, then go to the police. People do extreme things under pressure and a lot of people are feeling financially stressed."

"I don't need the negative attention. Police around asking questions, a crazy man complaining I cheated him, saying I conspired with a broker to commit fraud. It doesn't matter whether it's true. It would ruin my position at Stafford. Look at what's happened to the investment brokers accused of scheming to defraud investors. Those Ponzi schemes? Most people don't have a clue how they work, but they're more than happy to blame other people for their own poor decisions. One little hint of scandal and that's it for me. Ruined now and in the future."

"I can see you're worried. Why tell me?"

"Because this guy is determined. He's dangerous. I think he's been following me."

"Following you?"

"Followed me to your apartment. May have

even followed me here. He wouldn't know we're not together."

"Are you saying he might try to use me, or threaten me, as blackmail against you? To force you to give him money?"

"I don't know what he'll do, but you have to know, just in case." He put his hands to his face, massaging his temples.

Beth rose from her chair. "Is he here in Preston?"

"I doubt it. I haven't seen him here. I hope he didn't track me here, but I can't be sure."

"I'm calling the sheriff's office. I'm not taking any chances. Can you wait for them to get here? They'll want names, a description and all that."

He waved his hands. "Sit tight for now. I'm trying to raise the cash, and trying to reason with him in case I can't. I'm worried, but I'll work it out. I'm sorrier than I can say about involving you even this much." Stephen stood and moved toward the hallway. "I'll take off now. Just wanted to make sure...well, you know, be warned. But please, for now, don't take it to the authorities. I'm still hoping to have some kind of future. If I can find someone to loan me the money, I believe I can make it work out right for everyone."

"I understand. Thanks for the warning." She walked with him into the hallway. "You should go to the police when you get back to Fairfax."

The doorbell rang before they reached it. Beth opened the door.

"Michael. Hello."

He smiled and walked toward her. He stopped when he saw Stephen.

"Michael, this is Stephen." She turned to Stephen who was now leaning against the newel post as if he'd been visiting for a while and wasn't in a hurry to leave. "Stephen, this is Michael. Michael and I have known each other since we were kids."

Stephen said nothing for a moment. His face wore the neutral expression she remembered well. It was how he looked when sizing up an opportunity.

He stepped forward with a smile on his face and extended his hand. "Hey, Michael. Pleased to meet you."

Seeing the two of them there with her in Maude's hallway was indescribably odd. Caught in the crosshairs, but not quite in the crossfire. That was a weird, scary allusion.

Michael said, "Nice to meet you. Sorry if I'm interrupting something."

He didn't look sorry.

Stephen said, "I was on my way out."

Michael nodded and stepped aside.

"Beth." Stephen gave her a quick hug, nodded at Michael and left.

She could almost feel the molecules of air in the hallway separate in frantic vibration as Michael stared.

He said the obvious. "That's Stephen."

"Yeah," Beth said, confirming the obvious.

"What's going on? I thought you two—"

"He and I are done." She waved her ringless hand. "He had a problem and he wanted to tell me about it. Now he's gone on his way."

Michael pulled her into his arms. He brushed his lips along the line of her neck and gently kissed her. Then stopped. Beth looked around. Elise was standing in the kitchen doorway.

Elise looked puzzled. "Sorry. I wanted to check because, well...anyway, I'll go." She went back through the kitchen and out the back door.

"Who's that?"

"Elise. She lives in the neighborhood. She must've been curious, or concerned, about Stephen. He was in the backyard with her and James when I returned home."

"You've been out? Driving?"

"The sprain wasn't as bad as the doctor thought. It's much better."

"Don't rush it."

"Hey, life goes on. Things to do. People to see."

"I repeat. Don't rush it."

"Why?"

He leaned close and kissed her hair. "Because I'm smarter now than I was twelve years ago. I want to see where this goes, this thing between us."

He held her so close. Beth put her cheek against his chest and breathed in his scent.

Maybe they could get it right, this time.

Chapter Twenty-One

The town was buzzing. Word was the Markland people were coming back to meet with the mayor. The Preston gossips said Markland wouldn't return to Preston if they'd chosen another site because a press release would cover that. So, if they were returning, then it could only mean...

"...they must have decided on Preston," Ann Mallory said.

"They could be gathering more information."

"Possible. Doubt it. That young couple who viewed your house is coming back into town in a week and wants to see it again."

"They sound interested."

"Hopefully, they'll get anxious and make an offer without waiting to come back. With Markland coming back to town the property around here could get hot."

****

Beth took Clarissa out to the lake and settled herself in a chair with her feet propped up on the ottoman and a bottle of water on the armrest.

Clarissa agreed to stay at Bellingame Manor on a trial basis, still uncomfortable with the unconventional flavor of the duties. She dined with the family and found them dreary, but she enjoyed reading aloud to Edward. He was unexpectedly competent at chess, as if the board existed as fully in his mind as on the table. Edward was less comfortable getting around on foot.

"The roses are particularly lovely this season," said Madame Bellingame. *"Mr. Bellingame, in his later years —he was a good deal older than I—was a famous rose enthusiast and planted an extensive garden. I did not share his enthusiasm, but their beauty and scent are undeniable."*

She nodded at Clarissa. "Perhaps Miss Parrish would benefit from a turn in the garden, Edward."

"Mother, I do not care to walk in the garden. Miss Parrish's enjoyment will be all the better if unencumbered."

"Nonsense, Edward. She is quite peaked. I have kept her far too busy and she must take some air. There is no more pleasant walk anywhere in Woolridge than in your father's garden."

"Then, Mother, perhaps you should escort her yourself."

The silence grew long. Clarissa thought that if the absence of sound had color, this would be deep reddish purple. It emanated from Madam Bellingame and was reflected back by her equally obstinate son. Clarissa found their disagreement tedious and personally insulting.

"Please do not disturb yourselves. I shall happily take the air and enjoy the garden quite nicely on my own." She stood and Marston, the

butler, was quickly behind her, moving her chair. Her skirt rustled as it brushed past the table.

"Miss Parrish," Edward called out softly. "I apologize for my boorish behavior. If you will reconsider, I will endeavor to enjoy a stroll."

Madam Bellingame flashed Clarissa a look of triumph, but Clarissa kept her face carefully schooled. She had no wish to be embroiled in a tug of war between mother and son.

Clarissa walked alongside Edward as he tried to feel his way with his cane. She held back from interfering until he stumbled on a hidden rabbit hole or some such obstacle. She reached for his arm to steady him. He stiffened. She released him, sensing his annoyance.

"If I may trouble you, Miss Parrish, please direct me toward the house."

"Mr. Bellingame, please do not do so. I wish to walk further and prefer companionship."

"As you just saw, I am not fit to walk abroad."

"Mr. Bellingame, I wish you would oblige me by walking with me as my dear neighbor did back at home. Mrs. Walmsley was blind from birth and it did not deter her. May I have your hand, sir?"

He held out his hand automatically, still questioning. "My hand?"

She took his hand gently and raised it to her shoulder. "Place your hand so. Walk alongside me and slightly behind. It will feel awkward at first, but will become comfortable very quickly."

His hand lifted from her.

"Sir, will you at least try?"

She heard his breath draw in sharply and then he placed his hand lightly on her shoulder. She pressed his hand more firmly down.

"Shall we go?" She stepped out slowly, but surely, setting an even pace.

Her shoulder grew warm where his hand rested. Once they were moving forward, his fingers grasped more firmly than was necessary. She was sure he would relax with practice. She smiled to herself, unaccountably pleased with her small victory. She was so pleased, in fact, that she was quite unrepentant about lying. Dear Mrs. Walmsley had never existed and could not, therefore, be hurt by it, and yet had served her need very well.

"A hare, Mr. Bellingame. We've found the owner of the rabbit hole." She stopped short and his hip brushed hers, or would have if not for the fullness of her skirt and petticoats. She felt his nearness and froze for the moment. He made no effort to move away. She waited, not wishing to make him feel self-conscious, yet totally conscious of her own person.

"Mr. Bellingame, I must ask you about your trip on the Woolridge coach. How is it that you were able to travel so well then, but cannot traverse your father's garden which must surely be well familiar to you?"

Edward sighed. "A sad pretense of freedom, no more than that. I ride to the first stop and then return with the coach. Peters, the elderly man who shared our coach, is my father's retired valet. He was there to assist at the beginning and the end. Madam, you shame me.

I cannot even cross the road by myself, but—"
His voice grew stronger, "I knew it was you,
Miss Parrish, when you joined us at the table
for lunch that first day."

"Indeed? How did you know, sir?"

"By your voice, by the many small sounds
and scents, and by the way the air moved
around you."

Could he feel the quickening of her heart?
Her entire person seemed to tremble with it.

"I believe you are more keenly aware of such
things as a result of your blindness. Is that so?"

"Excuse me, please."

The stranger with the neon blue eyes
towered over her chair. Startled, she jumped,
fumbling the book.

"Sorry for disturbing you."

"I saw you yesterday. You saved me from
falling at the library."

"Yes, ma'am. It's a small world, for sure. I'm
in Preston looking at real estate. I saw the 'For
Sale' sign. You the owner?"

"Yes." She clutched the book to her chest.
The man had the same affable expression on
his face as before. Did he look like he knew an
inside joke? Was it her imagination?

"I'm only in town for a quick visit. I called the
agent listed on the sign, but got her voicemail.
I thought I'd take a quick look at the lot, which
is beautiful, and then saw you. Again, sorry for
disturbing you, but it's almost like fate taking a
hand, isn't it? I wonder if I could see inside the
house?"

This was against the rules, right?

"I don't think my agent would like that. Why don't you try calling her again?"

"Oh, hey, I'm sorry. No wonder you feel uncomfortable. You don't know me. I'm a stranger in town for a day. Maybe I can arrange to make a trip back again soon." He rested one hand on his broad chest and a ring on his hand flashed with reflected light.

She held her breath as something stirred in the back of her mind. Was she over-reacting? His size was intimidating. "Sorry, but you'll have to go through Ann Mallory."

He smiled. He had lots of teeth, all even. Wolfish. Like a white wolf.

She put the book on the arm of the chair and picked up the crutch. She walked with him back toward the house. "If you leave your number, I can have Ann call you."

"No need. I'll try her again on my way out of town. You know, I grew up in a house that looked a lot like yours."

"Really? It might have been a catalog home, too."

"Sorry?"

"Sears Catalog homes. They're all over. Mostly built in the 1930s, 40s."

"You know a lot about this."

"There are groups who specialize in these houses, like fan clubs. Owners who enjoy the uniqueness."

"That's interesting. I had no idea. My parents will be fascinated."

"Do they still live in theirs?"

"Oh, yes. They wouldn't give it up. They love it." He beamed, speaking of his family. Clearly, he loved his family and houses like this.

"That's so sweet." She wanted to feel okay about him. She shouldn't hold his size, his eyes, against him. He couldn't help his genetics.

"They're great people. They just celebrated their golden anniversary."

"I guess there's no harm if you'd like to take a quick walk through the house."

His smile broadened. "Are you sure? I'd like to."

"Go on in the back door. I'll meet you on the front porch."

"Alone? You sure you don't want to come in, with me?"

Beth almost agreed, but a tiny voice in her head warned her off.

"Please, go ahead."

He grimaced. "I'm sorry. I wasn't thinking." He walked up the steps, pausing again at the back door as if giving her one last chance to accompany him. She waved him on.

She waited on the front porch. She would've opened the front door, but it was locked. Mr...? She hadn't gotten his name.

It was only a moment's wait before he opened the door.

"It's amazing. Just like home." He stepped back into the hallway. "Can I ask you about the dining room furniture? I've seen some like it."

Instinctively, Beth stepped forward, crossing the threshold into the vestibule. Neon blue moved toward her.

"Hey, Miss Kincaid!"

Beth turned back and stepped outside onto the porch again. "Elise. Hi. What's up?"

Elise stopped, mouth open, staring at the large man filling up the vestibule.

Beth explained, "He's looking at the house. Moving to the area."

"Sorry. Guess I interrupted, huh?"

He looked at his watch and said, "I need to be go anyway. I promise I'll contact Ms. Mallory. Thanks again."

Beth and Elise watched him get into a black SUV and drive off. Something jiggled in her memory, but she couldn't quite pull it out.

"He's big."

Beth looked at Elise. "Yeah. By the way, how old are you?"

"Why? Did I do something wrong?"

"Just wondering."

"Sixteen."

"That boy who was here with you the other day, is he your boyfriend?"

"Sort of." Elise looked at her. "Who was that guy?"

"I don't know. He wanted to see the house." She didn't get his name, but it didn't matter. He had Ann's number.

Chapter Twenty-Two

The phone rang in the night. Its shrillness startled Beth and she knocked it off the night stand trying to grab it. She scrabbled on the floor in the dark and answered before the last ring.

"Hello?"

Silence.

"Hello?"

The breathing started.

She disconnected.

Beth went downstairs, forgetting her crutch, and limped around the ground floor in the dark checking the locks. Did the caller know she was doing this? Was he waiting outside, sickly amused, for lights to come on?

She found two unlatched windows. The window in the laundry room at the back of the house and a window in the dining room. She stood in front of each of the unlocked windows and tried to recall when she'd last touched them. They could've been unlatched by the people who'd looked at her house. Beth pulled the curtains tightly closed. She picked up Michael's flashlight, comforted by the solid weight of it and carried it with her. Uncertain and a little afraid, she sat on the Davenport, still in the dark. Teddy had joined her at some point in her journey. He bumped her leg and meowed.

"It's not time to eat, boy."

He jumped up beside her and pushed his way under her arm and onto her lap. He butted his head at the flashlight that was in his way.

"What am I going to do, Teddy?"

He meowed again. Beth put her head down on the arm of the Davenport and tucked her legs up, leaving Teddy to re-fit himself alongside her. She didn't intend to sleep, but eventually did. In the morning, she had a crick in her neck, an ache in her back, and anger fueled by the inability to deal out justice to the creep who had alarmed her in the night.

****

Ann called, "I have someone who wants to see the house."

"Is it a tall guy, really tall, with short light-colored hair and blue eyes?" Beth tucked the kitchen phone receiver between her cheek and shoulder and poured iced tea into her glass.

"I haven't seen him yet. I'm supposed to meet him there. Who's the tall guy?"

"He came to the house yesterday. He asked to see inside the house."

"You didn't let him, did you?"

"Don't get irritated. I know I wasn't supposed to let him in." She put the iced tea pitcher back in the fridge and shut the door. "I gave him a few minutes to do a quick run-through."

"This was a stranger, right?" Ann was stern.

"Yes. I didn't go inside with him."

"Are you kidding me? You must know how dangerous that could be? It's dangerous for real estate agents and we're used to dealing with strangers."

"No harm done. He said he'd call you."

"What's his name?"

"I don't know."

"He didn't introduce himself?"

Beth shrugged. "He talked a lot about the house, about his parents...."

"But no names."

She paused, momentarily silenced by the outrage in Ann's tone. "No, I didn't get his name, but I'd seen him the day before."

"How's that?"

"I was coming out of the library and I tripped. He caught me, stopped me from falling."

"Is that how he found out you had a house for sale?"

"No, we didn't talk, except to say thank you."

"And yet he showed up in your backyard the next afternoon, by chance?"

"Ann, what are you saying?" Beth stopped pacing and sat at the kitchen table.

"Could be coincidence. Could be a guy looking to buy a house. Could be a guy who followed you home."

Beth was speechless. It was true. But unlikely, right? "Why would he?"

"Use your imagination." Ann cleared her throat. "I'm sorry to be so harsh, but you're alone there. Don't put yourself at risk for the sake of politeness. Draw a line in the sand."

"What?"

"Know the boundary over which no one trespasses. That's what I do with lookers. Most are genuine. Some aren't. They all provide identification and have to pass my radar."

"What's that?"

"If my radar reacts, no matter how good the prospect looks, I don't do it. No business is worth risking my safety. Sorry for the lecture but please remember it."

"I will. What about the person you're meeting here? What time?"

"Two-ish."

"I'm going shopping, so I'll plan to be gone then."

"You must be healing well. Glad to hear it. We'll be there around two."

****

Michael called suggesting they go out to lunch. "Pearl's Diner at noon?"

"Sounds good. I'll meet you. I'm planning to do some shopping this afternoon."

"Perfect."

****

He waited for her outside the main entrance to Pearl's over by the newspaper boxes. Beyond the boxes and planters, the truck stop looked neater than she remembered. Smaller now, but now with a convenience store and a clean, inexpensive motel was across the street.

"I see the Camellia Motel is still around. Looks almost retro now."

"Most of the truck traffic stopped flowing through here years ago. Tourists and vacationers stray from the main routes and keep this crossroads alive. Unfortunately, they are passing through on their way to vacation, and spend most of their money, somewhere else."

She was still thinking about people passing through as they walked to a corner table.

"You seem distracted."

Beth laughed. "I am. I didn't sleep well and this morning, Ann gave me a lecture about strangers."

Michael took her hand. "Strangers?"

"Just a potential buyer yesterday who stopped on impulse and wanted to see the house."

"Male? Alone?"

She smiled and rolled her eyes. "Please. I didn't go into the house with him. I'm smarter than that." She saw Michael wasn't satisfied. She changed the subject. "Don't over-react like I did last night."

"Last night?"

"I got one of those calls in the middle of the night where no one talks."

"Wrong number?"

"Doubt it. Whoever it was stayed on the phone to give me a little heavy breathing."

"The number didn't display on your Caller ID?"

"No. It was my cell phone. It read Anonymous."

"Could've been a mistake. Somebody could have dialed unintentionally."

"Maybe. Even if intended, it was probably random. If it wasn't random, then I also realize people who make crank calls don't show up. They're cowards or passive-aggressive. They get their thrills operating in the dark."

"Call me any time. Don't wait until you're scared. If you can't get me or you need someone closer, call the sheriff's department. You have their number? You have my cell?"

"Yes, programmed into my phone."

****

It was a quiet evening, time to prop up the foot and give it a rest after an afternoon of shopping. After lunch with Michael, she went to Roanoke and bought a few things, nothing extravagant, but pieces that were more flattering than her worn out jeans. Her social life showed definite signs of picking up.

Teddy pushed up under the book and settled in her lap. Beth found her bookmarked page.

Clarissa and Edward had made those garden walks a regular thing. With Clarissa's help, he re-learned the steps to some of the simpler dances. He disliked dancing in the dark, but at her urging, he reappeared in local society and, before long, it became apparent which local lady Mama Bellingame had in mind for her son to marry.

Success with her 'pupil' meant heartbreak for Clarissa.

Clarissa stood quietly, pretending to examine the rose the gardener had cut for her, but the gardener, unwitting chaperone that he was, had departed. Edward was near to her. Her every thought and feeling was captive to his presence.

Edward slid his fingers from Clarissa's

shoulder lightly down the length of her arm until he grasped her gloved hand. He brought it slowly to his lips.

Did he know his effect upon her? How could he not? The familiar, intimate gesture was deliberate. Clarissa stiffened, torn between the nearly violent response of her body and flesh— and the knowledge that his actions showed how little he respected her dignity and reputation. "It is wrong of you to make love to me when you have made your intentions known elsewhere. It is unbecoming of you and unfair to me."

"Yet you do not withdraw your hand. I dare to hope you have some understanding, some mercy for my state."

"Your state? Please tell me, Mr. Bellingame, what of your state should sway my heart or head? Do you woo me with honesty or with a wish for pity?" She snatched her hand from his grip.

"I wished to say I was sorry, but I see I have done poorly. I do not seek your pity, but your kind regard. I must accept this marriage for the sake of my mother and family name. I may only say this once, else you will think still worse of me. I do not care for Miss Sinclair. She is doubtless a well-esteemed young gentle-woman, but my heart is firmly engaged elsewhere, but regardless of personal preference, I am honor bound to fulfill a promise made long ago between our families."

Clarissa held the rose too tightly and a thorn pierced her gloved finger. Tiny drops of blood slowly welled up through the fine white cotton.

Clarissa gave a small sob.

"My beloved. My dearest girl. Most darling woman who woke me from my dark enchantment." Edward stumbled forward seeking her with his hands. He found her silk skirt and sank to his knees. "Know that if I had the choice of sight or life with you, I would choose you. I curse the honor that forces my hand elsewhere."

Clarissa knelt with Edward and took his hands in her own. Tears wet her cheeks.

"Mr. Bellingame, Edward, I know this—we are responsible for our choices. Even when we submit to the demands of honor or love, these are yet the choices we make. These choices make our lives what they are. I do not have great money or title, but I will make my own life. I will not allow others to make it for me." She touched her forehead to his hands, brought them to her cheek. "I choose to be forward at this moment, dear Edward. It is unseemly, but I will never look back and wonder what may have been had I but spoken."

Madam Bellingame stood at the drawing room window. Her face, seen through the mullioned panes, was distorted and shocked in outrage.

"Stand with me, Edward, this one last time." She touched his cheek, then on tiptoe she pressed her lips to his cheek. Over his shoulder, she saw Marston emerge in haste from the house onto the terrace stair.

"Stand here for a moment." She released Edward's hands and stepped back. She walked

toward Marston and they passed at the foot of the stairs. She heard Edward cry out for her when he felt Marston's hands upon him, but she did not pause.

Clarissa and Edward...star-crossed lovers?

Was that what Maude had done? Had she made her choices and never looked back? Or had she settled for the choices she'd felt duty-bound to make and made up an entirely fictitious, vicarious life through her writing? She wished she'd known about Maude's secret career while she could've talked to her about it.

Beth was getting ready for bed upstairs, brushing her teeth, when her cell phone rang. She couldn't help the small chill that passed through her at the first ring, but it wasn't the middle of the night this time. She wiped her face quickly and grabbed the phone.

Long silence except for the breathing, then the heavy breaths mutated to something almost like chuckling.

Unnerved, Beth looked at the name displayed and again it was Anonymous. She disconnected, this time promising herself to check displays before answering. In the morning, she'd call the service provider and find out what to do.

She was determined not to spend another aching night on the Davenport. She'd sleep in her own bed and she'd do what she had to, to feel safe. Beth carried the heavy flashlight up to the bedroom with her.

Once she was in her room for the night, she

closed the door, locked it and pushed the bureau in front of it. It wouldn't stop a determined intruder, but it would slow them down long enough for her to dial 911.

Chapter Twenty-Three

"Beth. Listen, please. I need your help."

Stephen. Once again, he sat on the Davenport. His posture was tense, his voice earnest.

"If I could ask anyone else, I would. There's no one. This may be life or death. It's definitely life or death for my career."

"I understand it's serious, but I can't imagine what you think I can do for you."

"I need money. A lot of money. Not something you'd have sitting around. I know you, Beth. You try to sound hard, but you aren't."

Beth stood and walked to the front window. She crossed her arms and looked past the window sheers, willing him to leave. Why wouldn't he stay away? She couldn't help her emotional response to his request for help, but there was a difference between helping someone out of a tight spot and giving in to emotional blackmail.

"I don't owe you anything. Why are you coming to me? We broke up. Went our separate ways. If the problem is the investor who wants his money back, then go to the police if you can't work it out with him. If you're afraid the bad publicity will hurt your job, then get another job. You got involved in investing and areas of finance you don't know enough about."

"It wasn't my lack of knowledge. It was the market. Things are recovering. I need to get this guy out of my life. I'll pay you back. You know I will. You're my only hope, Beth."

She had loved this man—or had thought she did, at least enough to accept his proposal of marriage.

"Beth," his voice was almost a whisper. "A loan against the land, that's all. You won't have to sell it. The land will still be there and I'll have it paid off before it's even an issue. Or if it sells before I can do that, the price will more than pay off the loan, and I'll still be paying you back. This can't hurt you, Beth."

She wasn't obligated to help, but she could, and it was true she'd hardly notice until she tried to sell the land, and even then–

Make your life. Don't let it be made for you. It was silly of her to remember Clarissa's words at this moment—the words of a fictional gothic romance heroine. But they were true and could have been Maude's own advice.

In fact, those words were Maude's. They'd been written to her by Maude in the copy of *Clarissa's Folly* that was back at her apartment.

When she turned back toward him, his face showed he understood her decision. His shoulders slumped, but he seemed calmer, resigned, as he stood.

"Thanks for hearing me out, Beth."

"I hope you understand." She resisted the urge to explain, to make excuses about why she was throwing him to the wolves, if that was truly the case.

He took Beth's place at the window and pushed the sheers aside. "It's nearly dark out." After a long moment he let the sheers fall back into place and walked over to Beth. "I'm sorry I bothered you with my problems. You're right, my problems aren't yours."

She felt as if she should offer reassurance, but honestly, she was so grateful he was leaving without more pleading, she said nothing.

He walked past her to the door. Beth followed him into the hallway, but let Stephen go into the vestibule and to the front door by himself. He stood there with the door ajar looking back at her for several long moments.

"Stephen, go to the police."

Anger flashed across his face. It happened and was gone again so quickly, she would've missed it if she hadn't known him so well. He opened the door the rest of the way, then stepped across the threshold to the porch where he stopped again. He looked left, then right.

Beth joined him at the door and looked out. Elise and Aaron were on the porch near the music room window. They were sitting on the planks, their backs against the side railing.

"Well, hey there. I was saying goodbye to my friend. I'll be right back." She followed Stephen down to his car.

"I truly hope it will work out for you."

He sped off without another word.

Aaron stood and helped Elise to her feet.

"We were taking a walk," she said.

"Aaron, it's nice to meet you. I never thanked you personally for cleaning up the debris after that storm."

He nodded and didn't look too unpleasant.

Elise pushed her dark hair back from her face. "We saw that guy." She looked back at Aaron. "I told him about the weird guy with the freak eyes."

"Neon blue."

"Neon." She nodded. "Yeah."

"You saw him?"

"Yeah, a little while ago."

Beth tried to tell herself it wasn't significant, but Elise had thought it important enough to plant herself and her boyfriend on the porch.

"We were walking by the lake. He was in your back yard. He didn't see us, so we came up to the road through Mrs. Boyle's yard." She hunched her shoulders. "He gives me the creeps. I saw the other guy's car in your driveway. The Stephen guy from the other day?"

"I guess I'm popular?" She tried to laugh off the worry. It didn't work. "Do you think he's still in the back yard? He was interested in the house. Maybe he was taking another look at the lot?"

"No other car out here. Why's that?" Aaron's deep voice was unexpected.

Beth looked at the road. "He had an SUV before. Should I go look out back? I guess I should if you didn't see him leave."

"Aaron can go with you." She pushed against his shoulder.

Aaron was young, but he looked kind of scary in his dark heavy clothing. Not actually dangerous, Beth thought. It was getting dark fast.

"Okay. Thanks."

"Wait." Aaron held up his hand. "Elise goes with you around that side. I'll go the other way." He looked meaningfully at Elise.

Beth felt more alarm in that one suggestion, and the thought process which prompted it, than in anything that had gone before.

Elisa examined the bushes as they rounded the house. Beth knew Aaron was doing the same and was greatly relieved when he met them behind the house. They walked around the gazebo and the shed. There was no sign of anyone.

"Maybe he parked down the road and went back along the lake."

Beth invited them in, but Elise took Aaron's hand and declined. They looked like strange and unexpected protectors as they waved goodbye.

White feathery wings would be incongruous on them—her would-be guardian angels.

Chapter Twenty-Four

The arc of light from the sodium oxide bulbs overhead cast an unhealthy-looking yellow tinge everywhere it touched. Stephen and Cole parked at the far end, near the alley running behind the motel because it was the darkest area, yet light enough to be able to watch each other's movements.

Stephen said, "Those kids screwed it up, but we'll try it again."

"We. Interesting word. An anonymous word, don't you think?"

"What's wrong with you?"

Cole ignored the question. "Begging her for money. A corny signal at the window." He laughed and moved a few steps closer.

He tried not to move. Giving ground was a mistake with guys like Cole. He moved anyway, brushing at his face, pretending he was avoiding an insect. Cole smiled bigger. Stephen looked away. He couldn't think with those eyes drilling into him.

"Murder isn't something that comes naturally to me, so excuse me if I wanted to give her a chance to work with me first. We were engaged. I cared about her."

"She's pretty. Almost took a walk through the house with her yesterday. Open, not suspicious, but she's got instincts. And she's hot. Way too hot for you. Maybe you thought you could have her and the property, too. She's done with you, man." He laughed.

Stephen's stomach cramped. He deliberately hadn't eaten because he'd been having this intestinal trouble since he arrived in Preston. He crossed his arms and fought the impulse to groan. He hated having to work with such a low life. Large white smile, crazy eyes and so damned big Stephen couldn't even fantasize about breaking his face, but Cole's words about seeing the house shocked him. Panic overwhelmed his fear.

"You went there yesterday? How stupid can you get? You think neighbors won't notice a guy your size wandering the neighborhood, especially two days in a row?"

"I'm not a complex kind of guy, Wyndham, but don't mistake simple for stupid. Don't make me regret my patience with you."

"When we're done, you'll have your money and I'll have the pleasure of never seeing you again."

Cole threw back his head and laughed.

Stephen had a glimpse of the future. It was a dark place where Jack Cole, or someone like him, could show up anytime, anywhere. Stephen turned abruptly and walked away.

"Hey, Stevie, don't you want to talk me into some more sure-fire investments?"

Stephen suspected Cole would be just as happy not to get his money back because then he'd have an excuse to take it out on Stephen himself. Potential for violence emanated from Cole, cloying and suffocating. Stephen had to calm down and think clearly to stay ahead of him.

Beth had had her chance.

He headed back toward Cole with strong strides to mask his fear. "Let's get this done and stop the small talk. We'll go for it tomorrow. I'll be far away and with an alibi for the time of death. And you? Make sure nobody knows about you. Beth knows there's an angry investor, but she doesn't have a name so she can't have passed it on to anyone."

"This better pay off."

"I told you we each have life insurance policies and made wills when we were planning to get married. She hasn't had time to change the beneficiary yet." Stephen added softly, "Just be there tomorrow, and this time, we'll make the opportunity."

Chapter Twenty-Five

"He's in town," Ann spoke in a low, excited voice. "Mr. Markland is meeting with Ed Mason. It must mean they've chosen the site."

Beth was less enthusiastic. "I'm sure we'll hear soon."

"I'll keep you posted."

"Thanks." She hung up the phone. Ryan had no reason to come by her house, but she knew he would.

The doorbell rang an hour later.

"May I come in?

In the daylight, his skin was still very fine, but appeared less perfect and that added to his masculinity. The urge was strong to step closer to him, to touch him, but she resisted. She didn't understand the almost overwhelming attraction, but it was undeniable.

"I heard you were in town." Beth stepped back. "Come in."

"It's a beautiful day. Would you mind if we sat out by the lake? Or is your ankle still keeping you in the house?"

"I'm doing well." She was still using the one crutch, but taking most of her weight on the foot. "It's much better."

She poured them each an iced tea. Ryan carried the glasses and allowed Beth to make her way down the steps and across the yard on her own.

The lake was shimmering with the almost noon-day sun. Ryan moved the chairs closer together.

"The 'For Sale' sign is still out front. Any offers?"

"Not yet."

"You're not anxious so you must be thinking of staying. Have you decided against returning to your old life?"

"You already know I lost my job the day before I came here. The only thing I have in Fairfax is an apartment, and it's nothing special." She stole a look at him and saw he was looking at her hair. Self-consciously she reached up and smoothed some strands behind her ear.

Ryan spoke. "The development project is on hold indefinitely. I met with the mayor and explained."

"They're disappointed."

He nodded. "But not as much as I anticipated. The mayor seemed to think there are other plans being considered. Something more local." He gave her a steady look, but didn't pursue the question. "Markland's decision has nothing to do with the Kincaid property. It may not have been a problem for you with the local residents, but it was important to me that we were clear about it."

"That was very kind of you. Thoughtful."

"I am a thoughtful man most of the time. Sometimes business interferes with personal preference."

"Sometimes personal preference interferes with business."

He leaned toward her. "I don't understand."

"My job. The one I lost. I don't know why I'm telling you this, but apparently I am, so here goes. In appreciation for ten years of stellar work, they let me leave discreetly, saying that I was being laid off like the others. We all live with the choices we make." Shades of Clarissa again? Or Maude? Maude.

"That morning they told me they were letting my group go. They were fabulous people, hand-picked by me, and of course, I knew all their personal business, their fears, hopes for the future, and I argued for them. The other people slated for layoff were also professionals and had needs, too, but for my people? It felt personal. Intensely so."

Beth wrapped her fingers around the iced tea glass, feeling the smooth glass, the icy cool of the tea. She held it to her forehead.

Ryan said, "You lost it, didn't you?"

"In a big way. I knew enough about the executives so that when I reamed them, I did it thoroughly and personally. It was so stupid and unnecessary. If there was any hope at all of helping my associates, I blew it when I lost my temper."

"Why?"

"Why what?"

"Why did you lose your temper?"

"I told you."

Ryan smiled and shook his head. "Why did you lose your temper?"

Beth sighed. "I spent ten years being perfect. Exemplary. Always stable, reasonable, rational. I thought the life I'd made for myself would keep my temper under control. You don't know how it was when I was a teenager. My temper was…extreme. A lot like my father's. I thought it had to be controlled."

"Until one day it burst like an over-pressurized tire."

She nodded. "I let people think I was laid off."

"But now you're ready to own it. I'm glad you told me. You trust me."

She laughed. "I think I do, but I have no idea why."

"I'm glad you do. I have a question for you."

"About my land?"

"No, not your land. Remember what I told you about my role in Markland Enterprises?"

"That you do the fieldwork? You're the legs of the business." She smiled.

"Well, these legs have to do a lot of traveling in the next few months, but I'd like to make it a point to come to Preston, or wherever you end up, to visit you."

"Visit me? That would be…great."

"Michael Fowler seemed protective of you. Are you two 'together'?"

"Michael and I are getting to know each other after a long time apart. I don't know for sure where it will go."

Ryan smiled with a glow of understated confidence. "I've never minded competition."

He stood and offered her his hand. They

walked back to the house.

"This is only the second time we've met," she said. "We hardly know each other."

"Third."

"I don't think that first time counts." She preceded him into the house and they walked straight through to the vestibule.

"There's something I recognize in you. Maybe it's the love of a challenge." He was silent for a moment. "I'll be back in a few days. After that, I'll be on the road for a while."

He stepped very close to her and placed his hands on her arms, gently, lightly. "Thank you for trusting me with your story about how you left your job. I'll take it as a caution about your temper. I didn't realize it was true...."

"Didn't realize what was true?"

"About red hair and hot tempers."

She pushed against his chest. "I'm not a redhead. My hair is blond. With red highlights. Strawberry blonde."

Ryan looked doubtful. He put his hands in her hair as if examining the color and texture, until his fingers caressed the back of her head, her neck. Her breath came short. Lightly, he touched his lips to hers in a feathery kiss that stopped her breath before his lips moved on to brush her ear. "I'll be back on Friday," he whispered.

****

Beth was in turmoil. The physical attraction was undeniable.

She felt flushed. She put her hands to her cheeks. They burned.

Was it also the attraction of no personal baggage? No awkward, inconvenient history. Not a bad thing.

Teddy came to her, wrapping himself around her legs.

In a sudden frenzy of energy, Beth hopped and limped around the house emptying bureau drawers and closet contents onto the beds. How many boxes would she need in order to wrap this up? The china cabinet still held Maude's dishes and the everyday stuff was in the kitchen cabinets. She made a list of what to keep, and what not, including furniture. She made a list of what should be done regardless of whether she stayed and then a list of final tasks to be done if she were to clear the house altogether.

Ann called. "Can you believe it? They're calling off the project. But that young couple is back. They're thrilled Preston wasn't chosen and want to see the house again."

"I've been going through things, getting it ready to pack up, so it's a mess."

"Not a problem. I'll point out that you're packing up. It might even urge them along."

Beth knew in her heart, this was it. This was going to bring the decision to the point of no return. "I'll go to the park. Take your time here, but keep an eye out for Teddy, okay?"

Beth took Clarissa along, not certain if she could relax enough to read, but so close to the end of the book that she wanted to try. She found a bench in the dappled shade near the mill.

Clarissa endured the coach trip from Woolridge back to Hargreaves insensible to the bumps and jolts. The memory of her ignominious departure drove her thoughts as if she were still in the foyer seeing the maid bring down her hastily packed bags and the groom spiriting them out to the carriage.

Dismissed she was, and no opportunity to speak her mind to the proud, snobbish woman who had brought them all to heartache.

"Mum?" The boot boy offered his hand.

There had been no time to send a letter or in any way inform her uncle that she was coming home. The earthy scent of Hargreaves Common welcomed her. She left her bags by the dusty public roadside and crossed the lawn where the sheep grazed, to stand in the gazebo. What would she say to her uncle?

She didn't wish to be less than honest with anyone, and most surely not her loving uncle, but she had promised Madam when she first arrived in Woolridge that she would be discreet about the true nature of the role for which she had been engaged. Was such a promise binding? Her uncle would likewise be discreet. He might not ask, but he deserved an explanation for her abrupt return. This was especially true as it was possible unflattering gossip might find its way out of Woolridge.

Clarissa believed Madam or the servants would be capable of such tales.

She read a while longer, until Clarissa had

reached her uncle's home. Clarissa saw speculation in the eyes of the family, neighbors and staff. Unable to get past her unhappiness, she finally withdrew to her room where she stayed in seclusion for a fortnight.

Beth was disappointed and slightly disgusted. She'd become accustomed to Clarissa's spirited, opinionated behavior. What had Maude been thinking to have Clarissa run away instead of staying to fight for what she wanted? And then to shut her away in a room to mope?

She tucked the bookmark in and closed the book. She was near the end, but was sufficiently annoyed with Maude that she wanted to put it aside for a while.

Pure emotionalism. There was a lot to be said for a relationship uncluttered by sentimentality.

And it had worked so well with Stephen, hadn't it, Bethie?

Her cell phone rang as she walked back to the car. She answered it reflexively and was dismayed when no one responded to her 'hello.' The heavy breather was back and in broad daylight. The rock was back in her chest, and cold spread into her limbs.

She disconnected and then checked the call history. J. Kincaid.

Not Anonymous like before. Not the heavy breather.

Why didn't he speak? Why did he call her? How did he find the guts to call her? Had he gone back to drinking? She bit her lip, then selected the number and hit dial. It went straight to voicemail.

It was some measure of progress that she'd received a call from Joe and actually returned it. A good feeling, too, but she drove home distracted. She walked into the house still worrying over it. She called Michael and left a message. "Beth here. I got another call a few minutes ago where no one spoke, but this time the Caller ID said J. Kincaid. I hit re-dial, but no one answered. I don't understand why he would call me. Let me know what you think. Bye."

Done. She washed her hands of it.

The phone rang again. This time it was Ann. "Beth, if these people don't make an offer, I'll be surprised."

"Thanks for letting me know. I guess we'll wait and see."

"Beth, I've sensed ambivalence from you about selling the house. Think about this hard because once you've accepted the offer you need to go through with it."

"You're right on both counts. We'll see if the offer comes"

"In this market, and since Markland has nixed the development plans, there's no telling how long before another offer comes along."

"I understand. Thanks, Ann."

Teddy had crawled among the clothing items Beth left on Maude's bed. He was well-camouflaged by the various fabrics. He gave her a look that said these items are now where they belong and why hadn't she done this sooner?

Michael was coming to take her out to dinner. She felt vaguely guilty about Ryan's interest in her, but she and Michael had no commitment. They were only beginning to build this relationship into something that might go long-term.

She took extra care with her makeup and hair. She clipped her hair up and allowed the loose tendrils to fall as they would. It made her neck look long and elegant. She wore a fresh pair of jeans and a new, flirty looking shirt she'd bought yesterday.

Her cell phone rang on her way downstairs. She checked before answering and saw Michael's name.

"Hi, are you on your way here? You're a little early, but I'm ready."

"Beth, listen." He paused before continuing. "I got your message and went to the north pasture to check on Joe. There's been an accident with a tractor. He's seriously injured, Beth. The rescue squad is on the way, but it's got a distance to travel."

"How... What...?"

"Just listen. Do you think you can drive out here to the farm? I'll wait for you. By then the rescue squad should be here and I'll drive us both into town to the hospital."

"Wait, Michael. I don't understand."

"He's hurt. It's very serious, Beth. He was working on the tractor and it slipped off the blocks and tipped over. If you think you're too upset to drive, then wait there and I'll come and get you after the rescue squad has him on the way to the hospital."

"No, I can drive. I'll leave now."

"Good. Thanks. Be careful."

"I'll meet you at your house."

Beth changed her sandal to a sneaker for safer driving. She removed some layers of bandaging from her sprained ankle and slid that foot into the other sneaker without the laces. It was tight, but do-able. She'd manage with the one crutch for minor support. She grabbed her purse, fished out the keys and opened the front door.

Her cell phone. She hobbled back to retrieve it from the coffee table. She heard a noise and turned around.

He stood there, a waking nightmare, nearly as tall as the doorway and almost as wide, with uncanny neon blue eyes. For the briefest of seconds Beth thought, hoped, he was just overly-anxious to see the house again. He walked toward her, his white smile terrifying.

She stepped back, desperate for options. The tip of the crutch caught the edge of Maude's threadbare carpet. She stumbled backward, feet slipping and arms flailing.

He laughed as his massive hands grabbed her hair and throat.

Chapter Twenty-Six

Michael knew as soon as he saw Joe that he would not—could not—recover. No man could withstand the weight of the huge old tractor sitting on his lower chest and pelvis. And Joe was older, less resilient. The only reason he still lived, as far as Michael could figure, was that the ground was so soft he hadn't been crushed to death outright. He lay unconscious on his back, lips parted, his breathing faint, but thick sounding. His cell phone had fallen in the grass near his outstretched hand.

The smell of blood and earth mixed with spilled gasoline. It burned his eyes and nose and he coughed. He considered trying to lift the tractor by hooking it to the truck hitch with the tow chain, but feared lifting it might harm Joe further, or hasten his death. He saw no way that raising the tractor could save him.

Sam was down by the main road waiting for the rescue squad. He'd lead them straight out here to the north pasture. He wished they could've gotten a life flight, but the service was already engaged with some other accident.

He knelt on the ground near Joe watching his shallow breathing, hearing a faint bubbling. He hoped Joe would stay unconscious. He had no idea what to say to him, or do for him, if he woke up.

Words filled his head.

Lord, this man needs your help. I need your help. If he wakes up, I need to know how to help him. How do I comfort him? What can I do?

He rested his forehead against his hand as he knelt with his arm on his knee, stunned. He hadn't set out to pray. His knee felt damp as the moist earth worked through the fabric of his jeans.

I haven't prayed in a long time. Lord, I hope you remember me.

His mind had gone empty. He still didn't know what to do, but he felt more at peace.

And Beth was on her way.

She should be well on her way by now. If this was goodbye, and she had the opportunity, she needed to take it. She and Joe weren't reconciled, but she wasn't as angry as she'd been. If so, she wouldn't have called him to tell him Joe had called her. His heart contracted painfully at the thought of Joe's last call going to his daughter.

Vehicles rumbled in the distance. He rose and tried to see beyond the swell of the hill. Curious cattle moved in more closely from the near pasture, toward the sound. Vehicles to them meant food.

He backed out of the way as the emergency crew examined Joe and, at their direction, helped raise the tractor slowly and carefully using his truck and chain. When the battered orange tractor cleared Joe's body, the old man's eyes popped open. He screamed, or tried to, but it cut off quickly. The EMTs worked efficiently to get Joe into their vehicle. He was unconscious again.

From the expressions on the faces of these experienced rescuers, Michael doubted Joe would make it to the hospital. He followed as they pulled out and headed back toward the main road. He and Sam parked at the house.

"Go with them while I wait for Beth. As soon as she gets here, we'll be on our way."

"Don't drive crazy. Likely it'll be too late and it'd be a kindness if he passed while unconscious. I never saw injuries like that in someone alive."

Sam left and Michael fidgeted. He paced and checked the time.

Where was Beth? Maybe she'd had trouble? No, she'd call. He'd done his best to explain the seriousness of Joe's injury without freaking her out. What had he told her? He didn't remember exactly. He dialed her number again. It rang a few times and went to voicemail.

If she was being temperamental, or taking this lightly, then he didn't think there was any chance for them. It would hurt them both, but he couldn't see any future with someone who could never move forward.

He got in his truck. There was only one road she'd travel to get here. Maybe he'd panicked her, and she'd had an accident.

Chapter Twenty-Seven

"How nice of you to invite me in."

Beth's arms and legs felt like lead and her stomach had twisted itself up so badly she was queasy. She wished she could find some anger deep inside. Anything to counter the fear. She was scared, confused and disbelieving.

"Who are you? Why are you doing this?" She was in the living room, strapped to one of the kitchen chairs. He'd duct-taped an ankle to each side rail and her hands were taped together behind the chair back. He was wearing latex gloves, and the jewelry, too—a large leather wristband with gold studs. The sight of the gloves on his huge hands gave her the shakes.

The smell of the latex irritated her nose and she turned her head away. He placed a hand on either side of her face and forced her to look him in the eyes.

"Name's Jack Cole."

He didn't care if she knew his name. She closed her eyes. Shut it out. If only she could. When he removed his hands, she was able to breathe again.

"Why are you doing this?"

Cole said, matter-of-factly, "For money."

"I can give you money not to hurt me, to go away."

"Sorry. No can do. For obvious reasons."

She twisted at the thick, silvery tape that bound her. She couldn't stop herself even though her struggle clearly amused him. His teeth were so white. Big. And his eyes. She closed her eyes again.

"You can ask more questions. I don't mind. I like your hair. Is that the natural color?"

Her brain was a little slow to process his question. His nonsense question while she was worried about life and death. "What do you want? To terrorize me? Don't I look scared enough?"

"You look very scared. Good reason to. Smart. Under different circumstances..." Cole sat on the upholstered chair. He settled back, resting his massive, gloved hands on his thighs.

"Fate's funny that way, isn't it? But as it is, it won't work. But we can chat while we wait for Wyndham to call."

"Stephen? Are you the man who's threatening him? You are, aren't you? He lost money, too. A lot of it. I understand your anger."

"I'm not angry. Just want my money back." He picked up Beth's books from the table. He eyed the romance novel, gave her a doubtful, teasing look, then tossed it aside. He thumbed through the Sears' house book.

"Stephen and I broke up. Totally. We have no relationship, so there's no point in using me to get to him."

Without looking up, he said, "I knew, soon as I saw you on your balcony back in Fairfax, you wouldn't put up with a loser like Wyndham for long."

The man in parking lot. "You spied on me? Followed me?"

"Just getting to know Wyndham's life—just in case." He held the book up toward her and pointed to an illustration. "Hey, you remember what I told you about my parents' house? This looks like it."

"What?" What kind of conversation was this? "I'm sure your parents are proud."

"Not them, they're dead. Long time ago. Their house burned, too." He made a *tsking* sound with his tongue.

"My ankle hurts. And my hands behind the chair...it hurts my arms. Is this really necessary?" There must be a crack, even a hairline fracture, by which she could find her way inside his head and find a real person. Connect with him.

"It's just for an hour or so more. Until Wyndham calls. He needs time to set up an alibi."

"What?"

Cole smiled again.

"Don't smile. I told you it scares me."

"You're a pistol, aren't you? If I had my preference, I'd keep you and kill him, instead."

There, the word was said. Kill. "Who? Why? I don't understand."

"Not surprising that you don't. I've noticed that about honest people." Cole dropped the book lightly onto the table and stood up. "Wyndham needs the alibi." He walked closer and bent over, putting his face close to hers.

"Got any food in the kitchen?"

"Alibi?"

"So he can inherit."

"Inherit." She stopped suddenly. Inherit? He wouldn't. She'd never gotten around to signing the new will or changing the beneficiary for her life insurance. They weren't married yet and maybe, deep inside she'd had doubts. But if she told Jack Cole would he kill her now? Either way, her death seemed certain.

Cole stared at her intently. She couldn't read his face. He moved close again.

The doorbell rang. Hope lit her face. He shook his head very slowly in warning. His nose almost touched hers. His eyes were so unnatural she couldn't break away.

"Be very, very quiet. If you make a noise, I won't gag you. Instead, I'll break your neck here and now. You understand? You'll be dead before anyone can't get through the door."

He walked to the front window. Careful not to touch it, he peered through the slim opening between the window frame and the curtain. He spoke in a low voice. "It's that girl with the dark hair. She'll go away. If she doesn't, I'll invite her in." He grinned and arched his eyebrow as if teasing. "Should we invite her in? Just say the word. Any word."

They waited in silence. Beth's shock was so great she could hardly breathe for fear he'd seize upon a rasp of breath as an excuse to involve Elise.

Elise knocked again. They waited.

Finally, Cole said, "There she goes." He

picked up the roll of duct tape. "Sorry about this, but while I'm in the kitchen, it'll be a little insurance. Ha! Funny, right? Insurance?"

The thick, sticky feel of the tape and the dirty smell of his hand covering fully half of her face, his fingers pushing the duct tape over her lips, even over her nose had a nightmare quality. He wrapped it around the back of her head tightly before ripping it and neatly smoothing down the ends.

She struggled to breathe, wriggling her nose trying to loosen the tape. She wasn't likely to smother because he'd left a slip of an opening, but she felt like she couldn't get enough air. She beat back the panic, fighting to think clearly. She had no advantage in size or strength. Her only hope was to be ready if he got careless. As things stood right now, his carelessness would still provide no opening. She was strapped to this chair so thoroughly she was truly caught.

The Stewart Family Bible on the lower shelf of the end table caught her eye. She'd put it there a few days ago and dust had already started to settle on the cover. She realized her breathing had steadied and she worked to keep her focus on the Book. By breathing shallowly, she was able to get small amounts of air past the tape and into her nostrils.

Beth looked at the soft, torn edges of both the cover and the rumpled interior pages. This Book had been important to generations of her mother's family. Maude had believed it would be important to her.

She closed her eyes slowly. *Focus, Bethie, focus.*

She wanted to make her own life. She couldn't make it, not past this, without help. Praying was the only thing she could think to do. She tried to empty her mind and assemble a prayer. In the silence, the utter quiet of the old house, with her captor in the kitchen, Beth heard a small noise.

She closed her eyes more tightly and strained to listen. Please, God.

It was a scraping sound against the house shingles. She opened her eyes, looked to the left and caught a glimpse of James's face up in the window and down again.

Had James seen her? Had Cole seen him?

Elise at the door. James at the window. Was it foolish to hope? Emotion, warm and strong, surged in her chest, speeding up her heart rate.

"Hey, I think we're not alone. You hiding something from me?"

Eyes down, keep your eyes down. He'll see the hope. He's not expecting an answer, not with the tape across your mouth. Don't look up.

"I saw the cat bowl and litter box. I like cats. Mostly. Where does he like to hide? I'll fetch him out. No need for him to burn with the house."

Beth raised her head. This time she glared at him and allowed anger and disgust to scream in her eyes.

Chapter Twenty-Eight

Michael had almost reached Beth's house. No sign of her anywhere along the road stranded with a flat tire or by some other driving hazard. He became angry, but the anger didn't ring true and was edged out by apprehension. Beth might fly off the handle, but she wasn't petty and she wasn't a fool. His apprehension became tinged with fear creating darkness in his mind, a defined area of crystal clear thought with all emotion chilled and set aside. His thought processes had never felt sharper. By the time he saw the sheriff's cruiser parked outside of the Boyles' house, it seemed almost expected and reasonable.

Withhold judgment. Suspend conjecture. Get the facts. Assess the options. Breathe.

He stopped his truck near the cruiser where Deputy Tom Sims was talking to Martha and James. The people and their vehicles were hidden from Maude's house by the Photinia hedges.

"Michael, Mrs. Boyles' grandson, James here, said he saw Miss Kincaid tied to a chair in the living room. He only had a quick look—"

"Taped, not tied," James corrected.

"I called the sheriff," said Mrs. Boyle.

"Sergeant's on his way. We may have a hostage situation."

"Hostage? For what? Who's in there with her?" He knelt before James, clasping the boy's thin shoulders firmly. "Who's in there with her?"

"I don't know. Elise saw him. She calls him Neon. She saw him go into the house and she knocked, but no one answered. She boosted me up at the windows until I saw Ms. Kincaid in the living room in that chair, but I didn't see anyone else."

"Who's this Neon? Where's Elise?"

"She sent me to tell Grams to call the cops. She stayed over there to watch, you know."

"Whoa, Michael. Wait." The deputy said. "Don't go charging the house. If Ms. Kincaid's being threatened or held hostage you could precipitate violence. We have no clue who this guy is or why he's there. If he's there. He could've left. The sergeant will be here any minute."

"Why isn't he here now? How long are you going to just stand around?"

"There's a bad accident a few miles out of town, near the junction with the interstate. Multiple vehicle involvement with fatalities. We responded along with the county and state police. Michael, I understand your concern, but we can't rush the house and break down the doors. Not yet, anyway."

"Oh, no need," said Martha Boyle. "I have a key."

Chapter Twenty-Nine

With great care, Cole worked the tape loose from her lips and gently tugged it down to her chin.

"Hey, beautiful. Ready to go?"

"Where?" Her voice was hoarse.

"To your reward. Isn't that what they say? That's where my gramps used to say he was going back when I was a kid. He was a mean, old buzzard. Ha! But he could really swing that cane. You gotta love 'em though, don't you?"

"Please don't do this." Despite her anger, tears welled in her eyes.

"But I have to. Stevie didn't call and he's not answering his cell. There comes a time when you have to move forward. Staying ahead of trouble is all in the timing." He put a hand on either side of her face and pressed them against her cheeks. His gesture pushed her lips into the mimicry of a pucker.

"I'm ready to leave town. Time to go. Time to say goodbye."

He released her face and reached down near the floor. Beth felt the cold metal of a knife blade against her ankle as he cut the tape securing her right foot to the side rail. She hadn't seen him holding a knife. His hands were so fast. Her foot was cramped. Numb. He sliced the tape securing the other ankle.

"I'm going to cut the tape on your hands now. Be very careful what you do when your hands are free."

Sounded like a challenge. As if he wanted a fight or, at least, some struggling. "I think you'd like that."

His big, white smile again. He cut the tape binding her wrists.

Was this her moment? She couldn't stop him from strangling her or breaking her neck. He was too obscenely big. Her only hope was to delay until help arrived.

She stood abruptly, hoping to throw him off-balance. He tipped backward, his bluer than blue eyes widened. She moved without hesitation, but his reflexes were quick. Instead of trying to break his own fall, he grabbed her. He got her ankle, her healing ankle, and pulled her back, dropping her onto her butt. She kicked with her free foot, but he pushed it aside like swatting a fly. He got a grip on the tape still circling her neck and yanked. She screamed and screamed and–

His hand cut off her air. He kept his fingers wrapped around her windpipe until she began to see spots and her vision went red. With a quick wrap and snip, her wrists were taped together again behind her back. He stood yanked her up.

"Most home fires start in the kitchen."

One breath. Two breaths. Her vision was clearing. She hated him. If she was going to die, she wasn't going quietly, not if she could drag enough air through her damaged throat and into her lungs.

His arm was around her neck as he backed into the hallway. She tried to kick again, but her feet barely touched the floor. His chest and stomach pressed like granite against her back. She struggled against him anyway, knowing it was hopeless, knowing he was enjoying it. He could easily have finished her off in the living room. This was part of the thrill.

She tried to kick her heels into his kneecaps. He laughed.

A sound came from the back of the house, that of a door rattling or someone pushing, thumping against it.

His arm tightened around her throat, stretching as he turned toward the kitchen. The click-click sound of the front door lock mechanism turning heralded the front door bursting open.

He kept one arm around her neck, but his other arm reached behind his back and came back with a gun. She saw the gun and Michael coming through the door all at once and she knew someone was about to die.

She struggled, putting all of her strength into it, hoping to throw off his aim. He took a step back, then did a stutter step. Somewhere below them, out of her sight, Teddy shrieked.

Cole's foot, seeking firm ground, hit the corner of Maude's old hallway rug and slipped. Suddenly, airborne and weightless for one long second, she floated above the falling monster helpless to save herself. She hoped for a soft landing.

As they hit the floor, Cole's gun shook loose. Beth saw it spin across the floor with a whispery sound.

Michael filled her vision. Tom was on his heels.

Cole tried to shake her off, but Michael grabbed Beth and Tom put his Glock to Jack Cole's head.

****

"His name's Jack Cole. He's working with Stephen Wyndham. Stephen went to establish an alibi and left Cole to kill me. Murder me."

They were all in the front yard, a small crowd of citizens and law enforcement. The curiosity seekers milled around, like gnats attracted to the victim and the police.

"Her father is in the hospital. I have to get her there," Michael said.

"Stay where you are sir. I'll need to confirm," responded the officer.

"She's coming back here. She's not leaving except to go to the hospital."

The sergeant stepped aside with the officer. When they returned, he said, "Beth, we'll take a statement from you in the ambulance on the way to the hospital. In fact, I'm concerned you aren't under medical supervision already."

"Ambulance? I don't—"

"Not every injury is visible and I think the EMTs are concerned you're looking shocky." His eyes were on her neck. "The officer will take a preliminary statement on the way."

She put her hand to her throat where Cole's hands, and then his biceps, had choked her.

She'd have bruises, no doubt. The back of her neck tingled. She turned and saw him in the police car, his freakish eyes staring. He didn't look scared.

She shivered. "Michael–"

"Ambulance for you. Now. I'll be right behind you."

****

The rescue squad delivered Beth to the emergency room. Michael followed closely behind. Sam was already there. Apparently, Michael had called and filled him in and he'd prepared the way with the doctors on duty.

A dark-haired woman in blue scrubs appeared at Beth's side and said, "We transferred Mr. Kincaid to the ICU." She walked with her, speaking as they went. "Your vitals were normal in the ambulance, so we'll wait to admit you until after you've seen your father, but you have obvious trauma, so don't delay."

Michael snagged a wheelchair somewhere along the way to the elevator, but Beth wasn't ready for that. It would be too much like giving in and she couldn't afford that weakness.

Beth hesitated in the doorway to Joe's room for reasons she couldn't name. The floor seemed to move beneath her feet and her insides started shaking. She wasn't strong enough, after all. She pressed her hand to her forehead.

"Sit down, Beth." Michael put his arm around her.

"I never expected to be here. Not here in a hospital room with Joe. I don't know how to do this." She waved away Michael's wheelchair. "I'm okay. I'll be okay."

"I'll stick close by." Michael took her hand and walked with her to the bedside.

Joe was barely a rumple beneath the white blanket and about the same color. His vitality, all of the good and bad pieces that made up a human being, were gone, as if everything that made him who he was for the fifty-some years of his life had evaporated. The sight and sound of blinking monitors were the only testament to his living state. She waited for the old negative emotions to surface, but felt nothing. Nothing.

If the bad feelings were gone, what was left?

"Joe?"

His eyelids fluttered, but didn't open. Beth touched the pale hand lying atop the blanket. The enlarged knuckles and rough skin had smoothed as if their workday world was already a thing of the past.

"Beth," Michael said. "Speak to him. Say it for him, for yourself, or in memory of your mother, or you'll regret it the rest of your life."

Beth was shocked at Michael's words. It was too rigid a barrier—this animosity she'd nursed for years—to be overcome as if it were only a misunderstanding. Her next breath was jagged, nearly tearing her throat. Time drained away, each moment newly born and lost. Gone forever. How many moments were left?

She coughed. Her throat ached. "Joe?" She rubbed her eyes. "Dad?"

A man in hospital dress stood behind her. "He's sedated. He may hear you, but he isn't likely to respond."

Beth turned toward him and observed his double-take as he saw the marks on her neck.

"Why is he lying here? Why isn't he being treated?"

"Would you step aside with me?" He led her away, guiding her into the hallway. He pulled the wheelchair with them and gently eased her down into the seat.

"He is. We've treated what we can and tried to make him comfortable. Mr. Purchase assured us you were on your way."

"You can't do anything at all?"

"No. His internal injuries are too severe." He nodded and extended his hand to shake. "I'm Dr. Smith, on-call today, but I've treated your father before. Surgery might have repaired some of the internal injuries, but his organs were already in very poor condition and his heart is weak. His pelvis is shattered. I saw him about a year ago for another complaint. We discovered the compromised liver at that time. Given the state of his kidneys, heart and lungs, he isn't a candidate for transplant. He executed a DNR at that time. He also authorized me to discuss his health care and history with you, his daughter. If you have any questions, please ask."

Michael joined them in the hallway. He placed his hands on her shoulders in a gentle caress.

She brushed her cheek against his hand. "Will you push me back to the bedside? I need to finish saying goodbye."

****

The road noise, rough beneath the tires, filled the car. Beth didn't want radio chatter or other pointless noise to abate the emptiness. She wasn't ready to move on yet, but life, and inevitable death, were continuing on whether she was ready or not. When she'd been so angry with her father, she hadn't wanted to talk about him. Now, he was gone, and so was the anger, yet she didn't feel she could discuss him. It was too much for her to digest all at once.

Michael glanced her way a few times, but said nothing. Beth empathized. Her silence must be awkward for him. The subject of Joe wasn't an option, but there were other things they could talk about.

She threw out a few words as a test. "When I saw James's head pop up outside of the window I began to hope, but I was so scared for him. Jack Cole could've seen him." She massaged her forehead and pressed her hands against her eyes.

"Headache?"

"Only a little. There's so much I don't know. I'm so grateful, but I don't know who to thank."

"Probably your neighborhood. Your friends."

"I don't understand."

"Elise saw Cole. Neon, she calls him."

"His creepy eyes," Beth said.

"She saw him go into your house. Knocked on your door and when no one answered, she knew something was wrong. James was out back working on that old rowboat so she got him to help. She boosted him up. When he saw you in the chair, she sent him to ask his grandmother to call the sheriff's office."

"What about you? How did you find out something was up?"

"I came looking for you when you didn't arrive at the farm. Tom was in the street talking to Martha Boyle and James."

"Where was Elise?"

"She stayed around your house, watching the doors in case Neon, Cole, tried to leave."

She shivered again to think Elise might have found herself in Cole's path. "I'm so thankful. I owe them so much."

He reached over and grasped her hand. "We both have a lot to be grateful for."

"How did you get in the front door? I heard the key."

"Martha's."

"You and Tom both came in through the front, right? It happened so quickly. I remember Cole stumbling...over Teddy, I think. Who was at the back door?"

"Elise wanted to be the back door diversion, but Martha said it was too dangerous."

"Then who—"

"Martha Boyle herself. She took her shoes off and pounded on the back door with the rubber heels. Wanted to be loud, but not to dent the door."

Beth laughed, but ever so gently. She knew that's what Michael was hoping for and a little laughter did lift her spirits and didn't hurt her throat too much.

Michael said, "I didn't want to worry you

before, and I hate to do it now, but Martha and the kids took Teddy to the vet."

"What? He dashed upstairs and disappeared under the bed, right?"

"They called me while we were at the hospital. They tried to coax him out, but he wouldn't budge. Finally, they got him and took him to the vet. He has a broken leg."

"What?" Beth sat forward and faced Michael. "He has a broken leg?" Her voice rose, hysteria imminent.

"Beth, honey, he's okay. It's a hairline fracture. A cast for a couple of weeks. He'll be fine."

"He has–"

"Beth, it's okay." Michael signaled and pulled over to the side of the road. He reached across and popped the glove compartment open. "Here's tissues."

She cried through the whole travel pack of tissues. Michael held her at times, at times she pulled away, then returned. His shirt was soaked with her tears.

"I'm sorry, Michael," she said as the sobbing slowed.

"Don't try to talk, Beth. If you're feeling a little better, I'll get back on the road and get you home."

Home. The word didn't bring the feeling of safety it once had. "Did you know Stephen was working with Jack Cole?" She heard herself once again identifying him by first and last name. She couldn't help it. It was how she thought of him and when she did, she trembled.

"You told us. He needed your money, or whatever assets he could get his hands on, to buy off Cole. Why did he go messing in investment funds anyway?"

"Stephen was always on the lookout for an opportunity. He didn't think the rules applied to him."

"How do you feel knowing he's dead?"

"That he died driving out of Preston on his way to establish an alibi while Cole did the dirty work? To the woman he once professed to love? I'm hurt, but no more than that."

Michael nodded, but said nothing.

"The officer who took my statement in the ambulance asked about Stephen's family, next of kin and all that. I don't know who to notify. His employer, maybe. I guess I'll need to make funeral arrangements."

"No, for all sorts of reasons. The accident was extensive. Two fatalities and several serious injuries. Cars were incinerated. They identified his car by the plate found a distance away from the collision area. They were still picking the wreckage apart last I heard."

She had loved Stephen, hadn't she?

He lifted her hand and touched her fingers lightly to his lips. "Beth, you'll stay at the farm tonight."

Beth sniffled again and dabbed at her eyes with the tattered remnants of the last tissue.

"I appreciate the offer, but I'm going home...to Maude's house, I mean. The danger's over and I want to feel it in here." She laid her hand over her heart.

"I tried to tell the deputy Jack Cole was...either psychotic or a sociopath...I don't know what he is. I'm not a psychologist or a criminologist, but I saw him up close. He was detached from real emotion. He smiled at all the wrong times, almost like, instead of a smile, he was baring his teeth. An animal. No, not an animal. An animal can feel devotion, fear, and can share those emotions. Am I making any sense at all?"

"Yes, you are. We don't understand monsters like Cole. I hope we never can."

"Can we stop by the animal hospital? Is Teddy still there?"

"We'll drive by and see." He took her hand and kissed it. "Anything you want."

****

Dr. Hoyt said Teddy was stable. "Cats tend to suffer from shock and it can be fatal for them, more so than the leg injury. Teddy's been hydrated and has a very light sedative to keep him from fretting. I'd recommend you leave him here tonight."

"I don't want to put him at unnecessary risk, but I believe he'll feel better at home. I'll be with him."

The veterinarian stared at her throat. "I think you need him as much as he needs you."

Beth nodded. "I know I look awful."

"You're still standing and that's saying something given what Mrs. Boyle told me. I'll move Teddy into a box. You can carry him without causing him pain. Call me first thing in the morning to let me know how he's doing. It's very important he stay hydrated."

Michael toted the box across the threshold. Beth paused. She entered the house on shaky knees and stood in the hallway. Her heart tried to beat through her chest. She stared and saw...nothing.

Everything looked exactly as it should. A lamp had been left burning in the living room. It cast a low, soft-white incandescent light across the room and spilled into the hallway.

Mrs. Boyle, possibly with Elise and James, had tidied up so no trace remained of Jack Cole's visit. Not a rug was out of place, not a shred of duct tape to be seen.

"Michael, will you take Teddy upstairs? Into my room, in the front. I'll bring his litter box and dishes." But when Michael went upstairs, Beth's feet stayed glued to the hallway rug. She could see the doorway to the kitchen, but she couldn't see into the kitchen. She couldn't take a step in any direction.

Chapter Thirty

Michael came downstairs and saw her frozen in the hallway. He descended the last steps in a rush and took her in his arms. He tried not to crush her, but all of a sudden, he was afraid. How far were any of them from disaster? At any moment, you could look away and lose the most important person in your life forever.

After Teddy was settled, Beth finally climbed into bed. Michael sat with her while the medication the doctor had given her took effect. The bruises around her throat were dark and painful-looking.

She wore a t-shirt and sleep pants and still looked beautiful. The bruises gave her a battered, vulnerable air. The cat box on the bed with the assorted old clothing pushed up around gave the whole picture a bizarre air. Beth clutched a book in the crook of her arm— one of those silly romance novels.

"Want me to move some of this stuff?"

"Teddy is surrounded by Maude's old clothing and the reassuring smells and textures he loves." She reached across and touched his hand. "You look like you feel sorry for me. Don't. The bruises will heal."

"What about the ice pack for your throat?"

"I want to sleep. I can't possibly sleep with an ice pack around my neck."

He nodded. "A lot happened today. Do you

want to talk about it some more?"

"No. I've had enough of today. For now, anyway. I know it isn't over and we'll have to deal with it, and him, but not right now. I do want to ask you something."

"Anything."

"That day when we met out back, when I returned to sell Maude's house and you said you'd just gotten back into town, why were you here?"

"I was considering buying Maude's and Martha's properties. I don't have unlimited funds or credit, so I was caught between wanting to purchase, but concerned about getting in over my head with loans out on two properties. Martha was interested, but not ready. Maude said 'no.' When I saw you, it threw me. I didn't know what to say. You seemed so determined to sell, I decided to wait and see. Part of me wanted you to stay, and part of me was afraid you would stay."

"'Because I'd be in the way of your new 'venture'?"

"No. It was for a much more personal reason." He could feel the flush rolling up his face.

"You look nervous. Please don't be. I think I know now about why those marriages didn't happen. I want to say something, just throw it out so you'll know where I stand. I don't want anything from you that you don't want to give."

Her remark annoyed him. "You mean emotionally."

"Yes. I don't want anything from you

emotionally that isn't given with a whole heart—
that isn't fully committed. I'm done with settling
for less than the best, Michael, with playing it
soft and shallow with life."

She leaned forward and put a finger to his
lips. "Don't say anything now, please. Think
about it and when things are less dramatic, see
how you feel."

She slid down beneath the covers, rolled
over, and was asleep within minutes.

Michael was glad she'd insisted he wait
before answering. He didn't know the answer.

When he stood he noticed a small red piece
of paper had fallen from the book. A bookmark?
Or just trash? He picked it up and put it in his
pocket, then switched off the lamp.

He cared a great deal, but what she was
saying rang of permanence. He'd figure it out
later. Just now, there were more immediate
concerns.

Stephen Wyndham was dead, but Cole was
alive and well. Michael didn't doubt he'd hurt
people before. A murderer. How many times
over? He was far too cool for this to have been
his first attempt, and he was slick enough not to
have been caught or even to be wanted by the
law.

Beth would have to face him in court and
give evidence. Once she was past the worst of
the trauma, Michael didn't doubt she could do it
and do it well.

The doctor at the hospital hadn't been
thrilled when Beth declared she was going
home. The bruising, as bad as it looked, was

superficial. The doctor was concerned about shock or possible complications.

I want to go home, she'd said. She also announced she was putting aside the crutches. The doctor advised her to stay off her ankle as much as possible and keep it wrapped in an Ace bandage. Beth agreed she'd be careful, but that was as much as she'd concede.

Michael wondered if the idea of staying in the hospital while her father was in the morgue had been more than she could handle.

It was sad about Joe. He'd known Joe for as long as he could remember and while he was sorry Joe had died the way he did, he could've, should've, died any number of times over the years he was drinking. In those last moments of life, his eyelids had fluttered open, perhaps in response to Beth's soft words. Michael was glad for both of them that Joe had lived long enough to see his daughter standing at his bedside.

Exhausted, he thought he was too pent up to sleep, but not so. Taking time only to remove his shoes and socks before stretching out across Daniel's old bed, he fell asleep immediately. He woke suddenly in the night, disoriented, in the silent house.

He followed the trail of moonlight streaming through the window into the hallway and stood, listening.

A gentle creak came from Beth's room. The door was slightly ajar. Michael opened it. Moonlight highlighted the jumble on Beth's bed. He couldn't believe she'd taken Maude's clothing odds and ends dumped out of the bureau drawers the day before and placed them around Teddy in his box. A crazy thing to do. The box was in the middle of the bed and somehow Beth had curled up in the midst of it.

Michael was drained, but wide awake. He rubbed his face with his hands. What she said to him about commitment... He'd have to think about it. She was playing for keeps. If he was going to let her down, he had to do it now and not go along until he got cold feet.

He stepped quietly down the stairs. If she was aware of her surroundings on some subconscious level, he didn't want to alarm her. It was dark downstairs and he stubbed a bare toe against a table leg. He limped into the living room, whispering curses, and sat in the chair. His toe ached, but wasn't bleeding. When he stood, he noticed a vehicle, silhouetted by the moonlight, parked at the curb in front of the house.

He pushed aside the sheers. No reason a car couldn't park there, of course, but the shape immediately suggested a deputy's cruiser. Did they send a deputy to keep an eye on the house? But if Wyndham was dead and Cole was in custody, then who was being protected?

Not them. It was the house, surely. The story of what happened had likely spread across Preston. The house was dark and looked empty. It could be targeted by vandals or the merely curious. Law enforcement had parked a car there for the night to discourage trespassers.

Michael picked up the kitchen phone and dialed the sheriff's office. Nance usually took the night shift. "Hey, it's Michael. I'm over at Maude Henry's house on Lake. Have you got a car over here for security?"

"Did have two. Sims stayed at the house, but the other car got called off. He'll return as soon as he's cleared at the other location. We tried to reach you and Miss Kincaid, but no luck. You're back at the house now?"

"Yes, for several hours. Your cars must've arrived after we got back. Why were you—"

"Well, sit tight. The suspect broke free when they were bringing him in. Not sure what happened, but we think he had a pick in his belt or wristband. He put Whalen in the hospital."

"How serious?"

"He'll be okay. The State Police are out looking for Cole. Our deputies are patrolling around town and in the county."

Michael ran his free hand through his hair, thinking fast. "I'm taking her out of here. Let Tom know. I'm taking her out to the farm. Cole doesn't know about the farm."

"He's probably long gone by now."

"If he's not, Beth is a sitting target here. So is Tom. Let him know we'll be coming out."

"How long?"

"I don't know. Beth is sleeping. She's medicated. I'm not sure how she'll take it when I wake her to tell her."

"You're safe there, Michael. Stay inside."

"Can't."

"I'll raise Sims on the radio."

Michael paused at the window and saw a figure moving near the cruiser. It was only a shadowed form glimpsed in very iffy light. Could be anyone. Within seconds someone was knocking softly at the door.

"Michael? Tom Sims here. Nance called me. Can you step out?"

They stood in the deepest shadows under the front porch. The house blocked the rising, capricious wind.

Tom said, "They found an SUV parked about a block away. Reported by residents. Someone jumped the gun and towed it. It's ID'd as Cole's."

"So he probably came back this way to get his truck."

"I would have. He'd expect it still to be here. Wish it had been. Would've been good for a stakeout."

"So what would he do next?"

"Depends on how long it took him to get out here, I think. If he somehow got a ride out here, he's probably already stolen a car from the neighborhood and is out of the area. A guy like Cole doesn't strike me as someone who acts without thinking it out or puts himself in jeopardy if he's got options."

"Could be he's only just discovering his ride is gone."

"No telling. That's why I parked the car out front and got into the bushes to watch. The cruiser might warn him off. Or lure him in. I'd like to get back out of sight. Nance said you're taking Miss Kincaid out to the farm?"

"Yes. Come inside and go out the back door. If someone's out front watching, you're already spotted, but he won't know you're outside again. The house is dark. You can slip out the kitchen door and come around to the front keeping to the shadows."

They walked through the dark and silent house. When they reached the door, Michael spoke in a low voice, "It's a few minutes past two o'clock. A long time 'til morning. Be careful out there."

Tom slipped quietly out the back door. The wind was rising. He kept his grip on the storm door until Michael grabbed it and pulled it closed. Tom was briefly exposed crossing the moonlit area of the yard, then he vanished.

Michael was carefully latching the storm door when he saw a figure stumble back into the moonlight. At first he thought it was a bush or leafy branch that had blown loose, then realized it was the deputy.

Chapter Thirty-One

Beth stirred. She resisted waking, but something was poking her side. She reached down and found a book had worked its way under the comforter. Clarissa. The book was real. The terror earlier in the day seemed distant.

Kill her and burn her house, that's what he'd planned.

In cooperation with Stephen.

She shivered and pulled the comforter up around her neck.

Stephen's participation was the worst part. He was willing to sacrifice her to save his own butt. Over money. Stephen was shallow and self-centered, she knew that. Now she knew he was also a coward and worse.

And Joe. White sheets and cotton blankets politely covered his devastating injuries while his life slipped away. He'd died with her at his side and had known she was there.

A small tear rolled down her cheek and wet the pillow.

Teddy was sleeping soundly in the box with Maude's scent tucked all around him. He was so still she would've worried if not for the snuffling breathing noises he made from time to time.

He'd tripped the monster.

Good for Teddy.

Michael. Michael was here somewhere. Not only had he gotten her to her father's bedside, but he'd rescued her from Cole. Thank God.

And friends and neighbors.

Warm, if disjointed thoughts helped push aside the shaky scary feeling that wanted to creep out of the sleepy fog in which she was wrapped. The pain medication effectively diluted every strong emotion, including fear.

Slowly, Beth sat up in the dark. The clock said two o'clock. She stood carefully, lightheaded. She held on to the furniture and walls and made her way down the hallway to the bathroom. Bladder attended to, but she had a dry mouth and throat. Was it worth a trip downstairs?

Where was Michael?

Beth walked into Daniel's old room. Michael's cell phone and wallet were on the nightstand. His shoes were on the floor. The bed was hardly disturbed.

She'd managed by moonlight thus far and was reluctant now to turn on a light. If a light had been on downstairs, she would've seen a glow. The plumbing in this house wasn't silent, so if Michael was downstairs, he'd know she was up and around. Yet, no light was burning from below and no one was calling up the stairs to ask how she was feeling.

She couldn't just stand there, she thought, and she was right because she swayed toward the railing. A giggle tried to bubble up. She hadn't been sipping Lady Lisanne's laudanum, but she did take those pills. Beth tried to shake

the wooziness off and gripped the rail tighter.
She should go back to bed. Sleep it off.

And she almost did.

She walked back toward her room and,
again, saw Michael's wallet and phone on the
night stand. It struck her as fascinating how the
cold white light of the moon drained everything
of color. It made ordinary things look alien. Like
Michael's phone.

Where was Michael? She picked up his
phone. Where was her phone? In her purse, but
where was her purse? She had no idea.

Beth flipped open his phone and the little
window lit up. She'd heard about fast food
customers who'd dialed 911 for a lot less cause
than a missing Michael. Feeling silly, again, she
punched in the numbers, but then her thoughts
swam away and she was very thirsty.

She descended the stairs slowly on rubbery
knees. She clutched the railing and put most of
her weight on her healthy ankle. It was a slow,
careful process because she'd feel clear-
headed for a moment and then go right back off
into that hazy, drunken state.

Downstairs, she realized she was still
holding Michael's phone. She slid it closed and
dropped it on the kitchen table. She took a
glass from the cabinet and held it under the
faucet. Her night vision was sharp. It helped
that she was familiar with the house.

She sipped lukewarm water and felt the
brain fog lifting.

Outside the moon reflected off the lake and
lit the nighttime scene. Trees moved fitfully in

the breeze and the clouds gathering around the moon indicated the bright night would be changing soon.

Michael's phone rang.

She reacted instinctively, more to shut it up than to answer it.

"This is 911 emergency. We received a call from this phone number."

"I'm sorry." Her tongue was thick. "I think I did dial 911, but it was a mistake. I was confused. I took some pills. Prescribed pills. Had a really bad day."

A soft pause, then the caller said, "We have an officer on the way. He'll need to check."

Another voice came on the line. "Miss Kincaid?"

"Yes?"

"I'm Deputy Nance. Michael Fowler called about five minutes ago. He said he was going to wake you. Did he?"

"He called you? I don't understand. Where is he?" The first sharp edges of panic touched her.

"Miss Kincaid? Beth? Are you there alone?"

"I think so. I don't know. Michael was here. Where is he?" Adrenalin was clearing out the last of the medication haze.

"He may have stepped outside to speak with our deputy."

"Your deputy?" Beth was already on her way to the front of the house.

"Don't go outside, please. Stay where you are. We have another deputy in route to the house. He'll be there in minutes. Jack Cole escaped custody. We have every reason to believe he has cleared the area, but until we're certain—"

"Where is Michael?" Her voice rose in panic. She couldn't stand it. No more. No more loss. She ran from window to window. Outside, the night had darkened with onrushing clouds. Deep shadows shifted with the bushes and trees buffeted by the wind as the clouds scudded past the moon. It was impossible to identify anything specific.

Beth picked up Michael's hefty flashlight from behind the kitchen door. He would never have left her alone willingly, not under the circumstances.

"Tell your deputy to hurry because I'm going outside." She dropped the phone on the counter. She planned on using both hands.

She needed her temper. She fanned it so that the adrenalin surged through her arms giving her strength. Her temper could be her friend and asset.

God, please direct my strength.

The chill wind from the lake blew her long hair across her face. She clawed it away.

Everything looked normal considering she could hardly see with the dark and the hair whipping around her face. She tried to use all of her senses, but she might as well have been alone in this wild, blustery night. She hadn't thought to turn on the backyard spotlight and she was glad. It would only have made the shadows deeper and more impenetrable, and given warning. She scanned the yard, focusing on the outlines of trees, bushes and yard furniture, seeking any movement that didn't belong.

A strong gust hit her and she staggered backward as the moon broke free lighting the back yard. In the cold, silvery light of the moon a man stepped out of the black area near the shed.

Beth started forward instinctively, hefting Michael's flashlight as a weapon. The figure was about Michael's size and though she couldn't make out details, she guessed it was him and her heart thrummed, beating an urgent pulse throughout her body as he staggered and fell and a monster's dark form appeared. He moved quickly toward Michael, bent and grabbed him by the hair, pulling his head up as if to strike a fatal blow.

Already running forward, Beth gripped the barrel of the flashlight with both hands. Rage turned the dark night red. She jumped, swinging the flashlight like a bat as she flew toward Jack Cole. He saw her at the last moment and moved. That fraction of movement saved his life, but didn't stop the cracking thud against the side of his head.

Beth had put everything she had into her launch and she hit the ground hard jarring her shoulder and side. She gasped for breath as Cole continued kneeling silently for one long second, then fell forward.

Chaos ruled the dark. Lightning cracked around their heads as Michael struggled to rise, injured. Beth pushed herself up to her knees.

The next lightning flash showed troopers and deputies rounding the side of the house.

****

Beth sat with Michael in the hospital while they checked him out. He had a concussion, but not as severe as Cole's. Beth's blow had sidelined Cole long enough for the authorities to get him securely into custody. It was weird to think, and neither said it aloud, but Cole was probably at this hospital, under guard, getting treatment.

"Why did he come back to the house?" Beth asked Michael. Why didn't he leave town and keep going?"

"I think he tried to, but his truck had been towed. Maybe he thought he could get his hands on your car. Probably never expected you'd be back in the house tonight and thought it would be the easiest target. Even if he saw the deputy's cruiser, it would only mean one person to silence."

Chapter Thirty-Two

Beth drove Michael's truck down the narrow paved road that led to the hard-packed dirt of the Fowler Farm Road. Michael kept one hand around the door handle in a white-knuckled grip. From the corner of her eye, she watched him work the invisible brake on the passenger-side floorboard. When she didn't turn onto the neat, well-maintained road to the Fowler farm, but instead, took the rutted dirt road on the right, he sat up straighter.

"Where are we going?" he asked.

His question was clearly rhetorical since the destination was obvious.

"Do you mean why are we going?" She avoided a large rock and slowed to reduce the impact of an approaching pothole. She stopped near the end of the dirt track.

She waved her hand at the ruins of the Kincaid house, "I plan to build there, Michael. Knock it down, haul it away and start fresh." She pointed past him to the right, toward the trees and the low, scrubby growth. "I'll clear that for the lake view. Probably a boat dock, too."

Michael stared through the window out at the trees. He reached up, ran his fingers through his hair and winced.

"Still hurt?"

"Not much. I could've driven."

"Doctor said 'no.' That's good enough for me."

"Too bad you don't listen to advice as well as you enforce it." He opened the truck door and stepped out. He stood for a moment, his hand on the top of the vehicle, then walked toward the trees.

Beth cut the engine and followed him. They pushed through the brush and the crowding, grasping branches trying to avoid sticker bushes until they broke free where the foliage ended at the lake's edge. They stopped short of stepping out onto the rickety dock. When Beth touched her shoe to the first gray boards, Michael warned her off.

"Don't trust that. Looks like it could fall apart with the least weight."

She shrugged and smiled. "It's okay. I can swim. I'm not afraid of the water anymore and one day I'll be all the way past the bad memories, too. Take a look around us, Michael."

He turned, scanning the lake and the shore. She waited, giving him a chance to see her vision.

"There's more I want to say. Do you want to hear?"

"I'm listening."

"I want to do something with the acreage that's closer to town. I'm not exactly sure what, but something that fits the natural landscape. Camping areas, some guest houses...maybe like small bed and breakfasts, some with a few luxuries, available for families or a small organization to rent." She paused, looking for a reaction. "You aren't laughing."

"No. Go on."

"I want to attract a broad range of people, people who stay for a few days or a week or so. Families that come for fun, swimming in the lake or hiking, or to find solitude if that's what they want. Maybe stables."

"I heard word about town that you were working on your own development plans. Is this what they were talking about?"

"It burst out when I was trying to annoy Ed Mason. Not one of my better moments. I really hadn't given it any thought at that point, but since then I've considered and imagined it, and I think the idea has potential. Intimidating, but it can be done in stages. I'm a project manager by profession, but I'm lacking some expertise."

"Expertise?"

"For the practical side of planning and building." Beth struggled to hold her hopes quiet and still inside. This had to be his decision. "Last night, I asked you to think about commitment. Well, think about this, too, good and hard, and then I'd like to hear what you have to say."

"Last night you said you knew why my engagements didn't make it to the altar."

"I did."

"Why? What did you mean?"

She stared down at the hardscrabble earth and clumps of weeds. "I think you need to figure that out for yourself."

Chapter Thirty-Three

Michael had fought the urge to reassure her, to promise her he'd be a part of her dream, a part of her life, forever. She'd asked him to think about it and he would.

He sat in the kitchen of his farmhouse. He'd lived here all of his life except for that time in Iowa and while in college. Aside from having the occasional complaint, he'd never wanted to live anywhere else. Even when he'd gone on trips, he always looked forward to coming home.

Home. It didn't look all that different from when his parents had lived here. A comfortable sofa was a comfortable sofa. He'd upgraded the TV, had gotten himself a nice big flat screen, and added a few practical items like a dishwasher, but otherwise... Still, it wasn't like he was stuck in the past or anything. He'd always figured he'd make a move one day or marry a woman who'd want to make those changes...but then he hadn't.

Funny how, when he'd taken off for college he'd expected to...what? Travel? Get into business? Move somewhere exciting? College was okay and he'd spent a summer traveling in Europe. It was all good, but...it wasn't satisfying. He was always looking, always waiting, and in the end, he always came home to muddy pastures and cows who only got excited about meals.

So, maybe home was the farm, but the house? It had memories, but it was just a house. Sitting here by himself, with his head still aching from the blow Cole had given him, and from whom he'd been rescued by a beautiful woman with the amazing hair and the smile that lit the world, still he recognized it was a house, a pile of sticks. He sensed the years stretching ahead of him and they all looked empty. Without Beth, he didn't want to be here or anywhere and it scared the crap out of him to think he might be that dependent upon anyone.

He'd been in love before and it had never worked.

Michael looked up and stared at the fridge and the magnet holding the slip of paper with Beth's phone number. It had been joined by a worn red heart cut from construction paper. Beth's bookmark.

Always before he'd entered into relationships knowing he could walk away. This time was different. This time, he couldn't see any alternatives. His life, his future, was on the line.

He stilled his mind and tried to hear the words of his heart.

Chapter Thirty-Four

Beth took Clarissa with her out to the Adirondack chairs by the lake. As the doctor had foretold, she'd overused her ankle and it ached. She slipped off her sandals and propped her bare feet on the ottoman. The sun was bright, the sky was so deep a blue that it almost hurt her eyes, but it was a natural, wholesome blue. The breeze sealed the perfection of the day.

Beth opened *Clarissa's Folly*.

"Uncle, I must go back. I've been a coward, and now I must remedy my error, if I can."

"My dearest niece, I fear you will have your heart broken. And what of your reputation? I wish to see contentment and satisfaction in your future. There is no shame in contentment and is more than many a man or woman could hope for. Passion is fleeting and to seek it has led many a young person to grief and regret."

Clarissa looked closely into the kindly eyes of her uncle who had earnestly sought to guide her and educate her and she wished to please him and to put his concerns to rest. She leaned forward and clasped his hands in hers.

"Uncle, you and my Aunt have given me all that a beloved child could ever hope to receive from even the fondest parent. If I am too bold for a female of good repute, then do not feel

dismay, but rather admire yourselves for having grown a young woman of courage and uprightness. I must step out and test life. When I left before, I thought I was doing just that and yet, at the first trial, I failed. Instead of standing my ground when Madam sought to evict me, I ran away rather than risk my heart and person further. I cannot find self-respect and satisfaction in running away. I cannot settle for a convenient life."

He touched her cheeks and kissed her forehead lightly as he had when she was a child. "Go, then, with my loving regard. Remember, you may always come home."

"Thank you, Uncle. I believe, I hope, I am going home."

The groom drove her to the Hargreaves station to catch the mail coach for the first stage of the trip. She had only a small valise, not knowing for sure where she might find herself at the end of this day.

"Mum? The coach is here."

The boy carried her bag and handed it up to the driver atop the carriage to be stowed. He offered a slightly grimy hand to her to assist her to step up into the coach when a man suddenly filled the door apparently deciding to exit without warning. Clarissa stumbled back and the boy stammered in surprise, "Watch it, sir, there's a lady here."

Clarissa's knees nearly failed her. She put a hand on the boy's shoulder to steady herself lest she fall in the dust.

The gentleman paused midway out of the

door and after a long moment in which the earth itself ceased to breathe, he said, "Clarissa? Miss Parrish? Is that you?"

"Edward," she nearly sobbed, controlling herself only for the sake of not raising a scandal in her hometown.

Edward spoke in a formal voice, "Will you assist me away from the coach, Miss Parrish?"

"Indeed."

The boot boy caught the bag the coachman tossed down, as well as another small valise. "And this 'uns the gentleman's. Looks like both will be staying."

Edward crossed the grass with Clarissa as she guided him to the gazebo. Once there, alone and with at least a modicum of privacy, she asked, "How do you come to be here? Have you traveled so far by yourself?"

"I did not fear the travel, but now that I am here with you I must open my heart and that, my dearest Clarissa, terrifies me."

"Sit here next to me." She pulled him down to the seat beside her.

"I've come to beg your forgiveness for my weakness, for using my blindness and my family as an excuse."

"An excuse? Edward, what do you mean?"

"I feared taking a chance on life. I feared failing myself and you."

Clarissa took his hand and brought it to her lips. "And now?"

"Now I understand that life without living is but a shadow existence—and I'm not willing to settle for anything less than a long life with you."

Thank you, Maude Henry.

Beth wished she could thank her in person and with a heartfelt embrace. She hoped Maude somehow knew she'd gotten the message and how valuable and appreciated it was.

Lukewarm didn't cut it. Never had. Reality didn't always measure up to the potential, but potential was intangible, a wisp of smoke, a dream that could never live. Sometimes reality far exceeded imagined potential.

A deep, familiar voice said, "It's Friday."

"Ryan!" Beth jumped up from her chair to welcome him.

His eyes went straight to her throat and her hand moved there in response.

She said, "A lot has happened since you were here."

He moved to stand near her. He put one hand on her shoulder and with the other hand he touched her cheek as he more closely examined her throat.

"I know that hurt. Hurts. Are you all right?"

"Yes, I am. In fact, I've never been better." She sat back down in the chair and he sat on the footstool, their knees touching. He was as remarkably gorgeous as ever, but now his attention was focused and serious.

"What happened?"

It was as if she could feel the feathery touch of his eyes on her face, her throat, her bruises. "It's a long story, but someone decided I was more useful to them dead. It's over now, but it helped sort out my thinking, and understanding what's important to me."

"And what is that?"

"My intention is to build something here. With Michael's help, if he's willing."

"You don't owe me any explanations, but I'd like to know, why?"

"I found roots and commitments I never recognized before." She leaned closer. "I thought I'd put the past behind me so many times, that I'd made a new life. But I never really forgave. I ran away, instead. Does that make sense?"

He touched her hands. "It's human nature to run from hurt."

"It's more than that. If I couldn't forgive them, then I couldn't forgive myself either. Yet it kept me chained to the past. The harder I ran, the more completely I was trapped. I hope I'm smarter now."

Ryan said, "So you're staying."

She nodded.

"Preston and Michael are lucky to have you."

She felt his kindness filling the air between them. "So much for your reputation as a hard-hearted businessman. You're a romantic."

They walked to the front of the house, hand in hand.

"You are an amazing woman, Beth Kincaid. I wish we'd had more of a chance to become friends, to know each other better."

With a hug and a goodbye kiss on the cheek, Ryan added, "I'll be back to visit the next time I'm in the area, if that's okay?"

The only answer she gave him was a smile and she sent him off with a wave.

Beth turned around and there was Michael standing on her front porch, dark hair slightly tousled and his hands in his pockets. He looked uncertain as he watched Ryan's car vanish down the road. Her heart felt as if it might burst.

"Will you take a chance on me?" he asked.

"Will you break my heart?"

He walked down the steps and stopped close to her. "I figured out something about those women I thought I loved and wanted to marry, who, when it came time to say 'I do,' I didn't."

"What was that?"

"They all had something important in common—they weren't you." He walked slowly toward her as he spoke. "I believe I've been waiting for you for all these years and I can hardly believe my good fortune—that you're here and willing to take another chance on me."

She held out her hands and Michael was there in less than a heartbeat wrapping his arms around her. This time, she didn't wait for Michael to steal a kiss, but stood on tiptoe as she pulled his face to hers and claimed one of her own.

THE END

ABOUT THE AUTHOR

Stories of heart and hope ~ from the Outer Banks to the Blue Ridge

USA Today Bestselling and award-winning author, Grace Greene, writes novels of contemporary romance with sweet inspiration, and women's fiction with romance, mystery and suspense.

A Virginia native, Grace has family ties to North Carolina. She writes books set in both locations. The Emerald Isle, NC Stories series of romance and sweet inspiration are set in North Carolina. The Virginia Country Roads novels, and the Cub Creek novels have more romance, mystery, and suspense.

Grace lives in central Virginia. Stay current with Grace's news at www.gracegreene.com.

You'll also find Grace here:
http://twitter.com/Grace_Greene
https://www.facebook.com/GraceGreeneBooks
http://www.goodreads.com/Grace_Greene

Other Books by Grace Greene

THE MEMORY OF BUTTERFLIES
(Lake Union Publishing)

Brief Description:
A young mother lies to keep a devastating family secret from being revealed, but the lies, themselves, could end up destroying everything and everyone she loves. Hannah Cooper's daughter, Ellen, is leaving for college soon. As Ellen's high school graduation approaches, Hannah decides it's time to return to her roots in Cooper's Hollow along Virginia's beautiful and rustic Cub Creek. Hannah's new beginning comes with unanticipated risks that will cost her far more than she ever imagined—perhaps more than she can survive.

THE HAPPINESS IN BETWEEN
(Lake Union Publishing)

Brief Description:
Sandra Hurst has left her husband. Again. She's made the same mistake twice and her parents refuse to help this time—emotionally or financially. Desperate to earn money and determined to start over, she accepts an offer from her aunt to house-sit at the old family home, Cub Creek, in beautiful rural Virginia. But when Sandra arrives, she finds the house is shabby, her aunt's dog is missing, and the garden is woefully overgrown. And she suspects her almost-ex-husband is on her trail.

Sandra needs one more chance at regaining her self-respect, making peace with her family, and discovering what she's truly made of.

Thank you for purchasing

KINCAID'S HOPE

I hope you enjoyed it!

Please leave a review where this book is sold. It helps authors find readers and helps readers find books they'll enjoy.

I hope you'll visit me at www.gracegreene.com and sign up for my newsletter. I'd love to be in contact with you.

CPSIA information can be obtained
at www.ICGtesting.com
Printed in the USA
BVHW042156230320
575806BV00014B/765